The Couplets

Meant to be Together, Volume 2

Richard Alan

Published by Village Drummer Fiction, 2019.

Copyright © 2018 by Richard Alan and Village Drummer Fiction All rights reserved. No part of this book may be reproduced in any form without permission in writing from the publisher, except by a reviewer who may quote brief passages in a review.

This book is a work of fiction. Any names, places, characters, or incidents are products of the author's imagination or are used fictiously. Any resemblance to actual events, locales, or people is entirely coincidental.

All trademarks are property of their respective owners. Village Drummer Fiction is not associated with any product or vendor mentioned in this book.

Cover design by AuthorPackages https://www.authorpackages.com[1]

All trademarks are property of their respective owners. Village Drummer Fiction is not associated with any product or vendor mentioned in this book.

www.villagedrummerfiction.com[2]   ISBN-13: 978-1-970070-02-6

This book is available at most online retailers.

---

1.   http://www.authorpackages.com/

2.   http://www.villagedrummerfiction.com/

This book is dedicated to my wife and partner, Carolynn, without whom none of this would be possible.

I also dedicate this book to my father, Gerald, who was the greatest natural engineer I have ever known—even after forty years working with many engineers of all disciplines, he surpassed them all.

I would also like to dedicate this book to our three sons, David, Allen, and Isaac. Their humor, joy, character, and accomplishments have made the bad times better and the good times greater.

Chapter One ~ Anna Cardozo

Mrs. Heather drummed her fingers on the counter. She was still on hold waiting to talk to her insurance company after forty-five aggravating minutes. It was a gorgeous morning with an azure-blue cloudless sky and bright yellow sunshine. This was a typical March day in southern New Mexico.

Through the window, she eyed her front yard where she had placed her artists' crayon pastel pencils on a small card table and had set up an easel. Today she would attempt recreating the marvelous view she enjoyed from her home in the Organ Mountains.

When the call finally ended, she noticed a little girl standing on the sidewalk that led to her front door. It was five-year-old Anna Cardozo, the daughter of the restaurant owners up the street.

Anna was standing barefoot, looking down at the sidewalk with her head tilted to the side, as if she were studying something. She was wearing a cream-colored shift that came down almost to her ankles with a matching wide-brimmed hat. Both were wrapped neatly with a bright pink sash. Her lovely auburn hair tumbled out from under the hat.

Anna got down on her hands and knees, and much to Mrs. Heather's horror, she realized that Anna had taken her expensive artists' crayons and was drawing on her concrete walkway.

As she hurried outside, her thoughts were focused on how difficult it would be to get that stuff off the walk. Mrs. Heather scurried out. "Anna, stop that."

Startled, Anna quickly stood up. She looked like she was entertaining the thought of running away, but with the crayons still in her hands there was no denying what she had done.

Mrs. Heather ran up to her. "Anna, it will be impossible—it will take—those are very expensive."

Mrs. Heather was taken aback at what she saw there on the pavement. "Oh, my word. Anna, that's marvelous."

She became speechless as she regarded Anna's drawing. It was notebook-page sized, with a deep blue, almost black, background. Anna had created what looked like a night sky with the outline of a leafless tree in the lower-left corner.

After a few moments' pause to take in Anna's drawing, she asked, "What are you drawing, Anna?"

"My bedroom window." "Is that what it looks like?"

In a quiet mouse of a voice Anna told her, "I had to get up to pee after I went to bed and this is what my window looked like."

Mrs. Heather was shocked at the accurate view of the night sky. She even recognized some constellations. "Anna, I love to have company when I'm drawing. I could set up a portable easel on the table over there and we could draw together. Would you like to do that?"

"Sure!" Anna jumped up and down with enthusiasm.

So, Mrs. Heather brought out more art supplies and a tall glass of lemonade for each of them. Anna seemed to love the attention, not to mention an opportunity to draw another picture.

The little easel was parallel to Mrs. Heather so she really couldn't see what Anna was drawing, but as Mrs. Heather talked, she kept pointing out the different textures in the distant mountains and how the sun created shadows across the landscape.

Anna seemed to keep pace with the running account of the mountains that, she too, was so familiar with. Every now and then she giggled for no apparent reason.

After a conversation-filled thirty-minutes, Anna said in a laugh-filled voice, "Oh no, another one is running away."

"What's running away, dear?"

Anna's cheery voice replied, "Another tiny drop."

Mrs. Heather was confused, so she positioned herself to be able to see Anna's drawing. She had expected something good after seeing

Anna's sidewalk drawing, but still she gasped. "Anna, you have an amazing amount of artistic ability."

There on the small canvas, Anna had drawn a picture of her glass of lemonade. She had included the sweating moisture on the outside of the glass, and the ice cubes with the sun sparkling in some of them. She even drew the droplets running down the side of the glass, leaving a trail in the frost.

Anna had indeed portrayed the mountains, with a few strokes of color, behind the lemonade. Mrs. Heather could see the distorted view of them depicted through the glass.

"Lemonade needs a lemon," Anna said, giggling again. Then with only a handful of color-filled strokes, a slice of lemon appeared, perched on the edge of the glass.

"Anna, that's beautiful. That looks so real I can almost taste the lemonade and feel the wet glass."

Astounded by the ability of this young child, Mrs. Heather told her, "Artists usually put their name on their work, dear."

"I already did," Anna replied. "Where did you write it?"

"In the ice cubes," Anna stated in a casual tone.

Sure enough, Anna had darkened the edges of some of the ice cubes in a way that spelled out her name.

"Simply incredible," Mrs. Heather mumbled under her breath.

***

Anna Cardozo was the daughter of Carmen and Arturo Cardozo. The middle of three children, she was born and raised in a small town in southern New Mexico.

Anna's grandmother lived with the family, and although it wasn't apparent at a young age, Anna had inherited her grandmother's sense of grace and beauty. She had also inherited her great-grandmother's mathematical mind and high intelligence.

As Anna's mother was always busy working in their restaurant, she learned most of her values from her grandmother.

Anna's parents' restaurant was located on the edge of town and everyone in the family worked there, especially in the winter. That's when the snowbird tourists came to enjoy the flora and fauna of the warm, beautiful southwestern desert, escaping the cold of their northern homes. The restaurant earned the family an adequate living, but barely enough to get them through the slow summer season.

Unlike her brother and sister, Anna loved learning. She couldn't wait for the school year to start and was sad when it ended. She had many friends, until fifth grade when her friends discovered boys.

The other girls were developing physically, but Anna's physical development did not begin until her senior year of high school. She attained her adult height of five foot two in seventh grade.

Her parents had taken her to the doctor and he assured them that nothing was wrong. "Some girls just develop later than others," he'd told them.

This knowledge didn't prevent Anna from becoming the object of many mean-spirited jokes all through junior high and high school. At times, Anna became depressed and felt like an outcast.

She developed the facility of doing things on her own to minimize the chance of being hurt, although, she was easily angered when teased about her underdeveloped body. Even in college, when she did start to develop a woman's figure, she felt she was still treated like a little kid. Her own brother often referred to her as his skinny sister, calling her *hermana flaca* almost as often as he used her proper name.

Anna couldn't understand her now former friends' fascination with boys, so she just concentrated on her schoolwork and became a great student. When boys tried to talk to her, she was always on the defensive, waiting for some remark about her shapeless body. The only date she went on in high school had been arranged by her parents.

The local high school had purchased computers when Anna was a freshman. Anna immediately realized that the computer and the internet was a window to the world outside their small town. Her teacher had told her that computer programmers could earn an excellent living, and Anna thought that by having a well-paying career, she would never have to be dependent on anyone else.

***

On Parents' Day during Anna's sophomore year, the mathematics instructor told her mother and father that Anna should attend university and study engineering. "Anna has the mathematical and scientific talent, plus the work ethic, to become an excellent electrical engineer," he told them. "This is a career that will allow her to make a wonderful living for herself. I have a number of talented students in my classes, but Anna's comprehension and ease of learning math and science, combined with her great passion for science, is far beyond any student I have had the honor to teach. With Anna's abilities, you should definitely be planning to send her to college."

After a few more remarks about Anna's scholastic prowess the instructor stated, "I've noticed that Anna has incredible artistic talent, as well."

"Yes," Carmen told the teacher, "but it's just fun for her. She doesn't have a passion for it like she has for math and science."

While driving home after the conference, Arturo glanced at his wife. "Carmen, you know we can't afford to send her to college."

"You heard what the teacher said, Arturo."

"I heard. It hurts me more than I can tell you. Of all our children, I've known for a long time that Anna was the only true student."

"I have a feeling that God will provide an answer for that," Carmen Cardozo confidently told her husband. "I'm going to pray on it."

In a sarcastic voice, Arturo replied, "You do that, Carmen, and I'll check my bank account to see if *He's* made a deposit for Anna's education."

Six-months later, God's answer to Carmen's prayers arrived, after a man from Texas had just purchased many acres of land adjacent to their restaurant. He was going to build a huge RV campground and construction workers began showing up from all over the country to develop the site. At lunchtime, many of them went over to the Cardozo's restaurant for lunch.

With the extra money from the construction workers, they added a lovely shaded patio, nearly doubling the capacity of the restaurant.

When Anna asked her parents about money for university, they always told her the same thing, "You just worry about your grades. We'll manage the rest."

Anna graduated third in her high school class, had amazing SAT scores, and she received a scholarship that paid most of her tuition. When she received her acceptance letter from the university, she couldn't decide who was more excited—her mother or her father.

Arturo decided to leave the restaurant for a few days while he, Carmen, Anna, and Anna's grandmother, Perla, drove up to see the university campus.

Upon their return, Carmen commented to one of her friends, "Other than the times when the kids were born, I don't think I ever saw Arturo so happy. You know how tight fisted he is with money. When we went into the campus book store, he bought jackets, hats, bumper stickers, cups, pens, pennants, pencils, and t-shirts— everything with the university emblem. I couldn't believe it. He even bought a poster with the university emblem to put in the entrance to our restaurant. Everyone's going to know that Arturo's daughter is attending university."

Her face turned slightly, thinking about Anna's reaction. "My Anna on the other hand, just looked nervous the whole time we were there. She's not even in university yet and she's losing sleep worrying about being able to do the work. I was hoping that once she graduated from high school, she would be happier with herself. It hasn't happened yet. I'm beginning to wonder if she will always be alone."

Her friend reassured her, telling Carmen that Anna would come around. Carmen smiled and nodded, yet she still had her doubts.

***

When Anna talked to an advisor at the university, she realized she could double major in electrical engineering and software engineering, as many of the course requirements overlapped. She could finish her double major in nine semesters.

She rarely came home, except at holidays. Sadly, there wasn't much time to spend with family during those visits as they took place during the restaurant's busiest times.

Anna's social life in college mirrored her social life in high school and she concluded that most relationships were just "messy" and time consuming, preferring to focus on her studies.

Toward the end of her last semester, a number of corporations sent human resource personnel and engineers to visit the campus and conduct interviews with potential employees.

Anna was a nervous wreck at each interview. She was certain that none of the companies would want someone who interviewed so poorly. However, within two-days, one of the companies asked Anna to fly to Seattle, Washington for additional interviews. They sent her airline tickets and paid for her hotel and meals.

She was amazed that a company would do that for her. After the first-two interviews in Washington, Anna was shocked when she realized that the company was trying to make sure she liked them enough to ensure that she would come to work there.

With Anna's scholastic record, and obvious intelligence, she was given a job offer before she went home. She would start work in early March, giving her enough time to visit home after graduation and arrange to have her things moved to an apartment in Seattle.

Anna's parents were proud of their daughter, but they seemed sad too, as they realized that Seattle was a long way from southern New Mexico.

Chapter Two ~ Ruth and Oliver

TWO-YEARS AFTER RUTH Case received her master's degree, she found a teaching position at the University in Seattle. Ruth taught Russian, Italian, and Mandarin Chinese. She felt lucky that at twenty-six years-of-age she had found a teaching position at the university level. She thought that teaching language in a university setting was great, as the students tend to be more motivated than high school students are.

One morning, Ruth went out to find that her car wouldn't start. She called her department head to let her know she would be late. When she came back out, a guy was standing next to the front of her car. He had blonde hair, very bright blue eyes, and a slim build. He looked like he was about Ruth's age and was a bit taller than she was.

"Hit the key again, miss," he told Ruth.

She did, but the car just made a clicking noise. "I've got cables in my car. I'll jump it for you."

He opened the hood of the car. "Your negative battery cable is loose. I'll get a wrench and tighten it." And off he went.

He returned with a small wrench, which he used to tighten the cable. Ruth turned the key and the car started immediately. She thanked him for helping her and let him know that her university students would be thankful for his efforts.

"It's my pleasure." He smiled warmly.

That evening Ruth decided to study outside by the apartment complex's swimming pool. She donned a bikini with a very sheer shirt, which did little to hide her more-than-ample curves.

It was a warm evening, and many people were sitting around the pool. Many of them were highly-educated engineers, living in the apartment complex, who worked for a nearby software company.

"How's your car running?" It was the man from earlier in the day. He wore a t-shirt and swimming suit on his slim body. He sat down next to Ruth. "I'm Oliver."

"It's running fine, thank you. I'm Ruth." "What are you reading?" he asked.

"I am preparing an exam for my classes. I teach Russian, Italian, and Chinese languages at the University."

"Speaking a foreign language must be neat. I speak English and diesel." He chuckled.

"You speak diesel?"

Through a wide grin he said, "I'm a mechanic. I work on over-the-road diesel-engine trucks."

"It must be very nice to work with your hands all day, I'm sure." Ruth smiled, but inside she thought, *Drat.*

She had worked very hard to have an intellectual career so she could interact with intelligent and highly-educated acquaintances. She was disappointed that the first guy who talked to her, other than married colleagues, was someone who worked with his hands for a living. Some girls have good luck meeting guys and some have bad luck—Ruth thought she fell in the no-luck category.

"I'm having some friends over to my place Friday night," Oliver said. "Maybe you'd like to join us. We're getting a keg of beer, so it should be a good time."

"Thank you, but no. Drinking isn't my idea of entertainment, so I wouldn't be much fun at your get-together."

He looked disappointed. "Oh, I'm sorry. Well, you wouldn't have to drink," Oliver offered.

"I don't tend to hang around people who smoke either." "Oops," Oliver said, putting out his cigarette. "Maybe some other time."

"I really don't think so. I doubt that we have anything in common."

"I'm sorry to have bothered you. You seemed like a really nice person."

Oliver got up and walked away. After a number of steps, he looked back at Ruth with a sad expression on his face.

She wondered what he'd meant by "seemed" like a nice person. Was that diesel mechanic judging her? He didn't have the slightest idea who she was. Ruth had worked hard to progress to an intellectual level which that diesel mechanic clown could only dream about. She wondered how a drinking, smoking, diesel mechanic thought he could judge her.

When Ruth mentioned the incident to one of her colleagues, they had a good laugh that a mere diesel mechanic would have the nerve to ask Ruth to a beer party.

About four-weeks-later Ruth saw Oliver sitting at a Starbucks late in the day, latte in hand, reading a rather large paperback book. He looked up and smiled at her.

Deciding to be friendly, she approached him. "How was your party?"

"It was nice. You might have liked it."

"What are you reading? Wait let me guess—a catalogue of engine repair tools?"

The smile disappeared from his face. He stared at Ruth for a moment. "This is volume three of Shelby Foote's series, *The Civil War: A Narrative.*"

"I'm sorry. I didn't mean to imply—"

"Actually, you did mean to. And it worked. You've convinced me that you think I'm your intellectual inferior because I repair diesel engines for a living. Let me tell you something, Miss College Professor. Every time I fix an over-the-road truck, it puts some driver back on the road so he can continue to make a living for his family. I think the tool that a guy or gal uses to make a living is important. I'm the one who keeps that tool running properly and quickly repairs it when it breaks. I'm not working today because I was up all night replacing a burned piston on a husband and wife driving-team's truck. Their trailer is loaded with organic produce. If I didn't get them back on the road, all that produce would have spoiled and they wouldn't get paid. One of my fellow mechanics and I tore that engine down and repaired it so they were on the road again at six o'clock this morning."

Oliver returned his gaze to his book. "Have a nice day." He did not look back up, but started reading again.

Ruth felt like every eye in the coffee shop was staring at her, judging her. Who did this jerk think he was? She got in line to order, but by the time she got to the counter, she was so aggravated she couldn't remember what she wanted.

As Ruth was leaving the coffee shop she received a call from her father. As agitated as she was, she couldn't help but vent to him. After she told him what had happened, there was a long silence before he spoke.

"I feel sorry for you, Ruth. It must be terrible to have to put up with these intellectual midgets. Head back over to your university and talk to your scholarly equals. I'm sure they'll agree with you. Just don't tell them that your own father has dirt under his fingernails from spending most of his life repairing aircraft engines. Although I'm quite sure you won't—that fact must be awfully embarrassing for you."

"Dad, it's not like—"

"Shut up, Ruth," her father shouted. "You've been an intellectual snob since high school. Your university education has only made it worse. Before you call me again, you go back and apologize to that young man. I mean *sincerely* apologize to him." Then he hung up on her.

Ruth's dad had never done anything like that before. She was shaken up and went home as quickly as she could. When she got into her apartment, Ruth closed the door and collapsed into a sitting position on the floor. She cried her eyes out, thinking she had become so insensitive that her beloved father would call her an intellectual snob.

The worst part was he was right. She had been so blinded by conceit that she didn't even realize that while insulting Oliver, she was also insulting her father. Surrounded by colleagues in academia, they continually reminded each other how intellectually superior they were to the rest of the world.

What absolute hogwash!

Ruth realized she really would have to sincerely apologize to Oliver. It took her a few hours to get composed, and then she showered and changed into a lovely top and slacks. She checked the apartment complex list to find his apartment number, then walked over and knocked on his door.

He opened the door wearing denim cutoffs and a skeptical expression. "Yes?"

Humbly, Ruth lowered her eyes. "Oliver, I want to apologize for my behavior at the coffee shop this morning—and the pool the other day. It was absolutely inexcusable."

"Thank you. Apology accepted." He stared at her for a moment, as if considering something. "Would you like to come in?" Although she still had nothing in common with Oliver, Ruth thought it would be best to accept. Upon entering his apartment, she noticed many large maps on the floor and on the dining room

table. "What are all these?" she asked.

Oliver's eyes perked up as if she had hit on something important to him. "They're maps of various battles fought during the Civil War. I like learning about the Civil War. It's been a hobby of mine since I visited Gettysburg four years ago."

He walked over to the map that was laid out gingerly on his table. "A cousin of mine was in Louisiana at a used book store and he found this map and sent it to me. It has indications that it was drawn by a confederate general named E. B. Stuart, or someone on his staff. One of the history professors from the University is coming over shortly to help me verify if it's real. It's really in fragile condition. Once I realized how valuable it might be, I've only touched it with cotton-gloved hands."

"That would be quite a find, if it turns out to be real," she told him.

"If it is real, I'm going to give it to a museum." Oliver beamed.

"This should be available for everyone to see. There's also a good chance that it's a fake. The world seems to be awash in fake Civil War documents—would you like something to drink? I mean, non- alcoholic, of course."

"Water would be fine, thank you."

Oliver walked into his kitchen and returned carrying a glass of water with ice cubes, just as his doorbell rang.

As he opened the door, he welcomed, and then introduced, the history professor who would help determine the veracity of the map.

Professor Anderson was an older man who had spent most of his life in the History Department of the University. He looked over the map with zeal, and then set up a microscope.

He leaned over and studied intently. "My word, Oliver, this paper appears to be the right age. Of course, I can't be certain until we chemically analyze it, but the weave and coloring appear to be correct for a document of this age."

He unfolded a piece of paper that he had removed from his pocket. "I had a friend in Kentucky send me a copy of Stuart's signature from an authenticated document."

They all looked at the two signatures and they looked quite similar. Ruth could sense Oliver's excitement.

The professor spoke. "If this turns out to be real, well then, the three of us have been looking at an extremely valuable historical document. It could bring hundreds of thousands of dollars at auction."

"We have a long way to go before we have to worry about that," Oliver told him.

Professor Anderson looked at Ruth. "Young lady, we are in the presence of a genuine Civil War battle-historian. I can think of fewer than a dozen people who would have recognized the potential value of this map. There is little identification of the locations indicated on the map, but by observing the notes on the troop placements, Oliver recognized which battle the map referred to. I've been trying to get him to teach a course on battles of the Civil War in my department," he turned to look at Oliver, "but he keeps turning me down. Maybe you can help me encourage him?"

Ruth was overwhelmed, not only by her misjudgment of Oliver, but also by the suggestion that she would have any influence over his decisions. "We've just met, but I'll try."

Oliver laughed and waved the professor off with his hand. "If you need someone to teach truck repair, I'm your man. But teach history? I don't think so."

"Well, I keep hoping," the professor told them as he turned to leave.

When they were alone again, Ruth rather spontaneously asked Oliver if he would like to go for a walk.

"I'd love to, as long as you don't mind being seen with a diesel mechanic," he said, sounding only half-joking.

Ruth shook her head at her own blunder. "I am absolutely embarrassed to tears that I acted that way. My father spent nearly all his working career repairing jet aircraft. When I said those things to you, I was also demeaning him. I was mortified when I realized how I was behaving. He's always been a great father, husband, and provider for our family. My parents raised me with a great set of values, but I seemed to have lost some of them. Oliver, I am so sorry I acted that way."

Oliver smiled. "I won't bring it up again, if you won't." "It's a deal."

They ventured out, and on their walk they talked a lot about family and relationships. It was quite evident that family was very important to both of them. Ruth observed something else and decided to point it out to Oliver.

"I've noticed that you haven't lit up a cigarette," Ruth said.

"I quit, Ruth. The cousin who sent me that map is my age and he has smoked as long as I have. He was just diagnosed with lung cancer. He's having surgery in a couple of days to remove most of his left lung—I may not be the brightest bulb in the lamp, but I figure that's a good enough sign for me."

He shook his head. "It was murder for a couple of days, but I kept a picture of a diseased lung on the front of my locker at work, and on my refrigerator at home, to remind me why I wanted to quit smoking."

Ruth didn't really know what to say to that, and they walked in silence for a while until Oliver spoke again. "I was thinking about you the day after my party. I told you I was going to have beer there and you didn't seem to think that would be fun. I ended up having stomach flu earlier that day, so I didn't drink. And you know what? It *wasn't* fun. With me not being drunk, my friends didn't seem so funny. One of the girls got so drunk that she fell and dumped a full glass of beer on one of my favorite Civil War books. When I pointed out what she had done, she just laughed and said, 'Guess I'm drunk.' I was angry as hell that she thought getting falling down drunk and ruining a book was laughable behavior."

He stopped walking and looked at Ruth with a serious expression. "Also, I have to admit, I was angry at you, because I didn't want to like you, but you were right about the drinking."

Oliver was quiet for a moment as they resumed walking. His serious face turned back into a smile. "Well, Ruth, you may have to hang out with me now, because I may not have any friends left."

"I'm sure you'll find new friends."

Oliver stopped walking and turned toward Ruth again. "As long as you are the first of my new friends that will be fine."

They resumed their casual pace. "I'm worried that we don't have enough in common to build a relationship on," Ruth told him. "Let's just start by seeing if we can be good friends. I do think

we have shared values when it comes to family. That could be an excellent cornerstone for building a relationship."

They had dinner that night at Mama Michaela's Restaurant. It was served family-style on long rows of tables so everyone got to know each other. They had a wonderful evening sitting near a couple who obviously were very much in love. You could tell from the way they kept looking at each other and touching.

The guy was kind of shy, but told the funniest jokes about his software career. His girlfriend was from someplace in New Mexico. She told them many stories about growing up there and the hard times she and her family had. Everyone agreed that families got through the worst times by sticking together.

Oliver fit right in and Ruth felt very comfortable spending time with him. After dinner they went to a ballroom in Seattle for dancing. Neither was a great dancer, but the fun quotient was off the scale as they danced the night away.

When Oliver finally walked Ruth to her apartment door, she surprised herself. "I know we got off to a bad start," she said, "but I really had fun tonight and I hope to see you again."

As an answer, he put his hands on either side of Ruth's face and kissed her with one of *those* kisses—the kind you read about in romance novels.

"I had a fun day as well," he said.

Ruth felt certain she was experiencing enough fireworks exploding in her head to fill an entire Independence Day. She wrapped her arms around Oliver and held him as tight against her as she could.

They parted ways, but Ruth could hardly sleep that night thinking about Oliver—and that kiss. She kept thinking—if his kiss was so explosive, what would making love to him be like?

The next day Ruth's first class started at ten o'clock. She arrived to find a bud vase with a single yellow rose on her desk. The attached card read *Thanks for the great day—your favorite diesel mechanic.*

A few weeks later Ruth would receive a phone call that had the potential to destroy their growing and joy-filled relationship.

Chapter Three ~ Anna and Michael

ANNA SHARED AN OFFICE with another engineer and when she arrived the first day she was proud to see a placard at the entrance to their office with the words Anna Cardozo— Software Engineer on it. She was told her double major in electrical and software engineering were great majors, but she hadn't realized that companies would actually come looking for her, instead of her looking for them. After being raised in her small, southern New Mexico town, the Seattle area was certainly "the big city" for a small- town girl like her. It was taking some time for her to get adjusted to living there, especially to the weather.

It was cloudy every day, the temperature rarely got above fifty, and it wouldn't get much warmer until summer. March in New Mexico would be in the seventies and sunny almost every day. Anna's apartment was about one-mile from her office, though, so she could walk to work, regardless of the weather.

The group Anna worked for was developing a new electronic device for aircraft. She and her officemate, Michael Levin, were designing the software interface between the hardware components and the user interface. In the trade, it's called firmware engineering. They would also be responsible for testing the device's motherboard

to make sure it was built properly and worked as intended. They would be developing tests for all the software the department wrote as well.

While Anna worked for the company directly, Michael was hired as a consultant. He had done this kind of work since he was in high school and had developed many types of products, from dishwasher controls to satellite communication controllers. Michael was just under six-feet-tall, very nice looking, and five years older than Anna.

Anna learned that her immediate supervisor, Paul, wasn't happy to get an engineer right out of school for his eight-person engineering group. She knew that she would have to work as hard as she could to keep him happy. The others in the group were nice people, though, and pleasant to work with.

Michael had been especially nice to Anna. The first day she arrived he told her he had prepared an outline with the things she would need to learn. "Plus, here is a book on math algorithms," he said. "It will help get you up to speed with the rest of the group. If you have any questions, just ask."

Anna found that Michael was easy to work with, and he made her laugh. He seemed to make very funny jokes at his own expense. He was also an expert at malapropisms; after a member of the IT department gave them some absolutely worthless advice, Michael shook his head and told Anna, "We're certainly going to *illiterate* him from our memories."

Another time, after recommending a book to her, he said, "If you study this material you will easily *reprehend* it." He would drop words like that with a perfectly straight face—at first she thought he was serious, but soon realized he did it on purpose to make her laugh.

There were two other women in the group, and Anna started going to lunch with them. They let her know what to expect from different group members. No one seemed to like Paul. The general consensus was that his supervisory method consisted of tons of criticism and very little guidance.

Michael approached her with a project. "Anna, here is an outline of a module to code by the middle of next week. Our group will get together to review it. Code reviews are conducted to try to head off problems before running the code in an actual device. It also assures that the company's software quality standards are met."

Anna did the work on time, but she was a nervous wreck the day of the code review. It took place in a small conference room with whiteboards on the walls. Every time someone read a block of her code, Paul would find a reason to criticize it. Each criticism was accompanied by him saying, "If you had more experience, maybe you would know better."

After fifteen minutes of this, Michael gave Paul a look that was so cold it could have caused an entire ocean to freeze. In a strong, stern voice Michael suggested, "You've made your point, Paul."

Paul slowed down the criticism, but Anna still found it humiliating.

When they got back to their office Michael told her, "Your code was excellent. Don't let other people's remarks upset you."

"It's not that easy for me. This is my first job and I want to look good."

In a dramatic and ominous tone, Michael said, "Paul has a code review in two-weeks. Be sure you're ready for it."

Two-days before they went into Paul's code review, Michael handed Anna a copy of Paul's code with lots of little notes and symbols on it. The symbols came from the book on mathematical algorithms that Michael had given her when she'd started. Anna spent a number of hours studying the annotated code.

When they had all assembled in the conference room, Michael read the first six lines of Paul's code. He walked over to a whiteboard and turned back to face the group. Michael looked directly at Paul. "I'm not sure what you were trying to do, Paul. You only need two lines to get this done."

Michael proceeded to write the two lines on the whiteboard. Anna knew Michael was very good at writing code, but the two lines he put on the board were brilliant.

Paul still found a way to stick it to Anna, though. "With all your experience, I'm sure that's easy for you." Paul then looked in Anna's direction and gave her a disparaging look.

Michael ignored him and continued. "The next twelve lines are written in a way that uses way too many machine cycles. Code like this can drastically slow down processing."

Michael then looked at Anna. "Anna, please come up to the whiteboard and show us how this code could be written more efficiently."

Anna looked down at the code Michael had given her before the review. Applying what she had learned from the book on algorithms would enable her to compress Paul's code. Paul was glaring at her, practically daring Anna to challenge his work. She looked back at Michael, who was smiling at her. One of the other women in the group nodded to her.

That's all the encouragement she needed. Anna was nervous as she walked to the whiteboard and started writing, after she had the first line completed, she glanced back at the group. The other two women had huge smiles on their faces. Paul wasn't even looking at her. She compressed Paul's twelve lines of code into four and sat down.

"Thank you, Anna." Michael looked over the lines she had composed.

"That was excellent," Warren, the engineer sitting next to Anna said, as she sat down.

Twenty-six-year-old Warren was the quietest engineer in the group. Of average height and rather plain looking, he spoke with a rural Midwest accent.

Michael had said he was the best software engineer he had ever met. The word Michael used was "genius" when he described Warren's ability when it came to software. A compliment like that coming from Michael was huge praise, to say the least.

Warren then said to the group, "If there are no objections, I'll show how the next block of code could have been written more efficiently."

Anna couldn't remember details of the rest of the meeting, but she sure remembered how quiet Paul was.

At the end of the meeting Michael said, "Paul, before your next code review, why don't you stop by and see Anna, Warren, or me and we can review some better methods of writing code."

Paul mumbled a quick thank you as he headed out of the conference room.

When Anna got back to their office she thanked Michael.

"It's not me, Anna. It's you. I've been doing this kind of work since high school. I've probably met hundreds of engineers. One engineer was an old-timer who's probably long gone now. His name was Gerald. He was taught engineering course work in the Army Air Corps before and during World War II. He was the most gifted, most natural engineer I have ever met. Whether it was internal combustion engines, aerodynamics, electrical systems, hydraulics, structures made of metal, wood, or plastic—he had the ability to develop an abstract idea of how something should work. This enabled him to invent, build, or repair almost anything. The vast majority of engineers you will ever meet will never engineer something beyond what they learned in their textbooks."

He tapped the side of his head as if in illustration. "A *natural* engineer thinks of engineering at a high level of abstraction. This allows him to go beyond the textbook learning that he was trained with. His abstract thinking also allows him to develop concepts that have never existed before. It requires a mind that is capable of huge amounts of abstract thought. That kind of thinking is something you are born with—it can't be taught—Anna, that's how you think.

That book I gave you on algorithms would take most engineers months to learn. You learned it in a few weeks."

"Michael, it wasn't that difficult."

"That's what I'm telling you." Michael wore a joyous expression on his face. "It wasn't that difficult—for *you*, Anna."

While Anna was pleased at Michael's thoughts about her, she still felt like she was a beginning engineer who had amazing amounts to learn, just to become minimally competent.

When Anna went to the cafeteria for lunch that day she didn't see any of her usual friends. She was about to return to her office with her lunch, when she saw Warren sitting by himself next to a window that had a great view of the lovely green space next to their building.

"Hi, Warren," she said as she walked up to him. "May I sit with you?"

He looked up at her and smiled. "Please, sit down."

Anna hadn't noticed Warren's warm smile until now. He always seemed to concentrate on his work with such intensity, that he didn't smile.

He told her that he started working for their company right after college and that he loved software engineering. "I love creating applications for devices the average person will find useful," he said. "I knew how terrible Paul's coding skills were. But, I thought I was the only one who thought that. When you and Michael pointed it out, I knew that I could finally speak up too. Now, we are going to turn out a brilliant device with code that will execute like lightening. I live for that."

Warren took a bite of his lunch and glanced out the window at the lovely view. He swallowed quickly. "Oh, my God! Look at that gorgeous Great Blue Heron taking off from the marsh." Then, he leaned in to whisper. "I also live for birding."

"I'm from southern New Mexico," Anna told him. "You should come down our way. We have amazing, brilliantly-colored birds that you can see right from our backyard. My older sister, Chela, used her first paycheck to buy a feeder to put out there. Since then I think she is up to eleven different types of feeders. She also has nesting boxes for various birds placed around our yard. We call that part of our backyard Chela's Aviary. She joined a birding club and goes on hikes with them. Every year she goes out and does some kind of bird counting with them."

Warren perked up even more then and started telling Anna about the Varied Thrush that had just arrived at one of his feeders. He started going on and on, describing the beautiful bird and all the other birds that would soon be visiting. He probably talked for ten minutes straight. Anna hadn't heard that kind of enthusiasm about birds since she had talked to her sister, Chela, about last spring's bird count.

She wondered if Chela and Warren would be a good match. "Warren, do you have someone special in your life?"

His eyes quickly flashed down and his cheeks turned pink. "No, I don't. I'm so busy with software that I don't have time for dating."

"Good."

He looked surprised, so she quickly covered. "I mean, it's good that you enjoy your work so much."

As soon as Anna arrived back at her office, she told Michael they should have a party, sponsored by the firmware group, for all the project's engineers. "It would be nice to get together away from work," she said. "The building I live in has a community room that can be rented. We could have the get-together two or three weeks from now, on a Friday night."

Michael looked shocked, which didn't surprise Anna—up to that time, her behavior had let him know that she had no interest in social activities.

Anna hadn't dated that much, and she still found relationships with men confusing and kind of frustrating. In fact, she had only been on a couple of dates in her life, one of which was with a cousin, so she could attend her high school's senior prom.

Anna found her officemate good looking, and he was certainly a nice guy, but even if she wanted Michael to go out with her, she had no idea how to make that happen. She was afraid that she would not even know how to act during a date.

Besides, she had lots to learn to become proficient at her new career. She told herself this party was about getting her sister and Warren together. It had nothing to do with seeing Michael outside the office.

He smiled at her suggestion and agreed that a party for the engineers was a great idea. He said they could split the cost of the room, food, and drinks.

That evening an excited Anna bought an airline ticket and called her sister, who seemed thrilled, but being her beloved big sister, Chela also let Anna know that she didn't like the fact that Anna had spent money on an airline ticket for her. But after a brief discussion, she said she missed Anna terribly and would love to come for a visit.

Chapter Four ~ Warren and Chela

CHELA WAS THREE-YEARS-older than Anna. Their mother always teased that Chela was flirting with the boys in the newborn nursery right after she was delivered, and had been flirting with boys ever since. Anna always said that as far back as she could remember Chela always seemed to have a boyfriend.

Chela's only other interest was a love of birds. By the time she was eight she would go for long walks around their town looking at them. One day, when Chela was about ten-years-old, an old lady at an apartment building next to their family's restaurant must have noticed her staring intently at a hummingbird sipping nectar from a feeder. The woman came up to her and asked Chela if she knew the name of the hummingbird. When Chela said that she didn't, the woman returned to her apartment and then came back with a small paperback book of desert birds.

"That is a Rufous Hummingbird," she explained and gave the book to Chela. The woman showed her how to look up birds in the book, based on their families. She also showed Chela how to keep track of the date, place, and time of each sighting.

Chela couldn't believe her luck. She started walking past the woman's apartment on a regular basis and if the woman was outside she would show her what sightings she had recorded.

On a few occasions the old woman went walking with Chela and taught her about locating birds based on the sounds they make. One time, she even invited Chela to accompany her birding club when they went into the Organ Mountains. She said Chela could help with a bird count.

In late spring the old woman told Chela that she was getting too old to travel to New Mexico for the winter, so she wouldn't be coming back the following year.

"I have an extra pair of binoculars that I'm going to give you," she told Chela. "They're old, but if you continue to take care of them, they'll last you a long time. The instruction manual on using and maintaining them is in the box, so you just follow what the little manual tells you and you'll see a lot of birds through those lenses."

Chela was amazed at the old lady's generosity. She thanked her and walked directly home with her new treasure and showed them to her mom.

"You make a nice thank you card for her and then get busy in the kitchen baking her a cornbread," her mother told her. "Don't put too much spice in the cornbread. She's from up north and probably doesn't like chili as much as we do."

When the cornbread was ready, Chela and her mother walked over to the woman's apartment and Mrs. Cardozo thanked the woman for her generosity.

"You are certainly welcome. Thank *you*, Mrs. Cardozo, for raising a child who is so interested in the natural world. It is children like Chela who will make sure it is preserved for future generations."

Later, during high school, Chela organized a birding club. Her love of birds was only interrupted by whoever her boyfriend was at the time. While Chela had exquisite taste in nature, she had joined what her mother referred to as the "boyfriend bum of the month club." She had a lovely figure that allowed her to attract almost any guy she wanted, but she seemed to come home with one loser after another. From age-sixteen on, she seemed to have a parade of "serious" boyfriends. She even became engaged to one of those clowns.

Her parents were sick about it. She called off the engagement after she learned that he became so drunk one day that he tried to beat up his own sister. She was a big woman, and sober at the time he started to hit her. She managed to grab a tortilla press and beat the—well, let's just say he had to change his underwear.

By the time Anna was in university, Chela was spending most of her time helping at the family's restaurant. She had no desire to continue her education and attend college. Chela began thinking that her future would be like that of her mother, in that she would never leave the restaurant or her small town.

***

Michael and Anna sent out an invitation for their firmware group's party. Everyone in the group responded positively, except Paul, who told them he had plans that evening. Anna had personally delivered an invitation to Warren to make certain he would be there.

Chela arrived at SeaTac Airport in Seattle on the day before the party. At only five-foot-four, Chela's dark hair and dark eyes were completely defeated by the gaudy clothing she was wearing. It was pulled too tight around her full, slightly-overweight body, and Anna nearly died when she saw her sister.

After a quick hug hello, Anna told her sister, "You can't dress like that. You're going to meet my friends from work tomorrow and you can't dress like you're renting out your body parts."

"Anna, this is how I always dress."

"We're going straight to the mall so I can get you some clothes."

Chela pouted. "So my little sister thinks I have to dress like her college friends."

"I have to work with these people, Chela. It's important that
they respect me. You will allow me to buy you appropriate clothing. You wear what I buy while you are up here, or you can stay here at the airport and wait for the next plane home."

"Okay, little sister," Chela agreed. "I can use some new clothes."

"Also we're going to a place that will show you how to put on makeup properly. You look silly like that."

"Anna, please don't tell *me* about makeup."

"Someone needs to. Chela, I love you dearly, but you do what I say, or you can go home. I have a nice job up here and people like me. I can't afford to damage my reputation."

"Anna, I don't want to go home."

"Why not?"

"You remember Carlos Santiago? He's told everyone in our little town that I've promised to marry him. No one will ask me out now. I'm certainly not going to marry that drunk. I have no future back there. Besides, I really don't want to spend the rest of my life working at the restaurant."

"Well, Chela, there is someone in my software department that I want you to meet. He'll be at the party tomorrow."

"You're going to fix me up with one of your high-tech, college-educated friends? What in the world will I talk to him about? What will he have to say to a girl from a small town in New Mexico?"

"Chela, Warren is from a small town in Iowa. He's one of the nicest people I work with. He's really quite shy. He grew up in a big family like we did, but on a farm. I really think you'll like each other."

***

As Michael introduced Chela to their co-workers at the party, Chela heard many compliments concerning how nice it was to work with Anna.

"Your sister is the nicest person and a great engineer," Chela heard again and again.

Chela thought Anna was right about one thing—the clothes and makeup she insisted Chela wear, allowed her to look like she belonged with this group.

When Warren arrived, Anna pointed him out to Chela.

"He's nice looking," Chela said, "but I doubt if he'll want to have anything to do with a completely non-technical person like me."

"You might be surprised," Anna told her as they walked over to where he was standing.

"Warren, I would like you to meet my sister, Chela."

He smiled and extended his hand politely. "Hello, Chela. It's very nice to meet you."

Anna made some small talk for a few minutes and then guided them to a couch in front of a large coffee table. She walked away with a grin, but Chela could tell Anna was keeping an eye on them from across the room.

They were having trouble engaging each other in conversation, straining to find things to say. Anna clearly noticed the awkwardness between them, and after giving them a bit more time together, she walked over carrying glasses of wine.

Anna handed each of them a glass. "Warren, did I tell you that I saw a Spotted Towhee in my yard today?"

He immediately perked up. "I have yet to see one this year," Warren excitedly told her.

Chela sprung to attention, too. "What does it look like, Warren?"

Anna smiled.

Chela understood now why her sister wanted to introduce her to Warren.

"There is a *Birds of the Puget Sound* book in the middle drawer of the coffee table," Anna told them.

That opened the conversation like a floodgate opens a dam. Chela and Warren started chattering like—well—like a pair of small birds on a sunny spring morning.

Anna looked satisfied that her work was done. "Chela, if you look deeper in that drawer, you might find a book on birds of the southwest desert, just in case you want to show Warren any of the birds from home."

"Thank you, little sister," Chela said with a huge smile on her face.

From then on, all Anna had to do was keep filling their wine glasses.

***

Michael noticed that Chela and Warren were deeply involved in conversation and commented to Anna. "I thought you told me those two were having difficulty finding things to say to each other. Warren and Chela are talking up a blue fog over there. What in the world did they find to talk about?"

Anna shrugged and smiled. "Birds. They're talking about birds."

Michael started to laugh, but then realized she was serious. "I didn't realize that Warren had any interests in this world besides software."

"Well he does, and I think we should encourage him. You offered to take me to Tiger Mountain for a hike. Maybe we should go tomorrow and invite my sister and Warren to join us."

Michael was shocked again. Until then, Anna had turned him down on even the most platonic of activities that he'd proposed. But at the end of the evening, Anna told Chela and Warren they were planning on going for a hike the next day on Tiger Mountain.

"Would you two like to join us?" she asked.

"Yes." They answered in unison and then looked at each other, laughing.

After Warren left, Michael, Chela, and Anna cleaned up the party room. When Michael and Anna were alone, she asked him, "Do you think Warren had a good time with my sister?"

"I think they had a good time with each other. It was almost as if an invisible rope was connecting those two the entire night. I don't think they ever got more than ten-inches apart. Was this a setup?"

"Michael," Anna said, feigning an innocent tone, "whatever do you mean?"

Michael laughed, finished helping with the cleanup, and headed home.

***

Chela and Anna returned to Anna's apartment. "Well," she asked Chela, "What do you think of Warren?"

"He's very nice. He treated me like a lady the entire evening. When we went through the buffet line, he insisted I go first and made sure I saw everything that was available. He pulled out my chair for me at the dining table, and before he sat down, he asked if there was anything else I needed. I don't remember the last time a man treated me that nicely. And you can't imagine how much joy we got out of comparing our birding experiences."

Chela thought for a moment. "No. That's not accurate—you can't imagine how much joy we got out of *sharing* our birding experiences with each other. I could see in his eyes that he was imagining the birds in the surroundings that I described—but I'm still worried we will run out of things to talk about."

"Ask him about that. You might be surprised."

Chela planned to do just that.

The next day was cool but sunny. Michael and Anna squeezed into the back of Warren's two-door Jeep, Chela climbed in the front, and they all drove to Tiger Mountain.

When they arrived, Warren took out a pair of binoculars for Chela. "These are great birding binoculars," he told her excitedly.

Chela looked through them and commented that she was amazed at their clarity.

The group started hiking, but it really wasn't much of a hike because Warren and Chela kept stopping to listen to, or look for, yet another bird.

Michael and Anna decided to leave the birders behind and head off to the top of the mountain by themselves.

During their hike, Chela stopped and turned to Warren. "Warren, I want to ask you something. I have really enjoyed the time we've had together, but I hope that my lack of technical knowledge won't be a problem for you. Will it?"

He grinned at her. "Chela, I spend eight-hours-a-day, five- days-a-week, with technical people and I have never had the slightest desire to spend time with them outside of work. Your sister practically ordered me to show up at her and Michael's party. I couldn't refuse her because she's been so nice to me."

His smile grew. "I know now, it was a setup. I was annoyed at first that she thought a good-looking woman like you would want to spend time with an ordinary-looking guy like me, but when we started sharing our interest in birding, and the joy we find in nature, I saw your face light up. At that moment, I felt our relationship beginning. I think we will continue to see it grow from our wonderful set of shared interests. Besides all that, I think you're one of the nicest people I've ever met."

As they walked, Chela wondered if Warren was right. This could be a great beginning for a relationship, but she was concerned that the shared interests would not be enough. As smart as he was, Chela wasn't sure that Warren would need her.

When they arrived back at Anna's apartment after a wonderful day on the mountain, Chela announced, "Warren is going to take me over to his place in the morning to show me his birdfeeders."

Warren gave her a surprised look. "I am?" Chela stared at him for a moment.

He clued in then. "Oh yes, I forgot. We did plan to do that."

***

The next morning Warren picked her up after breakfast and they drove to his one-story craftsman-style-home.

Warren gave Chela a full tour. It had an L-shaped living and dining room with three bedrooms. The interior was tidy, but almost every horizontal surface, except the floors, had piles on them—piles of magazines, books, neatly folded clothing and towels, and various flyers and brochures that had been left at the front door.

"I apologize for the mess," Warren said. "I have trouble being organized at home, so I keep everything out where I can see it."

"You have nice furniture and lots of closets. Why don't you put things away in them? If you put the same things in the same place each time, you won't forget what's there."

"That's easy for you to say." Warren laughed.

Chela smiled. "Pick a room and we'll organize it together."

Warren seemed pleased that she would take the time to help him. "Let's start in the living room," he suggested.

"Okay, let's start by getting all your clothing into your bedroom."

As Warren moved clothing, Chela was filling the dressers and walk-in closet. She had Warren bring the dark colored towels into the master bathroom where she put them in the little linen closet. She organized all the soaps and things that were on the tops of the bathroom vanities.

"Warren," Chela asked, "where do you put your dirty clothes?" "I put them in the washing machine. When it's full, I run a load."

Chela had wondered why Warren's clothes were always wrinkled, and now she knew.

"Why don't we run what's in the machine now and we can put all your clothes away. You can start the week with all clean clothes."

"Chela, this is lovely. How can I thank you?"

"We girls from New Mexico are high maintenance. We need lots of hugs to get us through the day."

"I think I can afford that." He wrapped his arms around her and they engaged in a long embrace.

Then Chela pushed away. "That's enough for now. Breaktime's over."

Warren couldn't help but laugh at her remark. "I can't remember the last time I laughed so much."

They went back to the living room and Chela asked about all the piles of magazines. "Most of these don't even seem to have been read," she told him.

"I stack them up when they come, figuring I'll get to them later, but I only read one of the birding magazines, plus one fly fishing magazine."

"If you're not reading them, why are you continuing to pay for them?"

Warren replied with excitement. "I have a great system with my bills. As soon as I receive a bill, I write a check for it the same day and put it in the mail. That way I'm never late." He paused or a moment, as if pondering what he had just said. "That's not too good, is it?"

"We'll worry about that another day. Meanwhile, why don't you take the magazines you're not reading out to the recycling bin? That will just about clear out the living room. How about if I start on the kitchen? Maybe I can make us some lunch."

He agreed and started sorting through the magazines as Chela walked into the kitchen.

She checked inside the refrigerator, but all she found was a container of orange juice that looked so old, it might have crossed the ocean with Columbus. The countertops were covered with prepackaged food and canned goods. She also spotted a beautiful set of high-quality German kitchen knives, in a lovely wood block. They looked unused. There was a nice food processor and a large mixer, both of which still had their price tags attached. The can opener, however, looked well-used.

Chela noticed a gorgeous set of pots and pans that looked like they were stainless steel with a copper core, but the only ones that looked used were a pasta strainer and small saucepan.

When she moved some things off the barely-used stove, she was surprised to find that it was a Viking, like her father had in his restaurant. She knew she could make some incredible meals in this kitchen, but had to do some shopping for fresh ingredients first.

When Warren had the magazines removed from the living room, the space was usable again.

"Off to the market," Chela declared.

They returned with seasonings, crab, shrimp, three types of cheeses, two different types of peppers, salad fixings, limes, onions, a bottle of white wine and soft drinks. Chela rinsed a cup of rice and started it cooking in Warren's never-used rice cooker. She used the limes and fresh cilantro to prepare shrimp ceviche.

Then she directed Warren to prepare a salad for them while she stuffed Ancho peppers with pepper jack cheese, *queso blanco*, and crab. She dipped the peppers in an egg mixture and then fried them.

Warren cleared off half the dining room table and set out plates and silverware for the two of them. He opened a bottle of wine and was filling two wine glasses when Chela started bringing in serving platters of the food they had prepared.

"Chela, I don't think my house has ever smelled this wonderful before," he said.

During lunch they talked about food, birds, and relationships. The more they talked, the closer they grew. After that they spent a couple more hours organizing Warren's house and then proceeded out to his backyard to observe his aviary. They sat together on an Adirondack styled loveseat.

"I love having someone to share my aviary with," Warren told Chela.

She beamed back at him. "I love that I'm the one who gets to share this with you."

Suddenly they heard a sound like that of a very angry bee— except that it was a hummingbird.

"Oh my," Chela said, amazed to see a Rufous Hummingbird at Warren's hummingbird feeder.

"They migrate up here all the way from Mexico," Warren reminded her.

"He's certainly enjoying your feeder. I wonder if he stopped at my feeder in New Mexico on his way up here." She giggled. "Maybe I was a Rufous Hummingbird in a previous life and that's why I came up here."

Warren laughed. "That's a good enough reason for me."

As the afternoon turned into evening, Warren suggested that they have dinner at a little family-owned Italian restaurant that was within walking distance from his home.

"It's a fun place with a fixed-price. There's no menu but you get whatever Mama Michaela feels like cooking that night. There are at least seven courses and the desserts are to die for. She serves it all family style."

As they entered the restaurant, Chela observed two rows of tables set end to end. As people sat down at the tables, bottles of wine were placed on them. Warren leaned in and whispered that he was glad that Chela could make friends with the people around them and engage them in conversation so easily. He joked that it took pressure off him to make conversation with the strangers.

Chela smiled and gave his hand a little squeeze. She loved the group setting. The conversation was light and lively. She was proud every time shy Warren added the occasional remark. He even made a few very funny jokes that made fun of his software career. The only interruptions to the happy banter occurred when Mama Michaela brought out the next course.

Chela noted the wide range of tastes and textures presented with each course. She was also quite pleased that Warren had

suggested a restaurant with a social atmosphere that she would enjoy. Chela felt that he had her in mind, thinking that Warren wouldn't choose a place like this for himself. She gradually, and thoughtfully, brought Warren into many of the conversations. Warren, she decided, had a great sense of humor but was generally too shy to use it.

As they walked home, Chela thanked Warren for taking her to Mama Michaela's. "It was a wonderful meal and we dined with so many nice people. I know you're not a social butterfly like me. The idea that you took me to a place that you wouldn't necessarily go to, but thought I would enjoy, made the evening extra special for me."

Warren was glowing from her praise.

He told her, "I'm glad you enjoyed it. I've enjoyed our entire day together."

On the way back to his house, Warren was quiet, as if he was wracking his brain trying to think of something. Chela wondered if it was the same thing she was thinking about.

When they returned to his house, Chela suggested that they sit outside for a while. Since it was getting cold, Warren got a blanket and carefully wrapped it around Chela as she sat down on the Adirondack loveseat again.

With a big grin, Chela stated, "I'm sorry, Warren, but I won't be warm enough under this blanket by myself." She held up one side of the blanket, inviting a smiling Warren to get under it with her.

He sat down next to her and she tucked the blanket around both of them. Warren put his arm behind her head and across her shoulders. She looked up at him and they shared a long kiss.

"Chela, I was thinking about tomorrow and I was wondering—"

She was glad they were on the same page. Chela smiled.

"Thank you for asking me, Warren. I've been thinking about it too, and I would love to spend the night with you, so we can get an early start on tomorrow."

Warren looked a bit surprised. "Chela," he began, "I wasn't— I mean, I didn't mean to sug—"

Chela suddenly realized that Warren was too shy to actually ask her to stay the night, he must have been thinking about planning a date for the next day. Still, she knew what she wanted and decided to read his hesitation as agreement. "You mean, you didn't mean to suggest we had to start work first thing in the morning?"

Warren's cheeks flushed red, as he seemed to catch on. "Oh.

Yes, right. We should plan a hearty breakfast first."

That may not have been what he had meant, but Chela was glad that Warren had the good sense not to try and get a different answer. They stayed outside for hours watching the stars in the incredibly clear night sky.

Then as they got into bed, Chela saw that Warren appeared nervous. When they started making love it was obvious to Chela that Warren had had few, if any, partners before her. Instead of caressing her, it was more like his hands were exploring her.

If Warren hadn't had many partners, Chela knew that he would be concerned about his performance with her. She had enough experience, however, so it was easy to guide him to do the things that she enjoyed.

As their lovemaking ended, Chela was pleased to see that Warren continued to hold her. "Warren, that was amazing and I love how you hold me." Chela placed little kisses all over Warren's pleased face.

They fell asleep holding each other—two small town kids who found joy doing simple things with each other, in and around a big city.

Within a few weeks Chela moved all her things from Anna's apartment to Warren's house. They were two people that you would never pick out of a crowd, unless you could somehow see the glow which emanated from the joy their relationship created.

Warren let Chela take over paying his bills, and she made regular use of his lovely kitchen appliances to create a never-ending feast of daily meals. Each day he came home from work and told her how much he always looked forward to the smells that permeated the house when he arrived home. He also told her that he loved seeing her warm smile greeting him each day, too.

Chapter Five ~ Anna and Michael

LONG AFTER CHELA moved in with Warren, Anna arrived at work to find a birthday cake on her desk. She wasn't aware of any one at work who knew it was her birthday. The cake was decorated with two lovebirds kissing each other and the words Happy Birthday surrounding them. Anna thought it was odd to decorate a birthday cake with lovebirds.

There was an envelope with a letter inside that read.

Dearest, Anna,

There might be a couple in this world that is happier than we are, but we have yet to meet them. Thank you for bringing us together. Have a great day. Please don't be late to your birthday dinner which will be served at six-thirty tonight at our home.

All our love, Warren and Chela.

Anna looked back at the cake and noticed that one of the lovebirds had a C on its chest and the other a W. Anna was really happy for her sister and Warren.

Lydia, Anna's department administrator, walked by the office and came in. "What a lovely cake, Anna. But they put the M on upside down on the one lovebird and the C should be an A."

"What?"

Lydia smiled warmly. "M and A..."

"Oh. No." Anna felt her cheeks warm. "That's not for Michael and me. That's for Warren and Chela—my sister and her boyfriend."

Lydia grinned and drew out the word, "Right." She peered closer at the lovebirds. "Warren and Chela. Sure."

"Lydia, stop that. Help me get this out to the common area so everyone can have a piece of my birthday cake."

As Anna put out the cake, plates, and forks, she was thinking about Michael. She knew that a number of women in the company had all but begged him to go out with them. Various friends had told her that he let it be known that he was only good for a one-night stand and had no interest in having a long-term relationship. There was a rumor that Michael had been engaged to someone a-number-of-years ago, but she died suddenly, and he hasn't been serious about anyone since.

Anna was curious, but thought it was probably better that she didn't pry into Michael's personal life. He could have all the one night stands he wanted. As long as they could work together, that's all she cared about.

Over the next few months, Michael took Anna to a few concerts and plays. Anna thought it was nice to get out occasionally and Michael always treated her with respect. They occasionally went on walks with Chela and Warren, but that was the extent of it. Or so Anna thought.

It was Lydia who pointed out the change in their relationship. Initially, if someone acted in a confrontational way toward Anna, Michael would explode and direct a nasty verbal tirade in the direction of the individual involved.

After their first couple of months working and spending time together, however, Lydia said she was shocked to watch Anna step between Michael and someone who was about to be the object of his anger.

Anna had looked at Michael and calmly said to him, "Michael, I'll take care of this."

Everyone looked like they were waiting for Michael to explode at Anna. Instead, he said, "Okay, Anna," and calmly walked away.

On one such occasion, Anna turned to the individual who started the problem and quietly told him, "There is never a reason to talk to someone like that. We all have to get along."

The guy apologized to Anna and said he would walk over and apologize to Michael as well. Lydia then told her that not only was she a brilliant engineer, but she thought Anna was going to be a great leader as well.

She was the only person in the department who dared to get angry with Michael. Instead of arguing with her, he would just tell her he was sorry he had made her angry and would do his best to make sure it didn't happen again.

What amazed Lydia more than anything else was that the whole world knew that Michael and Anna belonged together—the whole world, it seemed, except for Anna and Michael.

***

The project was nearing the end of its six-month development-phase. The firmware that Anna and Michael were creating was complete. Only testing remained. Michael would be leaving for a new contract job in four weeks.

The consulting agency that represented Michael called and asked him to consult for a client's new firm, to help get their new avionics device running.

The agency also contacted Anna and asked if she would consider consulting for them, too. She told them that she had only been at her current job for six months and certainly did not have enough experience to consult.

Their reply was quite direct. "Ms. Cardozo, they asked for you by name. Apparently they worked with you at your present job. The client didn't just call up and say we need an engineer. They called up and said they needed Anna Cardozo. The client in Boise said he had never seen two engineers whose skills complimented each other like you and Michael Levin."

"But it's only a six-month-contract," Anna complained. "If I take it, I'll have to find another job in six-months."

"Ms. Cardozo, Michael Levin says you're one of the best engineers he's ever worked with. If he's only half right, it will be easy for me to find you another job in six months. Michael believes in your engineering ability, so I'm willing to pay you double what you're earning now if you take this job. At that rate you can work for six-months and wait six-months before you start another job."

Anna couldn't believe her ears. "Ms. Cardozo, are you still there?"

"Yes, I'm sorry. Did you say that you'll double my current salary?"

"That's what consultants receive. It will actually end up being more than that. You will be paid by-the-hour for as many hours as you work. Michael tells me you work fifty hours every week. That means you'll get double your current rate, plus twenty-five percent additional, if you work the same hours you do now."

"I need to think about this."

"Great. I'll overnight a contract to you. When you receive it, look it over, and let me know if you have any questions. I'm going to talk to Michael in an hour and I'll send both of your contracts out after I speak with him. Thanks, Ms. Cardozo. I'll be talking to you tomorrow."

Anna hung up the phone—her head was spinning. This was too much, too fast. She hadn't even had her first performance review at her current job. And what did Michael say about her? Would she be working with him on the consulting position? Why would someone pay her that much money?

That evening she called Michael to ask him some questions. He assured her they would be working together if she took the contract.

He told her that they would be doing the same thing at the new company as they were doing now, but it was smaller, so they would have more responsibility.

He also promised that she could find a short-term lease on an apartment in Boise that was one third the cost of her Seattle apartment. He also mentioned that Boise gets what he called real winter. Being from southern New Mexico, Anna wasn't sure what the phrase "real winter" meant.

Next, Anna called Chela. She described everything and told Chela that she wasn't happy about moving to another town where she wouldn't know anyone.

"Anna, Warren and I will come and visit you," Chela told her. "Besides, Michael will be there. You're always telling me how he watches out for you. I think this is a wonderful opportunity."

"Chela, Michael *only* watches out for me when it comes to business. That's all."

"Beloved sister, you sound like you're trying to convince yourself."

The next day, as promised, Anna received her contract. She went to Michael immediately. "My contract has a mistake," she said. "They didn't get the money right."

"Let me see it. They better *not* be trying to take advantage of your lack of experience."

Anna hated when Michael got that angry tone in his voice, accompanied by an ugly look on his face. Generally, however, she only heard it when he was protecting her from someone or something, so she let it go.

After reviewing the contract Michael chuckled rather raucously. "It's correct."

"Why are you laughing?"

"Because when you said the money was wrong, I thought you meant they were shortchanging you."

"But, Michael, that's more money than the agency and I talked about."

"Well, you deserve it, Anna. Besides, I told them that we were a team and if they wanted us, they had to pay us as a team. The company and the agency both agreed to that."

Anna looked down at her desk and smiled. He was treating her like a business partner. She filled out her contract and returned it to the agency. Then she wrote out a letter of resignation and handed it to Paul.

He gladly accepted it, which didn't surprise Anna. "Good luck on your new job," he told her.

In her nicest voice and with her biggest smile she told him, "Thank you, Paul. It's been wonderful working here and it's been a real *education* working under your supervision."

She reached out and shook hands with a surprised-looking Paul. She figured he was probably wondering if he had just been mocked, but was sure that he thought that she was too nice to do something like that.

Anna was able to smile a genuine smile—she was thinking that she was grateful that Michael had taught her that if you mock someone in a nice enough manner, they won't know what happened.

He'd told her this when she had asked about a sign he had over the desk at his apartment. It read, TACT—the ability to tell someone to go to hell and make him feel happy to be on his way.

"Good luck to you too, Paul," Anna said. "Have a nice life."

Chapter Six ~ Oliver and Ruth

OLIVER AND RUTH HAD been dating for a number of weeks, and Ruth thought they seemed to have a great start on building a strong relationship. One Saturday morning they were going to go to a car show together in Puyallup, Washington and then over to Gig Harbor to attend the annual art show.

They were having breakfast together at Ruth's apartment, when she received a phone call that would change her life.

"Ruth Case?" "Yes, this is Ruth."

"This is Sandra Hollings, from the State Child Welfare Agency."

Ruth's heart jumped into her throat—it couldn't be.

"Yes, Ms. Hollings. May I ask what this is regarding, please?"

"Ms. Case, I'll be direct. Twelve-years-ago, you gave a child up for adoption. That child has been returned to the foster care system. To make a long story short, her adoptive father abandoned the family when she was two-years-old, and her adoptive mother died of pancreatic cancer about four-weeks-ago. As you are her birth mother, we were hoping that you might consider making your daughter part of your current life. Not many people are willing to adopt a twelve-year-old child."

Ruth couldn't think—couldn't speak.

She was so stunned; she just stared at the phone.

"Ms. Case? I know this must come as quite a shock. Your mother gave me your number, but I didn't tell her why I wanted it. I just told her that there was some paperwork I needed from you."

"Oh."

"How about I give you a few days to think about this, and you can call me back?"

"Okay."

Ruth shook her head and released the breath she had been holding. "Give me your number please, Ms. Hollings."

She wrote down her number and hung up the phone. Only then did she realize that Oliver was staring at her, looking very concerned.

"Dare I ask who died?"

She slumped down onto her chair. "Oliver, this is difficult for me to wrap my head around, let alone tell you. I don't know what to think—I think I need some time to myself."

"You mean we've been good partners for a while, but now that something difficult has come along, you don't think you can share that with me? I thought you told me we were building a good relationship."

"Oliver, please. Try to understand. This is very difficult for me and you may not like what I have to say."

"I thought we agreed that partners work together in the good times *and* they especially work together in the bad times."

Oliver crossed the room and sat down next to Ruth, placing his arm around her shoulders.

Confused and scared, it was difficult to get the words out. Ruth opened her mouth silently a few times before she could actually utter the words out loud. "Oliver...I became pregnant when I was fifteen.

I gave the baby up for adoption. That phone call was a woman from Child Services asking me if I wanted my daughter back. Apparently her adoptive mother just died and her adoptive father abandoned her when she was two-years-old."

He gave her shoulders a squeeze. "So, when can we meet her?"

"What?"

"When can we meet your daughter?"

"Oliver, I don't think I'm ready to be a mother. I have to think about this."

"Ruth Case, there is a twelve-year-old girl out there who just lost the only mother she's ever known and she is living with strangers. She's probably scared out of her mind and there is a good chance that she is thinking about meeting *you* right now. You are the sweetest, nicest person I have ever met. I have no doubt that you would provide a loving home for this child, if that's what's needed. We don't even have to decide about that today."

He moved back to his own chair and sat down, leaning in toward her as he spoke. "We haven't talked much about it, but when I was a combat soldier in Iraq, I learned that there isn't always time to debate the merit of a solution, or worry about our own feelings. Sometimes, we just have to get busy *doing* to help someone else. Besides, now you have a partner to help you."

Ruth stared at Oliver. She allowed a nervous smile to spread across her face. "Thank you, Oliver. I agree with you. We should at least meet her."

Ruth made the necessary phone calls and then Oliver drove them over to the home of Holly's foster parents. She had been there for a little over six-weeks. They had been informed that Holly knew she was going to be meeting her birth mom, but didn't really care. Ms. Hollings had told Ruth that Holly viewed her as just another stranger in her life, just another person who had abandoned her.

When they saw Holly, Oliver looked as amazed as Ruth felt. Holly's face was an absolute copy of her own face—even Ruth could see it—although Holly didn't smile much. She was slim built, wearing a plain top and jeans. Her face was framed by dark, straight, shoulder-length hair.

The foster parents suggested the three of them walk up the street to a burger restaurant to have lunch. While they were in line waiting to order, Holly pointed out one of the neighborhood boys from her class at school.

He saw her and walked over. "Hey, it's Hollyhock, the new kid." He then swung his fist as if to hit Holly in the shoulder.

Holly grimaced in expectation of the blow, but it never came. Oliver had caught the boy's fist in the palm of his hand. "Hey, punk.

You ever lay a hand on her and I'll be on you like stink on shit. You got that?"

Ruth realized that she had never heard Oliver use such an angry tone and was shocked at the expression on his face. After years of turning wrenches, Oliver had forearms like steel and Ruth could see his grip was like a vise.

The boy clearly realized that Oliver had such a tight grip on his hand that he couldn't move it. "I was just kidding," the boy pleaded. "Remember me, punk. You don't ever touch her. You got that?"

Everyone stood there watching the exchange between Oliver and the boy, who seemed very frightened now.

He replied politely. "Yes, sir. That won't be a problem, sir. I'm sorry, Holly."

Oliver released the boy's hand and he hurried off with his friends.

Holly looked up at Oliver. "Thank you. He's been banging on me for the last few days. I imagine that will be the last time now—thanks to you."

The angry expression evaporated from Oliver's face and was immediately replaced with a kind smile. He looked warmly at Holly. "No problem, kiddo."

Holly looked at Oliver in such a way that Ruth supposed that was the first time she'd had a father figure to stand up for her. That made Ruth both sad and happy at the same time.

As they were eating, Holly told Oliver and Ruth that she enjoyed reading stories. "I like to write as well, but I'm not too good at that."

"I can certainly help you write, if you like," Ruth told her. "I'll think about it. I especially enjoy reading stories about family."

Holly got a flash of some emotion across her face when she said that. Anger? Remorse? Ruth wasn't sure.

Then Holly looked directly at Ruth. "I think I enjoy those, because I never really had a complete family. Not that I can remember, anyway."

Ruth's heart sank. It wasn't her fault. She had done the right thing—the only thing she could at the time. She had been just a child herself.

They engaged in more awkward conversation for a while, then returned to the foster family's home. Ruth suggested that Holly come over to her apartment on the following Saturday so they could continue to get to know each other.

Holly didn't seem too excited about that, but agreed. As they were about to leave, Holly stopped Oliver. "Thanks for...well...you know."

"I do know, and I'm looking forward to seeing you next Saturday."

Holly produced her first real smile of the day as she looked up at Oliver. "Me, too."

"I'm so glad you were there today," Ruth told Oliver as they drove back to Ruth's apartment. "I was so nervous. I couldn't think of things to say to her. I'm not sure I would have known what to do when that boy tried to hit her. Obviously, you did."

"It's simple. I'm a guy and I understand guy stuff. As young as he was, he might have thought that was cute."

"I was struggling to find things to talk about," Ruth said, "but it seemed easier for you. I think Holly likes you. I hope she begins to like me, too, and we can become close."

"I suspect that she's been through a lot of crap, the likes of which you and I probably can't imagine. She could be full of an amazing amount of anger. If she feels she's been repeatedly abandoned, it could take some time for her to trust us."

***

The following Saturday the threesome gathered at Ruth's apartment and went out for a walk. As they wandered, Ruth spoke from her heart. "Holly, I hope we can become friends. I know it will take time."

"All the adults in my life have abandoned me." Holly seemed to be speaking from her heart too—an angry one. "Starting with you!"

"I like you, and I haven't abandoned you," Oliver pointed out.

Holly seemed surprised by his answer. "How do you know you like me?"

"I'm a people person, and I like people until they give me a good reason not to like them."

"Aren't you just here to be with your girlfriend?"

Oliver stopped walking. "I didn't have to come today, but I liked the person we met last week. But if you're going to continue to talk in a rude manner, we can end this visit now."

Ruth was shocked at Oliver's words, and Holly looked the same.

"You don't know what I've gone through," Holly shouted.

Oliver calmly replied. "And you don't know what I've gone through, little lady, but I'm still managing to talk to you in a nice and respectful manner."

Well, that really seemed to surprise Holly. "What have you gone through?"

"Quite a bit actually, but it doesn't give me the right to speak to anyone in a rude manner."

Ruth was getting scared. She worried that if Oliver made Holly angry, it would ruin her chance of having a relationship with her daughter.

Holly stared quietly at Oliver for some time. She appeared to be realizing he expected good behavior from her and didn't mind telling her so. Her face softened into an *almost* smile. "I'm sorry I was talking that way," she said.

"Fine," Oliver told her. "Now, I think we should go down to the waterfront and see if we can get a ride on a sailboat."

"Great," shouted Holly, smiling at Oliver.

As they walked, a very-much-relieved Ruth held tight to Oliver's arm. Conversation the rest of the visit was rather generic, but Holly looked like she thoroughly enjoyed the wind and the waves during the sailboat ride.

***

The next few visits were similar in the sense that there was little conversation of anything meaningful. There was a schism between Ruth and Holly that neither one of them seemed to be able to bridge. Holly mostly went with Ruth to get out of the foster home. Gradually, she discovered that she looked forward to spending time with Oliver, though. No matter what she asked him, he gave her an honest answer—even if it was an answer that he knew she wouldn't like. Also, after he answered, he would ask her what *she* thought and always listened carefully to her response.

Holly was enthralled that Oliver respected what she thought. She wondered if all fathers listen to their daughters, the way Oliver listened to her.

In all her anger, Holly hadn't realized that whenever they talked, Ruth was listening to her as well. She simply saw Ruth as someone who had abandoned her and Holly wasn't going to give her a chance to do that again.

But Oliver...it was so weird with him. Whenever they picked her up, Holly loved seeing how happy he looked as soon as he saw her. He joked with her and made her laugh. He teased her and she could tease him back. He reprimanded her when her manners were lacking, and probably weirdest of all, was that she was starting to feel so uncomfortable when he reprimanded her, that she actually tried to behave nicer when she was around him. She didn't want to disappoint Oliver.

Chapter Seven ~ Michael and Anna

MICHAEL AND ANNA HAD agreed to drive to Boise together to start their new job. He drove to her apartment on Saturday morning to help her load things.

It was a beautiful day for a road trip. The weather was shirt-sleeve warm with a cool breeze blowing.

At the appointed time Anna looked out at the parking lot and saw Michael pulling in. He was driving his motorhome, which was towing a huge enclosed trailer. Michael opened one of the doors on the motorhome's storage bays and removed a little two wheeled hand truck that he wheeled up the sidewalk.

Anna opened the door. "It will be easy to follow you to Boise when you're driving that monster."

"Follow? I guess I didn't explain myself properly. Let's take some of your boxes down and I'll show you what I meant. I have an empty storage bay in the motorhome for your things."

They carried boxes down to the motorhome and Michael opened one of the storage bays. It had a movable tray in the bottom. The tray was as wide as the bay. Michael pulled it out and started loading boxes. Then he led Anna to the back of the trailer behind the motorhome. He inserted a key into a switch and the back door of the trailer started pivoting down until it reached the driveway.

"You can put your car in here for the drive down if you like," Michael explained to Anna. "I will secure your car with the straps hanging on the walls. It will be safe in here. You can see how I secured my little car on the upper level. I'll do the same for yours. Also, you can see that we will have space in front of your car, so we can put your furniture in there. That's why I told you not to sell any of it."

"I guess I had pictured you showing up in one of those rental trucks."

"No, the motorhome has a big diesel engine, lots of room inside, and incredible towing capacity. When I take jobs out of town, I always try to take her with me. I especially want her with me when I'm near the big National Parks. If you love mountains, we have the chance to go camping and visit some of the world's most majestic mountains while we're working in Boise."

Anna had to admit to herself that she was nervous the way he used the word *we*. She certainly didn't think they were a couple and she intended to keep things that way.

They loaded the rest of her boxes and then wrestled the four pieces of furniture out of her apartment and into his big trailer, which swallowed Anna's car and furniture with ease.

Michael pointed out that the rear bedroom of the motorhome had a lock on its door. He told Anna she could sleep in there and he would sleep on the convertible sofa in the living area.

Michael had never done anything disrespectful toward Anna in the six-months she had known him, so she figured those sleeping arrangements would be okay. It would only be for one- or two-nights anyway.

Chela and Warren stopped by to see them off. Anna screamed when she saw that Chela was wearing an engagement ring, and Chela bounced with excitement telling Anna all about it.

"We went to dinner last night at a lovely restaurant on the edge of Puget Sound. Warren proposed to me right in front of the whole restaurant. *Hermana*, it was so romantic!"

Anna gave her sister a big hug and then gave Warren one too.

He blushed.

Michael shook Warren's hand and then gave Chela a hug. Anna noticed Chela whisper something to him and then he whispered something to her.

"Congratulations. You guys are going to continue to be a great couple," Michael told them.

"Let us know when you're settled in Boise and we'll come out to visit," Warren said back.

Anna closed up the apartment, and then Michael gave Chela and Warren a tour of his motorhome.

Chela commented that she was amazed at how luxuriously appointed it was. With cherry wood stain on the interior walls and cabinets, plus supple cream-colored leather on the couches and chairs, the motorhome was a cross-country traveler's dream.

She sat in the co-pilot's seat. "Wow, Anna, you're going to feel like a queen riding up here."

Michael wore a Cheshire-cat-grin on his face. "Warren, I know we've been really busy at work and you haven't shown Chela your *camper* yet. Why don't you drive over to the storage garage after you leave us? If Chela likes your camper, you should bring it out when you visit us."

"Great idea," Warren said, grinning too.

The two sisters shrugged and looked at each other as if to inquire what all the grinning was about. Then as Anna said good- bye to her sister, she asked what she had whispered to Michael.

"I told him to take good care of my sister. He said that would be easy, because you take such good care of him."

Anna was shocked that Michael had said that. She didn't think she did much to take care of him.

Chela and Warren drove off and Anna and Michael got into his motorhome. Their journey began with Anna's head in a state of confusion over Michael's remark. She finally decided that he must have been talking about their business relationship, although it was obvious that her sister thought he was talking about more than that. She reclined her seat and quickly fell asleep.

Chapter Eight ~ Warren and Chela

WARREN AND CHELA DROVE over to the storage garage. "I'm sure I've told you there is a big RV campground next to my parents' restaurant in New Mexico," she told him. "I was amazed the first time I saw one of those little campers— a popup I think they called it. A small SUV was towing it into the campground. When it was parked, I saw six children and their parents get out of the SUV. I couldn't believe that they were all going to stay in that flat little camper."

She shook her head. "Then they unhitched the small trailer and the father got out a crank. He started cranking and the top of the camper started rising. When it was fully raised, the father and mother started pulling out the ends and zipping up the sides. Suddenly, there was room for everyone in there. It was like magic. I always thought that would be a wonderful way for a family to travel together."

"I'm sure that's nice, Chela, but my camper is a little different than a popup. I hope you'll like it too."

Chela smiled at him. "Warren, as long as we're together, I don't care what your camper is like. I'm certain we'll have a good time traveling in it."

Warren drove up to a tall, wide door at the storage garage, parked his Jeep in front it, and put a key into the lock. As the door retracted, Chela didn't find a popup camper, but instead she found a forty-foot motorhome, identical to Michael's, but with a different exterior paint scheme.

"I accompanied Michael when he was shopping for his motorhome," Warren told her. "I knew nothing about these monsters, but thought it would be perfect for camping, and big enough to tow my Jeep and little boat for birding and fly fishing. We bought them used and paid cash. Michael has been incredibly gracious with his time teaching me how to maintain it properly. We bought the motorhomes last winter. We've only been camping with them once, just before I met you."

Chela was floored. When she got over the shock of seeing that Warren's camper was a beautiful motorhome, she gave Warren a kiss on the cheek and began exploring the interior. She opened every cupboard and drawer. She was glad to see it was organized better than his house.

"Chela, my new license plates arrived," Warren said. "Will you help me put them on the motorhome?"

Chela thought it was strange that Mr. Fix It wanted help to do something as simple as installing license plates. She followed him around to the front of the motorhome. He handed her the envelope with the plates.

"Go ahead and take one out for me, please."

She pulled out the first plate. It read 4MYRUFUS. "Warren, I can't believe you did this for me."

Poor Warren must have nearly suffocated she kissed him so long and hugged him so hard.

After they installed the plates, they went back into the motorhome. Chela glanced around at all the windows. "There's really a lot of light that gets in here with all these windows. When you're parked in a campground at night, you don't leave the windows open like that do you?"

"No, watch this." Warren opened a panel and moved a switch.

Gradually, curtains covered all the windows.

"That provides a lot of privacy," Chela said with a twinkle in her eye and a big grin on her face. "Maybe we should start practicing now, so when we really go camping, we will know how to do things in here."

Warren started giggling like a little kid, took Chela's hand, and led her back to the bedroom.

The following weekend they took their "camper" out to Lake Chelan where Warren started teaching Chela fly-fishing. She was in heaven, even though she didn't catch anything her first time out. She did learn a secret that all fly-fishermen know—God put the best fly-fishing streams in the most beautiful places on His green earth. Chela was absolutely entranced by the scenery she observed while they fished.

During the return drive Chela commented, "Just think, when we have a family we will be able to drive out to wherever Michael and Anna are living. Our families, with all our children, will be traveling together to visit gorgeous places. We're going to make our own family wagon train."

Chapter Nine ~ Oliver and Ruth, plus Holly

ONE SATURDAY MORNING, HOLLY finally asked Ruth the big unspoken question. "Why did you give me up for adoption?"

Ruth sighed. "Well, Holly, I was just fifteen-years-old. I thought it was best that you be raised by adults in a loving family, rather than by an inexperienced teenager."

"You didn't even take the time to get to know me. You just dumped me with some strangers."

"I didn't just dump you. They told me you would be adopted by a loving family. I had no idea what happened to you until child services called me."

"But how could you give away your own daughter?"

Ruth's face began turning red. "Believe me, it wasn't easy. I have agonized over that decision for years. I did what I thought was the best for you."

"You didn't do anything to see if I was okay! If you did, you would have known how awful it was."

"The adoption agency wouldn't let me do that, even if I wanted to."

"But you never even tried to find me."

"Holly, I was told that you had been adopted by a loving family. I had no way of knowing what was going on in your life."

"If you cared, you would have found a way," Holly shouted.

Ruth began crying. She covered her face with her hands, stood up, silently walked to her bedroom, and closed the door.

Oliver looked at Holly in a way that made her tremble inside.

He unleashed his thoughts on her.

"Well you've certainly learned how to hurt someone's feelings in your young twelve-years! Now you listen to me. Ruth Case is the nicest, kindest woman I've ever met. She's not an immature fifteen-year-old anymore. She is one fine woman. I know you're angry about what's happened in your life. You have every right to feel that way, but now you have a chance to finish your childhood with someone who is amazing. She is more than ready to teach you how to live by her wonderful values, which will allow you to choose a nice life for yourself."

Holly stood there motionless, unable to speak.

"I'm sad about what happened to you during the last twelve-years too, Holly, but starting today you can have a nice life with someone who would do anything for you. Not many children are lucky enough to complete their childhood with a loving family after experiencing all the crap you've gone through. You told me how easy it was for you to learn Spanish. Did you know your mother is a language professor at the university and she teaches Russian, Italian, and Chinese? She's also fluent in three other languages and is learning yet another one."

Holly's eye's opened wide in surprise. She hadn't known that. She realized she hadn't really taken the time to get to know Ruth.

"That's right," Oliver continued. "You get your language ability from your mom. More important than any of that stuff, however, she's willing to provide you a place in a loving home. You haven't even met your grandparents, and let me tell you, Ruth's parents are some fine people who will be dying to meet you. That

woman in the other room is crying right now because of what you said to her and how much it hurts her that the last twelve-years turned out so badly for you."

Oliver paused as if he was letting the words sink in.

"She did what she thought was best for you—she was just three-years-older than you are now. Do you think it was easy for her? She'd do anything for you. Now she's willing to make you part of her life. You should be sick and ashamed of how you just acted. I can take you back to the foster family right now, *or* you can go apologize to your mother, because she cares about you and would like an opportunity to make a great life for you."

Holly was deeply saddened by Oliver's obvious disappointment in her. With tears in her eyes, she slowly stood up and took a few tentative steps toward Ruth's bedroom. She looked back at Oliver. "Would *you* do anything I ask?"

Oliver looked at her, still serious. "No. I would do whatever I thought was in your best interest, whether you liked it or not."

Holly turned her face away from Oliver for a moment, and then she ran back and threw her arms around him.

"Thank you, Oliver," she told him. "I believe you. You *do* want what's best for me."

Holly slowly walked down the hallway and knocked on the door to Ruth's bedroom.

***

Oliver gave them some time to be alone so they could talk and cry, and when it sounded like they had cried as much as they could and probably hugged a few times too, Oliver yelled down the hall.

"Ruth, we need to get going if we're going to buy an outfit for Holly."

They came out and Oliver drove them over to the big mall in Bellevue. Holly looked in heaven trying on dresses, and Ruth looked equally enchanted to be helping her. Oliver couldn't help but smile, as he saw the seeds of a relationship forming between Ruth and Holly. He observed Ruth listening carefully to whatever Holly said. Holly was surely realizing that her thoughts and ideas were important to Ruth too.

Every time Holly tried on another dress, she modeled it for Ruth and Oliver and asked how she looked, still focusing on what Oliver thought. He realized Holly felt close enough to him that she was genuinely concerned that he liked the clothes they buy for her. He remembered what the father of a Jewish friend had once told him.

He'd said, "When my wife smiles at me, its sunshine, but when my daughter smiles at me, it's heaven." Oliver was starting to know what he meant.

When they had finally settled on a lovely dress, Oliver asked in an innocent tone, "Doesn't she need a matching purse and shoes?"

"Well of course she does," Ruth exclaimed.

She seemed so happy and it looked like she was having as much fun shopping as Holly was. She mentioned to Oliver that she hoped they would continue to enjoy their time together, so afterwards they went to a small cafe for lunch.

When they had first met, Holly didn't have much in the way of table manners. But now, Oliver watched with joy in his heart, because for the first time Holly was starting to imitate Ruth's impeccable table manners. She started sitting up straight like Ruth did, she kept her left arm in her lap, and she unfolded her napkin and put it on her lap as soon as food arrived at the table. Holly started using her knife and fork just like her mom. Oliver realized that it was only now, after their long talk in the morning, that Holly seemed to interact with Ruth.

After loading all their bags in the trunk of their car, they headed to a movie theatre and enjoyed the afternoon matinee. Then after dinner at Ruth's, they prepared to take Holly back to the foster home.

"Could I leave my new clothes here?" Holly asked, "I don't want the kids at the foster home to mess them up."

"Of course, Holly. I'll put them away for you."

"Holly, next week Ruth and I are going to a very nice restaurant for dinner. We won't be home until late, so we would like to ask your foster parents if you can stay the night. That is, if you think you'd like to do that."

"I'd love to go to a nice restaurant and spend the night," Holly said.

Oliver suspected, based on everything she had told him so far, the small Greek café where they'd had lunch the first day may have been the nicest place she had ever eaten.

Chapter Ten ~ Michael and Anna

AS ANNA AND MICHAEL passed the desolate desert-like areas east of Yakima and began driving south through vineyards on their way to Richland, Anna was thinking that she was quite proud of her relationship with Michael. It was strictly professional, and it seemed clear to her that she could have her engineering career and not have to worry about having another person in her life.

She was proud of her independence and intended to keep it that way. Although she did remember feeling momentarily lonely when she found out that Michael was going to be leaving their former project. Anna had reprimanded herself at the time for thinking that she would miss him. She'd reminded herself that she was an educated, independent woman who didn't need a man in her life.

Anna tried her best to ignore her developing feelings toward Michael. No matter how hard she tried, however, those thoughts and feelings just kept creeping back into her mind. More and more often, Anna found herself looking at Michael's body and wondering what it would be like to hold him against her. She attributed that to being young and tried to convince herself she should be more mature.

A few weeks before their trip to Boise Anna had awakened one morning in a sweat. She had been dreaming of Michael making love to her, and she'd jumped out of bed and showered in water that was as cold as she could stand. That really didn't help much. She kept remembering how much she enjoyed the warm sensation of Michael holding her naked body against his in her dream. For the next three days at work, she couldn't look directly at him.

As Michael pulled the motorhome off the interstate, Anna was amazed to find they were in yet another beautiful part of Washington State. The area was surrounded by soft rolling hills and was very unlike the jagged Cascade and Olympic Mountains she was used to seeing around the Seattle area.

Michael drove slowly over to the office of the campground where he registered them for two-nights and secured a pull-through campsite that was located next to the wide and fast-flowing Columbia River. It was midafternoon by then. Michael leveled the motorhome and hooked up the water and electric lines.

After they were settled, he and Anna went for a walk around the campground and along some trails that paralleled the Columbia River. Then upon their return, Anna directed Michael in helping her make *posole* soup for dinner. Michael was in charge of chopping vegetables and filling the soup pot with chicken stock.

Instead of the pork she grew up with, Anna cubed grilled chicken breasts along with Ancho chilies, porcini mushrooms, hominy, black pepper, garlic, shallots, and lots of cilantro to make the *posole* soup.

"This soup is perfect for cool days. If it's not hot enough, you can add green pepper sauce," Anna teased Michael.

"I'm sure it will be spicy enough for me," Michael replied.

Michael's idea of spicy and Anna's idea of spicy were worlds apart. Michael referred to Anna's preferred level of spiciness as Flame On, and she constantly teased him about his inability to enjoy spicy southwestern dishes. However, when she cooked for the two of them, she always made sure that Michael could enjoy what she had made.

Her grandmother had taught Anna how to cook and how to vary the level of spiciness. She certainly wanted Michael, and all of her friends, to appreciate her cooking as she felt it was an honor to serve her grandmother's recipes.

As the early evening air was cooling off and a light breeze began blowing across the Columbia and into their campsite, they dressed in sweaters and headed outside to have dinner on a picnic table at their campsite. While Anna set the table, Michael brought logs out and placed them in the fire pit and then set up two folding chairs right next to it.

Michael sat down at the picnic table and tasted the soup. "Anna, this soup is perfect for a cool evening like this."

Anna was pleased. "Thank you, Michael. I'm glad you like it."

After dinner they remained in front of the campfire. It was a clear evening and the air continued to cool off.

She decided to bring up what Chela had told her before they left. "Michael, you told my sister that I take good care of you. I really don't think that's true, except in a business sense. We work together as a team. That's all."

"Anna, I have lots of rough edges. You smooth them out for me. Whenever you get angry with me, I know I've done something wrong and I feel bad that I've upset you. You're the only person in the last two-years, since my fiancé Sharon died, that can make me feel like that. In fact, from the moment I met you, I had a feeling deep inside me that I should do whatever I could to make your life easier. I also honestly believe that Sharon put us together."

"Michael, the only time I get upset with you is when you do something that could damage our business relationship. That's all we have—a business relationship."

Looking into the fire, Michael's expression went from neutral to a small smile. "Yes, Anna."

As the air was getting chilly, Michael went back into the motorhome and found two thick Pendleton wool blankets that they each used to wrap around themselves to ward off the cool evening air.

While he was inside, Anna thought about what Michael had just said. He returned with the blankets and draped one over her. "Michael," she said, "maybe it's time that you tell me about Sharon."

***

"Well, the funny thing is, I actually dated her friend Janet first. We got along great, but we had different religious backgrounds. She had invited me to help with a party at Sharon's place. We all went out for a walk that afternoon—I discovered later, that was Janet's attempt at seeing how Sharon and I interacted before telling me."

"Before telling you what, Michael?" Anna asked.

"Before telling me that Sharon and I were more suited for a relationship together than she and I were," Michael replied. "Janet told me she thought she and I didn't have a future together, but that she believed Sharon and I did."

"Really? You mean to say she wanted you to date her best friend?"

"Yes, exactly. I was annoyed at first, but after Sharon and I talked about it, and we spent more time together, I realized Janet had done something incredibly unselfish and she had a point about the religions. Sharon and I did have many values in common and we decided it was worth trying."

"At first, I wasn't comfortable acting like Sharon and I were a couple in front of Janet, but it didn't seem to bother either of them, so I vowed to get over it too."

"That would be strange," Anna agreed.

"After a week together, we both felt like we'd known each other all our lives—like we were meant to be together. Two-weeks after that, Sharon moved in with me."

"That was fast," Anna said.

"It was," he agreed. "We got engaged six-months into the relationship and started planning a wedding to occur around the anniversary of our first year together."

Michael got quiet then. He was having a hard time recounting the story. It had been such a difficult time for him, but he felt Anna deserved to know.

She sat silently, giving him the time he needed before continuing.

"Three-weeks before our wedding, we were out running. About half way through the run, Sharon stopped and put a hand on each side her head. I could tell she was in a great deal of pain."

He felt his eyes getting moist and he turned to look away. "We didn't know it then, but Sharon had a genetic defect that had caused a wall of an aorta in her brain to be abnormally thin. A tiny tear had occurred—Sharon barely felt it—but when she stopped running, her heart had to suddenly work harder to get blood from her legs back up to her heart. The extra pressure caused the tiny tear to become much larger in the weakened aorta."

"Oh, Michael. That must have been so horrible."

He nodded and swallowed down the lump in his throat. "Sharon felt a tremendous pain in her head, collapsed, and was dead before she hit the ground. She had no pulse and wasn't breathing. I thought she had suffered a heart attack, so I started CPR, waiting for the ambulance to come. By the time we arrived at the hospital, I could tell from the paramedics' faces that she wasn't coming back."

He managed to look back at Anna then. She was wearing such a look of compassion, Michael felt able to finish the story.

"The doctors told me she had died from a major rupture of a vessel in her brain. They assured me that there was nothing I could have done. Then I made the most difficult phone call of my life, to inform Sharon's parents that their daughter, the light of their lives, had just died. Instead of a wedding with Sharon—I attended her funeral."

Anna shook her head in disbelief. "Oh, Michael, how did you ever get through that?"

He shrugged. "I did what I had to. I sold the house we had shared and moved to a smaller place. I boxed up the audio system— it reminded me of Sharon. Then, the *Seder* plate, the *Shabbat* candleholders, the *Havdala* candle, the spice box, the *Hanukah* Menorah, and the other *Judaica* that we had purchased together, went into cartons, so I wouldn't have to look at them. I went out of my way to avoid doing anything that reminded me of our time together. I tried to make myself as numb as possible. I wasn't happy. I wasn't sad. I just existed."

Anna was speechless. She looked at Michael with such sadness in her eyes. He knew that he was doing the right thing in opening up to her.

"My father started giving me regular lectures about getting on with life. He was right, of course, but there was no way that I wanted to open my heart up again...until I met you, Anna."

Chapter Eleven ~ Oliver and Ruth

ON THE DAY OF the special dinner Oliver stated, "You know, Holly, I think you need to help Ruth buy an outfit. I've seen her closet, and she needs something new to wear tonight."

"Oh wow, that would be fun. What do you say, Ruth? Can I help you pick out something?"

"Well, we're going to a really fancy dinner, so I think it would be nice of you to help me."

Holly was in heaven—amazed, and quite pleased, that Ruth would try on outfits that Holly thought would look nice.

Oliver commented that Holly had an excellent sense of style and color and that he knew that was quite rare in a twelve-year-old. He said Ruth always dressed beautifully and had an amazing sense of style as well. He told them that at times he thought Ruth and Holly sounded more like sisters, than mother and daughter.

Ruth appeared jubilant with her growing relationship with Holly as they headed off to the hair salon for Ruth's appointment. When they walked in, Oliver told the receptionist that they had an appointment for Case.

She looked at her appointment book. "Yes, Ruth and Holly."

Holly's eyes opened wide. "I can't believe this. You even set up a hair appointment for me. Thank you, Ruth."

"Don't thank me," Ruth said. "My head has been spinning the entire day because I've been so busy shopping for my clothes. Oliver must have called and added your name to the appointment."

Both of them looked at Oliver, who shrugged his shoulders and feigned innocence.

Holly was nervous and wondered if Ruth realized that this was the first-time she had ever been to a hair salon. She and Ruth looked through some style magazines until Holly picked out a haircut she liked.

When Holly got out of the stylist's chair, she immediately turned to Oliver. "Well? How do I look?"

With a huge grin on his face he declared, "Sophisticated lady, I like that look."

Holly turned to Ruth, who also told her how great she looked. After the appointment, they returned to Ruth's apartment. While Ruth was deciding which shoes to wear with her new dress, Holly expressed a concern to Oliver that he and Ruth weren't married. "I don't want to be a part of a family that comes apart again."

"I understand your concern. There are no guarantees in life. We really don't know what will happen tomorrow, let alone in the future. We can only do the best we can each day and plan our lives for a successful outcome. Besides, you need to get ready for tonight. The three of us are going to have a wonderful evening."

Holly was so happy that Oliver said the three of us. She was thrilled that he wanted her to be part of a special evening that he had set up for Ruth many weeks ago.

They went to a lovely restaurant and their table had a romantic view of the gradual sunset over Puget Sound. Oliver was wearing his nicest suit, which Ruth had helped him pick out. He said he was quite proud of *his girls* and how lovely they looked.

Many people in the restaurant turned to look at the two girls who were holding Oliver's arms as they walked to their table. After they were seated, the waiter came over to ask what they wanted to drink.

"For you, ma'am?" he asked Ruth.

She asked for a glass of Riesling to drink with dinner. "And for your sister?" he said looking at Holly.

Holly ordered a soft drink, thinking that she looked so sophisticated that the waiter thought she was her mom's sister.

Oliver smiled. "The waiter just earned his tip on that one," he whispered to Ruth.

As Holly had never been to a fancy restaurant, she was a bit con-fused by the menu. Ruth must have noticed the consternation on Holly's face so she began suggesting different menu items that Holly might enjoy.

"It's okay to try something new. If you don't like it, just leave it and we'll take it home for one of Oliver's lunches."

Holly laughed and was relieved Ruth was watching out for her. She made sure Holly dressed as fine as anyone else in this restaurant. She had to admit to herself that Ruth was as nice a person as Oliver had told her.

And Oliver wasn't even her dad, but he treated her so nice from the first day they met. He wasn't even afraid to get angry with her when she had hurt Ruth's feelings.

When it was time for dessert, Holly told Ruth that she was full and didn't want any.

"Why don't we all share a dish of ice cream?" Oliver suggested. As three spoons and a lovely pewter dish with vanilla ice cream were placed on the table, Holly realized they were even sharing dessert like a family. She was starting to feel like she belonged with them.

***

Two-weeks-later they were at a lovely, small, Italian restaurant in Is-saquah. They were dressed in casual, but stylish attire. This time Hol-ly realized that heads were turning as she and Ruth entered the din-ing room. She walked as straight as she could with her head held high, like Ruth had taught her. Holly thought that Oliver was right. She is a sophisticated lady.

"I love this place," Oliver stated. "My folks used to bring me here when I was Holly's age."

They were seated at a table in the middle of the dining room, and the waiter brought a beautiful bouquet of flowers over to the table, setting them in front of Ruth.

"These are lovely," Ruth said. "I wonder why our table is the only one with flowers on it."

She gasped as Oliver took a small box out of his jacket pocket, kneeled at her side, and said, "Ruth Case, will you marry me?"

Ruth looked at Oliver, positively beaming. "Yes! Definitely, yes."

The people at the tables around them started applauding as Oliver placed the ring on Ruth's finger and he briefly kissed her.

Holly was nearly as excited as Ruth. She couldn't remember a day when two people who cared so much for each other, obviously cared so much for her, that they would make her a part of one of the most important days in their lives. Holly's eyes got teary.

Ruth asked, "What's wrong?"

"Nothing," Holly replied. "I'm happy. You guys make me feel so special. Thank you."

Oliver told her, "Believe me, little lady, having you with us makes every day we're together a special day for us."

Ruth added, "Holly, we're certainly full of joy that you're part of our lives."

As Oliver drove them home, Ruth said to Holly, "Your foster parents told me that you could stay the night with me you like."

"I would enjoy that," Holly told her mom.

When they arrived back at Ruth's apartment they said goodnight to Oliver and he headed back to his own apartment after giving Ruth a long kiss.

"Do we have to go to sleep right away?" Holly asked Ruth. "I'd like to talk to you about some things."

Ruth smiled. "I'll make us some popcorn and you pour us some cold drinks, just like I used to do with my college roommates when we stayed up late to talk."

Holly talked about her childhood and how difficult it was for her when she realized that she had been given up for adoption. She thought her adoptive mom, Candice, tried hard, but never really listened to her. Candice's idea of being a parent primarily consisted of giving orders.

"When her husband abandoned us, she had to take two-jobs. That left very little time for me—I know that's selfish and I really do respect what she tried to do for me. When she got sick with cancer, I had to go into foster care. That was the worst time because I had no idea what my future would be. It made me feel like I had been abandoned again."

Ruth, in turn, talked about the pain of not knowing what happened to her child.

"You were a part of me every day for nine-months and then you were gone. I felt you moving and growing inside me. I remember your little cry when you were born. But then you were gone. It was almost as if you had died, but I knew you were still alive. You probably won't know how painful that was until you have children of your own. Meeting you, after all these years, almost makes me feel like I have a chance to right a great wrong."

"How did you meet Oliver and how did you know he was the one for you?"

"Until I met Oliver, I really never had a relationship that meant anything. Ours started out in a terrible way. I feel guilty about it to this day. He had helped me with my car and then invited me to a party. Briefly, I dismissed him because he worked with his hands and I was this genius intellectual, who shouldn't be seen with someone like him."

Ruth took a drink of her soda and continued. "My father— God love him—explained in no uncertain terms how wrong I was. I went over to Oliver's apartment to apologize. I still didn't think we had anything in common to build a relationship on. Oliver could have balled me out for an hour, and I would have had it coming. Instead, he just said thank you and that my apology was accepted. He invited me into his apartment. We went for a walk later that day, and I found how easy it was to talk to him. That's not always easy with guys."

"I know what you mean. Sometimes I think boys are from a different planet."

"While we walked, Oliver talked about family and how important it was to him. I knew we shared that value, and that's where our relationship started to grow."

"How did he feel when you told him that you had a daughter?"

"Holly, let me answer that by telling you that when the social worker called, I was scared to death. I thought it might destroy my still-new relationship with Oliver. I thought you would hate me. I was so shocked that I wanted a day to get my thoughts together. Not Oliver, God bless him. When I told him about you, he only wanted to know how soon we were going to meet you. He told me that there might be a little girl out there who needs me, and that is what I should be concerned about rather than consulting my own fears. He was absolutely right, of course. I was so scared that first day that I could hardly think of things to talk about."

"I remember thinking it was odd that Oliver talked to me more than you did. Remember that morning when I said those awful things to you. It was Oliver who told me what I had said was awful and told me to apologize to you. He sent me to your room to talk to you."

"He didn't tell me. I didn't know that."

They were quiet for a while and then Holly asked, "Are you still scared?"

Ruth laughed. "Yes, but in a different way. Now I'm scared that my wonderful, kind, intelligent, and beautiful daughter will have a mother who can provide her the kind of life she deserves."

"You shouldn't worry about that. I think I believe in you, and I know I've believed in Oliver for some time. I've been hurt so many times that it's hard to get close to anyone."

"Thank you for taking a chance on us, Holly. You know we're going to have arguments and fight about some things and I'm going to make mistakes."

"I know. I'm still a kid. The difference is you both listen to me. That's really new for me. It makes me feel important and I like that."

Ruth looked at the clock. "It's getting late. Do you want me to fix up the sofa for you to sleep on?"

"Would you mind if I sleep with you? I'd like to wake up and see you there. Is that silly?"

"That's not silly, and it would be fine."

Ruth turned out the room light and slid into bed.

"This was a really great day," Holly said. "Thank you, Ruth." "You're welcome, and thank you for being a part of my day."

They both fell fast asleep and the following morning when they awoke, Ruth asked Holly if she liked to cook.

"I only know how to do cleanup," Holly replied.

Ruth quickly showed Holly how to prepare the ingredients for Oliver's favorite omelet.

As soon as Oliver arrived at Ruth's apartment, Holly casually asked if he would like a spinach, mushroom, and Swiss cheese omelet for breakfast.

"That's my favorite. How did you know?"

"Oh, no." Holly put her hands on her hips and a coquettish look on her face. "We girls have our secrets."

Ruth guided Holly in cooking and folding the omelet.

After Oliver tasted it, he told Holly, "If you can cook my favorite breakfast like this, you guys can have all the secrets you want."

Holly looked at Ruth with a broad smile on her face due to Oliver's praise. Holly and Ruth decided to spend the day going for a long walk together around Lake Washington. Oliver said he was getting a headache and didn't feel like going with them. He headed back to his apartment.

Ruth told Holly that she was getting concerned, as Oliver's headaches had been occurring more frequently. She knew they started after his time in the Army. She said she would make a mental note to talk to him about that.

At the end of the day, Holly agreed to get together for breakfast at Ruth's apartment the next Saturday morning.

Chapter Twelve ~ Michael and Anna

SO NOW YOU KNOW about Sharon," Michael told Anna. As they sat in front of the campfire, Anna's eyes were filled with tears. "Just when things were the best, they became the worst. I could never provide that kind of love for someone—like Sharon did for you."

Michael left his chair, kneeled in front of Anna, and took each of her hands in his. "You can and you will."

He leaned forward and kissed her lips. Anna's mind was spinning. She tightened her grip on Michael's hands with as much strength as she could. She knew that business partners shouldn't act this way but...

It was heaven to be kissed by Michael. Anna closed her eyes. "Michael, I'm scared," she said in a quiet voice. "I've never even had a boyfriend, and sometimes just the thought of you does things to me that I don't like to think about. That frightens me. I'm not sure—"

Michael stood up in front of Anna. "Please stand up, Anna."

"Michael, please listen."

Michael lifted her arms, slowly pulling her to a standing position. He guided her arms around his neck, and in a soft voice told her, "This is how to get rid of that scared feeling."

Michael wrapped his arms around her, pulling her body tightly against him and put his cheek against hers. Anna's arms slowly tightened around his neck.

Anna thought that having Michael's arms around her was even better than her dream. With the warmth of the fire pit, the cool evening breeze blowing on her, and the heat from Michael's body against hers, Anna didn't ever want to let go.

After a while Michael asked her, "Does this help you feel better?"

"Yes, Michael," she whispered.

She heard a *pop* from the fire pit and over Michael's shoulder Anna saw glowing embers floating up into the evening air and into the night sky.

Michael kissed her again and then gently let go. "I'm going to put out the campfire and put the chairs away. We need to be up early to get over to the guided birding tour on Bateman Island. I promised Chela and Warren that I would try to take pictures of any birds we saw."

As Anna folded the blankets and stored them inside the motorhome, she thought that Michael was right—when he was holding her, she felt so safe. She felt warm and secure, from the top of her head to the bottom of her toes.

She had so little experience with men, especially very little physical experience, that she wondered if all women feel that way when they are held. She was afraid he might want her to do something that she didn't even know how to do.

Michael entered the motorhome. Anna snapped out of her thoughts and turned to him. "Michael, I'm worried that my lack of *physical* experience—"

"I understand, Anna. That's why we're going to take this very slowly. Anytime you're scared, you can tell me and we'll hold each other. From now on, anytime you want me to hold you, just tell me, or just put your arms around me. I'll hold you for as long, or as little, as you want. That's good enough for now. If you feel confused about where this is going, or anything else, talk to me. We'll work it out. That's the most important thing now. You were put into my life for a reason. I have a feeling we will discover that reason during the next few weeks and months. I'm still going to sleep in the living area tonight and you're going to sleep in the bedroom. When you're ready to do more than embrace, you'll let me know."

Anna was happy about how easy Michael was making this for her. She realized he had been protecting her since they first started working together, and he was still doing it. She prayed for the Lord to please love and take good care of Michael.

With a huge smile on her face, Anna walked up and put her arms around him. "I get to hold you like this, anytime I want?" Anna asked.

"Anytime you want." Michael relaxed into her, pulling her tightly against him.

"When I was a little girl," she said, "my father always kissed me on the forehead when he put me to bed."

"Did he do it like this?"

Michael leaned down as if he was going to kiss Anna's forehead, but she stood on her toes and met his lips with her own.

After a long kiss, she pulled back. "Not exactly like that, but I think what we just did was nicer."

Michael went and closed the window curtains of the motorhome, a warm content look on his face.

***

The next day started warm and sunny. Michael pulled Anna's car out of the trailer and he drove them to Bateman Island, which is a small island that is surrounded by the Columbia River.

As they hiked a short trail, away from the car and out to the island, Michael reached out and took Anna's hand in his. She held his hand in both of hers, as tightly as she could.

"Easy now," he told her. "I think my fingers are turning blue from lack of circulation."

Anna laughed, but still held on tightly, thinking that it's probably silly, but she loved the feeling of just holding his hand.

The walk itself was fascinating. It was led by a member of the local Audubon Society who gave a detailed description of the amazing bird life that populated the island and its surrounds. They probably saw thirty different species of birds. Warren had lent a special long-distance camera lens to Michael so he could get close- up photos of the birds they saw on that bright and sunny day.

As Michael was scanning along the river looking for birds, he suddenly exclaimed, "Oh look, a couple of red-sided kayaks."

The inexperienced birders, including Anna, immediately pointed their binoculars in the direction that Michael had his camera pointed.

Anna saw two people in red kayaks paddle into view and realized what Michael had done. "Michael, be nice." She started laughing.

Following the morning's birding adventure, they had lunch, and then visited some of the numerous sights that Louis and Clark had explored during their epic journey west to the Pacific Ocean.

Anna loved seeing the birds on Bateman Island and visiting such historically significant locations. She could see that Michael loved it as well. She watched Michael's face light up as he observed the same view that Louis and Clark might have seen as they looked across the Columbia River.

Anna realized that she was getting joy from Michael's happiness. She remembered Chela telling her how much better life's experiences were because she had Warren to share them with. She'd thought that was romantic nonsense when she'd heard it, but now she knew it was true.

Michael noticed Anna smiling at him. "What are you grinning about?"

Anna stopped smiling and put on a sad face. "I'm not grinning. I'm scared."

Michael looked around. "Scared of what?"

"Hey, buddy." She smiled, while putting her hands on her hips. "That's not the deal. When I tell you I'm scared, you're supposed to hold me."

Michael grinned and put his arms around her. "You are the lady who brings so much sunshine into my life."

An older couple was standing near them as they embraced. The man told them in a distinctly Upper-Midwestern accent, "You two keep hugging like that and you're going to need a nap."

Anna blushed.

Michael just grinned. "It must be the clouds or something," he told them. "They tend to blure one's mind."

The woman smiled. "Seeing as we haven't seen clouds all day, I can accurately guess what's blurring your mind."

They all laughed and began walking together.

The older couple introduced themselves as the Gersons, and said they were from Wisconsin and lived near Lake Oshkosh. They had a great sense of humor and it was fun talking to them.

Turned out they were camping at the same park as Michael and Anna, so Anna invited their new friends to a northwest-style dinner in their motorhome. The older couple agreed on the condition that they could bring wine and a dessert.

It didn't go unnoticed that Michael beamed when Anna had said *our* motorhome when inviting the Gersons.

That night Anna prepared a lovely dinner for the two couples, consisting of a spring salad mix with cranberries, walnuts, crumbled grilled salmon, lightly dressed with honey vinaigrette dressing. The main course consisted of Rainier cherry and apricot stuffed pork chops, roasted Walla Walla onions, and fresh steamed asparagus. Anna wanted everything to come out as perfect as possible for their motorhome's first dinner guests—their first dinner guests as an official couple.

While Anna prepared dinner, Michael went out and torqued the wheel nuts on the motorhome in preparation for their early morning departure to Boise. When he re-entered Michael was greeted by the delightful aromas of Anna's culinary efforts.

"While I was walking around the motorhome," he said, "I thought it was smiling, but I didn't know why until I came inside.

Anna, it smells wonderful in here. I'm just amazed at the fabulous meals you create in this tiny kitchen."

"Thank you, Michael." Anna smiled then gestured to the dishes she'd set out. "Will you please set the table? Dinner will be ready in a few minutes."

The Gersons arrived promptly and brought over a lovely Washington State Cabernet Sauvignon. The full-bodied wine was redolent in blackberry and bright tannins.

Anna mentioned that she was surprised at the quality of the wine and Mr. Gerson explained, "Not many people realize that the southern Washington State wineries are at the same latitude as the best grape growing regions in France."

Mrs. Gerson had also brought a dessert of apple pie. It was seasoned with cinnamon, allspice, brown sugar and ginger and Anna was impressed at how well the spices balanced the tart apple flavor. She made a mental note to try adding ginger the next time she baked an apple pie.

What's next on your tour of the northwest?" Michael asked. "We're off to see northern Idaho, then down to southern Idaho through Crater of the Moon National Monument, then over the mountains to see the Tetons," the Gersons told them. "We are scenery junkies and love touring."

They enjoyed a wonderful meal and good conversation, then said good-bye to their new friends.

"Anna, everything was wonderful." Michael put his hands on either side of her face and kissed her. "Our guests loved your cooking. I think they had a great time talking with us, too. Why don't I clean up the table and kitchen and you can relax."

"I'd prefer that we do things together whenever we can," she told him.

"That's my partner—my sunshine partner." Michael smiled and they started cleaning up together.

After everything was put away, they cuddled up and watched a movie. They were sitting on one of the motorhome's J-shaped couches, and Anna positioned herself so that Michael could put one arm around her and she could lean back and rest her head against his chest. She had never thought just lying against someone could feel so nice. She was certain she could feel Michael's love for her whenever they were touching.

After the movie, Michael reviewed the map his cousin had sent him that would get them to a scenic section of a national park. It was located a few hours' drive from where they were parked. It was a slight deviation from their planned route to Boise, but Michael's cousin had assured him it was worth the detour.

Then as Michael turned out the last of the lights in the motorhome, Anna, with a little apprehension, whispered her thoughts to him.

"Michael I think we should sleep in the same bed tonight. I mean, you know, just so you can hold me if I get scared."

Michael grinned mischievously. "I generally don't wear anything to bed but my briefs."

"Oh." Anna paused, thinking. "Well, that will be fine then." Once they were in the bedroom on opposite sides of the bed, Anna turned away from Michael and removed her clothes, except for her bra and panties. She pulled on a pink nightshirt that went down to slightly below her hips.

She turned back toward Michael as he was getting under the blankets, and a wave of warmth flashed through her body. He looked so sexy just wearing his tiny briefs.

They engaged in a lengthy embrace and kiss, then Michael suggested to Anna that she lay on her side, facing away from him. He snuggled up against her, spooning.

Anna put her arm over the one Michael had wrapped around her and held it tightly, as if it were a beloved teddy bear. She thought the warmth of Michael's body against hers was the nicest sensation she had ever known. Although part of her longed to pull his hands up to her breasts—her body was aching, she wanted him so badly. She wriggled around, trying to shake off the feelings of desire.

"Are you comfortable, Anna? Can you sleep like this?" he asked her as he kissed the back of her neck.

She sighed. "Yes, Michael, but I may not want to get up in the morning."

Chapter Thirteen ~ Oliver and Ruth, plus Holly

THE FOLLOWING WEEK, AFTER a lovely breakfast where Holly learned how to make crepes, Ruth suggested they go visit the farmers' market in Issaquah. "I want to make *Bolognese* sauce for tonight's dinner," she said. "It takes lots of work, but it is an incredible sauce. I'm also going to make ravioli, polenta, and some green vegetable, depending on what's available at the farmers' market. Would you like to help?"

Holly perked up. "Oh, Ruth, I'd love to."

As they arrived at the farmers' market, Holly was excited to see so many vendors in row after row of small white booths. As they walked, Ruth started calling the produce by their Italian names. She then added little words like good, pretty, please, and thank you. Holly caught on quickly and really seemed to love the language game.

Then the game took on an added dimension when they stopped to look at bouquets of fresh flowers. The proprietor must have overheard Ruth teaching the Italian names of the flowers to Holly. He came over and Ruth conversed with the man in Italian for a while and explained that she was teaching Italian to Holly.

"*Sei carina,*" the proprietor said, smiling at Holly.

Holly seemed to understand this. She replied, "*Grazie, signore.*"

The man looked most pleased and immediately handed Holly a lovely bouquet of flowers. "That's for starting to learn my language," he told her.

Then they drove over to an Italian deli and butcher. By the time they arrived, Holly was able to ask for beef, pork, and Italian bacon. She practiced the words. "*Manzo, e carne di maiale, e pancetta.*"

Ruth observed that Holly's mind could absorb new words in a foreign language like a sponge soaks up water. She realized that Holly had a good ear for languages as well, because she quickly imitated Ruth's accent when she spoke Italian.

When they arrived back at Ruth's home they started making cheese ravioli and *Bolognese* meat sauce—*sugo Bolognese*—from scratch. In addition, Ruth showed Holly how to prepare vegetables for a stir fry. "We will use Zucchini, onion—*cipolla*—and mushrooms—*fungi*. Ruth continued speaking Italian to Holly, as they cooked.

Holly quickly picked up the terms and even learned a little about the region the sauce comes from. Fresh basil, oregano, garlic, and lemon juice went into the sauce. Ruth told her in Italian, "So we don't need as much salt."

At lunchtime, Oliver had returned to Ruth's apartment and was immediately sent out to buy sandwiches, as the kitchen was too busy to make lunch. Instead of sandwiches he came home with a Sushi tray from the Japanese market.

Oliver taught Holly how to use chopsticks—*Ohashi* he called them.

Holly seemed excited by every little new thing she learned. "It seems like I'm always learning new things when I'm with you guys," she said. "I think my head likes that a lot. I think my head likes that one heck of a lot."

During lunch, Ruth received a phone call from her parents inviting her and Oliver over for dinner. She put her hand over the receiver and spoke to Holly. "My parents are on the phone. Would you like to meet them tonight?"

Holly hesitated a brief moment, then with a huge smile on her face, nodded yes.

Ruth told her parents that she and a friend were preparing an Italian meal and they should come over to Ruth's apartment for dinner instead.

They agreed and Ruth hung up the phone, turning to Holly. "When they find out who you are, they're going to cry and want to hug you."

"I figured that. I'll be okay," she assured Ruth. Turning back to the meal preparations she asked, "How long do we cook the sauce?"

Ruth was glad that Holly felt comfortable meeting her grandparents. She had come a long way in a short time. She recognized that Holly's switch in topic was just her way of dealing with things. "We let it cook, long and slow. It won't be ready until just before we eat."

"The kitchen smells heavenly already. I can't imagine how great the whole house will smell by dinner time."

Ruth took a bowl out, added flour, and then she had Holly make a well in the center of the flour and break a few eggs into it.

Holly started mixing the dough with her hands. "I like mixing this by hand," Holly said. "It felt powdery at first, but then started to feel spongier as I worked the eggs into the flour."

"I agree," Ruth said. "I feel somehow more connected to what I'm making when I use my hands. I get a similar feeling when I'm kneading dough for bread. It's like I'm closer to the creation of something we're going to enjoy together."

Ruth taught Holly how to greet her parents in Italian so she would be ready when they arrived late that afternoon.

They arrived right on time, and Ruth's mother immediately commented how much Ruth and her young friend looked alike. When Holly greeted her in Italian, she seemed even more amazed. "Ruth, your young friend speaks lovely Italian."

Ruth smiled proudly at Holly. "She just started learning today. She is nearly fluent in Spanish as well."

Holly then engaged in a brief conversation with Ruth's mother in Spanish.

Ruth felt it was time, and she spoke to her parents. "Holly and I have a surprise for you two," she said, "but you need to sit down first."

As her mother and father sat down on the couch in Ruth's living room, her mother was intently starring at Holly. Suddenly, as if a light bulb had turned on, Ruth's mother let out a little scream, put her hands over her face, and started crying.

Ruth almost teared up, too, seeing her mom's reaction. She breathed deep. "Mom. Dad. I want you to meet my daughter— Holly."

Holly walked over to her grandparents and hugged them. They embraced her for a long time.

Ruth was quite pleased that Holly took the initiative to hug them first. She took her aside afterwards. "Thank you for that."

"It was easy," Holly said. "They looked like they needed a hug anyway."

Ruth's parents seemed nervous around Holly at first, but were certainly overjoyed to meet her. Ruth's mom kept smiling and shaking her head. While they talked, she kept reaching out and touching Holly, almost as if she wanted to be sure she was real.

When Ruth, her mother, and Holly moved to the kitchen to bring dinner to the dining room, she heard her dad speaking to Oliver. "I'm amazed how much she looks like Ruth."

"Not only that," Oliver said, "but she has Ruth's sense of style. She's also a real thinker like Ruth. But best of all, I think she has Ruth's sense of feeling for people. When I couldn't accompany them on their walk today because I had a headache, Holly immediately asked Ruth if they should stay home to take care of me. I mean, we're talking about a twelve-year-old here with those kinds of thoughts and feelings."

During dinner, Ruth's mom asked Holly what it's been like to spend time with Ruth and Oliver.

Holly looked at Ruth.

"Be honest," Ruth told her. "I know it hasn't been easy and it took a while to start building our relationship."

Holly nodded. "At first…I didn't care at all about meeting Ruth. I know I have some stuff to work out, but Ruth, and especially Oliver, help me with that. Sometimes I feel like I should be angry with them, but then they treat me so nice and respect what I say, that I can't stay angry. Even when I say something that's not too nice, Oliver just says, 'Holly,' in that tone of his. I know I've gone too far and immediately apologize. I've never been around an adult guy for any amount of time. Oliver is definitely not what I expected."

She shrugged her shoulders. "I didn't think girls learned lessons from their fathers. If Oliver is any example, I couldn't have been more wrong. Even when he gets angry with me, I always have the feeling that what he tells me is for my own good. Also, I think that getting to know Oliver is making it easier for me to talk to the boys at school. I'm starting to see how Ruth and Oliver are like partners. I know they love each other, but it's almost as if they're best friends too. They laugh with each other all the time. Even when they have arguments, they're not mean about it. I like that. They both listen to me. I mean really listen to me. It's still hard to believe, but they really want to know what little me has to say."

Then Holly related the story of her schoolmate trying to hit her the first day she met Ruth and Oliver. "Oliver said if the kid ever hit me again, he'd be on the kid like stink on…well…poop. You should have seen the kid's face when he heard that. He's been real nice to me ever since."

Holly expressed her fear of abandonment, and the difficulty believing that she can depend on the adults in her life.

"As I've told her repeatedly," Oliver stated, "when there are problems, she's got two people on her side now."

"I know," Holly grinned at Oliver, "you'll be there to help me like stink on you-know-what."

Everyone laughed with Holly. Then Holly got quiet for a moment, thinking. "That might be the best part you know—we laugh a lot."

Chapter Fourteen ~ Michael and Anna

GOOD MORNING, SUNSHINE LADY," Michael called to Anna as he got dressed. "I'm going to get your car into the trailer so we'll be ready to leave as soon as we clean up after breakfast."

As he did that, Anna prepared them a lovely southwest-style scrambled breakfast consisting of chorizo, eggs, potatoes, onions, chopped garlic, cilantro, and a finely chopped Ancho chili.

He appreciated how she took his preferences into account when she cooked. She also prepared coffee to a strength that he preferred, and these small gestures taking care of him made him feel so loved.

Every day before they started out, Michael walked around the motorhome and trailer, inspecting them to make sure there weren't any obvious problems. That morning Anna called out to him as he got up to do his inspection.

"Wait for me," she said. "I want to learn what you do in case we have an emergency and I have to take over the driving duties."

He was very pleased that Anna wanted to learn more about taking care of the motorhome. He also noticed that as she put the dishes away, she put them in a more convenient location than he had originally set up. She seemed to feel some ownership of the motorhome and Michael loved that. It was one more thing he felt that they were sharing and one more thing that brought them closer together.

Anna was different from Sharon, but he was able to appreciate her in her own ways. That was something no other woman could convince him to do since losing Sharon.

Sitting down in the driver's seat, Michael brought the big diesel engine to life. Within a few seconds all the engine's gauges were in the green. He looked behind him to tell Anna that everything was ready to go. She was walking toward the front of the motorhome with a non-spill container of coffee for each of them. As she placed the coffee in the cup holder next to his seat, he stood up and gave her a hug.

"Are you scared?" She grinned at him as she teased.

"I'm scared that I might forget to thank you for taking such good care of me."

Anna wrapped her arms around him. "You're welcome, Michael. I love taking care of you."

Anna smiled, placed her coffee in the cup holder, and sat down in the co-pilot's seat, while Michael checked the engine gauges and placed the motorhome in gear. From thirty-five-feet-behind them, they listened to the muffled rumble of the diesel engine's eleven-hundred-foot-pounds of torque, as it began gently propelling them forward.

They pulled out of the campground around six-thirty in the morning and were soon merging onto the interstate highway. It was a glorious sun-filled day with mild temperatures and a near- cloudless sky.

As they left the tri-cities area, the terrain changed from rolling hills to the incredibly beautiful forests of northeast Oregon. Anna didn't seem to have much interest in the natural world when Michael had first met her, but she seemed to become more involved with the scenery as they traveled.

As they passed through the Blue Mountains of Oregon, Anna commented that the forests were full of stately trees. "They look like an army of soldiers guarding the forest," she said, "standing at attention in uniforms of gray and green."

Noticing Anna's interest in the scenery made Michael more aware of his own interest as well. While cruising in a comfortable leather-covered seat in his air-conditioned motorhome, he was thinking of the immigrants that crossed those same mountains to try for a new life in Oregon.

What was a steep section of twisty highway for him must have been nearly impassable for them. He decided that they must have been rugged individuals and that one day he would like to have the time to learn more about them.

I guess I'm at that time in my life where I can occasionally stop to smell the roses. He looked over at Anna and smiled. *Or maybe it's because I have someone in my life that inspires the desire to smell the roses with her.*

As they entered more mountainous terrain, Michael was happy to see the motorhome faired quite well going up and down the mountains. Anna started asking questions about how he was driving the motorhome and Michael hoped it wouldn't be long before he would be giving her driving lessons.

"It's a good time to start watching the map to see where we should get off the interstate," Michael suggested.

She agreed and began scanning it to find the National Forest that Michael's cousin had recommended. An hour later, they were exiting the interstate, then they followed some two-lane roads for about forty-five minutes before pulling into the parking lot of the ranger station, which was located at the base of the deep green, forested mountains.

Anna and Michael entered the station and he told one of the rangers where they wanted to visit.

"The trailhead is at a large paved parking lot that we use as a base for search and rescue," the ranger told them. "The road to drive up there is paved, but steep. There's only one tight turn, but we get semi-trailer trucks up there. You shouldn't have any trouble getting your big rig up there too. There's no camping allowed, but you can park there during the day and take the trail down to the viewing area. The parking area is clearly marked with a search and rescue base sign."

Michael told the ranger that they would be up there about noon, walk down to the viewing area, and they would probably be leaving around an hour or so later.

"It's a steep trail down to the viewing area," the ranger warned. "It will take twice as long to climb back up as to get down. The soil is sandy and loose, so stay on the trail. Don't attempt to walk down the sides of the mountain to take pictures—there is a sheer drop-off about one-hundred-feet below the trail, with a two-hundred-foot drop if you go over it. But if you stay on the trail, you'll safely arrive at one of the most beautiful scenic vistas in the northwest. You won't have cell service, and you should try to be out of there by three o'clock this afternoon as we expect rain then."

They thanked the ranger for his help and told him they would be out of there shortly after one. Then they started out onto a beautiful little road that was quite steep, but the motorhome maintained a constant fifteen-miles-an-hour for forty-five minutes, until they saw the sign announcing the entrance to the search and rescue area.

They drove in and found a huge paved area, probably the size of two football fields. Michael parked near the entrance to the little trail. Then after changing into jeans and wool shirts to combat the cool mountain air, they filled canteens with water and packed some simple snacks in day packs. As it was going to be such a brief hike, Michael opted for his running shoes instead of changing into hiking boots.

He looked at the emergency-supplies-kit. It was filled with medical gear that he had put together using recommendations from a book on mountaineering medicine, as well as what his family doctor had advised. It would be extra weight and they were going on such a short hike that he debated bringing it.

Then he remembered what his Vietnam-vet father always said—you can never be too safe—and he tucked it into his pack.

The trail was indeed quite steep. It curved down and to the left from the parking area, following around the side of the mountain and they quickly lost sight of the motorhome. To the left side of the trail, the mountain was going up so steep they could almost reach out and touch it—and the drop-off to the right was as precipitous as the ranger had warned.

Michael walked in front of Anna in order to check out the trail ahead. The view was spectacular and Michael couldn't wait to get to the viewing area.

About halfway down, as Michael was forging around a curve in the trail Anna shouted out to him. "Oh, my God, Michael, the view is incredi—"

She screamed.

He spun his head back around, just in time to see her plummeting away from the trail. Anna was cartwheeling and tumbling down the steep side of the mountain and Michael's heart was in his throat as he raced back to where she had fallen and started down after her.

The side of the mountain was so steep he had to slide on his back and stomach. As he skidded down after Anna, he grabbed at anything he could—plants or small trees—to try to slow his descent. Mostly they just pulled out of the ground, and if they did give him a grip they scraped and tore at his hands along with the jagged rocks that were biting into his body.

But none of that mattered. All that he cared about was getting to Anna before she plunged over the steep cliff. Thankfully her tumbling was arrested by one of the few sturdy trees on the side of the mountain—just before she would have gone over the precipice.

Michael grabbed onto the tree with his bleeding hands. Panting and full of adrenaline, he quickly assessed Anna's condition. She was moaning and in obvious pain with a huge gash bleeding profusely just above her right knee.

Upon realizing that she was no longer falling and that Michael was there with her, Anna managed a small smile. "I think I stopped my fall with my face," she mumbled.

Michael kissed her head half-a-dozen-times, then sprang into action. Her face had many scratches on it and was starting to look puffy. He carefully straightened out her bleeding leg, and she groaned loudly against the pain.

"Sorry," Michael said reflexively. "Hang on, lady. I need to stop the bleeding and then we'll get you out of here."

Anna nodded and lay back against the forest floor.

Michael tore into his first-aid pack and got out some sterile gauze bandages. After applying as much pressure as he thought Anna could stand, he took some water and rinsed out the deep gash.

Anna screamed in pain.

"We have to clean it—I'm sorry, I know it hurts like hell." He applied more pressure to the wound but when he lifted the gauze to check, it was still bleeding freely. It would have to be stitched closed. Michael thanked God—and his father—that he had his safety-kit with him. For the first time he was going to use the lessons he had learned from studying the mountaineering medicine book. He had Anna lay back against the hill and raised her leg, hoping that would help minimize some of the bleeding.

"What are you going to do?" Anna asked.

"The good news is the bleeding doesn't appear arterial. The bad news is there is a still lot of it and I have to close your wound. I promise this will hurt worse than hell, but I have to do it. It's the only way."

He wound some sterile gauze around a stick and handed it to her. "Bite down on this if you have to. I know it sounds impossible, but try to relax. Lay back and close your eyes. I'll get this finished as fast as I can."

Anna nodded, tears pooling in her eyes. She sucked in a big breath and placed the stick between her clenched teeth.

He positioned himself with one-foot against a tree to prevent them from sliding farther down the mountain. Then he tore open some surgical wipes and cleaned the area around the wound. He applied some surface anesthetic, which he knew would barely dull the area, but it was all he had. Still, every time he put pressure on her leg, Anna moaned in pain.

Michael injected some painkiller at a few points above and below the wound. Anna didn't say a word, but had her teeth tightly clenched on the stick and her arm over her eyes.

He broke open the package with the sterile u-shaped needle and thread. Using a needle holder, he gently began lacing up the opening, putting in a row of stitches to pull the tissue together over the deepest part of the wound, and then a row through the skin to close the surface. All the while he kept telling himself he was just darning socks, not Anna's leg.

Alternately he wiped his brow with the back of his arm and dabbed at the wound with the sterile gauze to keep the surgical area from disappearing under all the blood flow. Finally, the last suture was carefully tied off, as he had been shown by his doctor.

"You can look now," Michael told Anna.

She slowly moved her arm, pulled the wet, gauzy stick from between her teeth, then peeked her eyes tentatively at her leg. Anna let out a loud breath, almost as if she'd been holding it the entire time.

"Well?" Michael smiled nervously.

Anna returned his smile. "If that leaves a scar, mister, I'll sue."

"You have to be in lots of pain and you're making jokes? You *are* one tough lady techy."

Michael covered the wound with a bandage and tape, then took some surgical wipes and cleaned the dirt off the scratches on Anna's face, neck, hands, and a few other places where her clothing had torn open and she had been scratched.

Then, the reality of their predicament set in as he looked back up the mountain. It was steep as hell. He'd have to get Anna out by going across, rather than up, the mountain to the trail. He looked down at his running shoes, wishing he hadn't been too lazy to change into his hiking boots. They would have given him better traction on the slippery parts of the terrain.

With help, Anna got up to a standing position on her non- injured leg. They tried to move together, but that was hopeless. As if to mock Michaels's anxiety about getting Anna to safety, the clouds started to block the sun. He glanced at his watch and quickly realized they had been down there over-an-hour.

"You won't like this," he told Anna, "but I'm going to carry you over my shoulder, at least until we can get back to the trail."

Anna smiled weakly and Michael could tell she was frightened, but trying to hide it. "Do what you think best."

He appreciated her efforts. He needed all the confidence he could find to perform the feat ahead of him. He used a fireman's carry he had learned back in Boy Scouts. Then he started out across the side of the mountain.

It seemed like every-fourth-step broke free and they slid a bit. It was nerve-wracking and after a few-minutes Michael was covered in sweat and panting from the exertion of trying to keep his balance while carrying Anna.

After what he estimated to be one-third of the distance they needed to cover to get back to the trail, he had to stop for a break.

Michael gently lowered Anna to the ground and sat down. It took a few minutes to get his breath back so they could talk.

"I can't do this much longer," Anna said. "Your shoulder is digging into my stomach."

Michael nodded. "I'll try to carry you for a shorter distance and put you down more often."

He hoisted her up and set out again. His muscles were straining and getting sore, but he had developed an economy of motion by taking smaller steps, which also provided a steadier ride for Anna. He stopped four more times before they finally reached the trail.

As he lowered her to the ground to stand on her good leg, she cried out in pain and collapsed.

Anna had her foot twisted on its side and she brought all her weight down on it as he'd set her down on her good leg. She couldn't stand on it without a lot of pain.

Michael's legs were aching, too. The clouds had completely covered the sun and it was rapidly getting colder. He had to find another way to transport Anna out of there. Then he felt something cold against his neck.

Are you kidding me?

"At least, it's not raining." Anna smiled and tried to lighten the mood as she looked at the light snow that was beginning to fall.

Michael surveyed the sides of the mountain. There were a few three- and four-inch-diameter trees. He knew what would have to be done. Using another lesson from Boy Scouts, he would fashion a litter to get Anna up the trail to the motorhome.

He dug into the emergency kit and pulled out a small flexible saw that had rings on each end, and then proceeded to use it to try to cut through one of the trees.

Anna watched him intently. "What are you? A Boy Scout or something?"

"Lucky for you, I am."

The saw was by no means speedy, but it got the job done. Then, using a pocket knife, he stripped the bark from the trees, and used the strips of bark to tie two long poles together with two shorter poles. As the trail was narrow, he tied what would become the bottom ends of the poles closer together, resulting in somewhat of a V shape formed by the side poles.

The thought of having one side of the litter slide off the edge of the narrow trail was something Michael didn't even want to contemplate. He lashed a poncho across the poles and picked Anna up, gently laying her down on the litter. She was getting cold and the blood loss didn't help. Michael helped her take a long drink of water.

He gingerly lifted the ends of the litter and started up the trail, taking slow, even steps to keep the motion of the litter as smooth as possible. The trail had started getting slippery from the snow, so to maintain traction, he cut the size of his steps even further. The snow was coming down like cotton balls now, and Michael stopped to brush as much of it off of Anna as he could. She was starting to shiver.

As he picked up the end of the litter again, he cursed his running shoes—they were providing very little purchase on the snow-covered trail. His hands, arms, and shoulders were beginning to ache. He thought about trying to make a shoulder strap out of his belt to help with the load, but with Anna shivering so badly, he decided it was better to continue on the trail.

The ranger had been right—going back up the trail was much more difficult than going down, especially with the slippery conditions. The next time he stopped, Michael looked at his hands. There were blisters on his palms and some of his fingers, not to mention all the scratches he had sustained when he had slid down the mountain side after Anna.

Anna got an apologetic look on her face. "Michael," she started, "I have to pee. I'm so sorry."

"It's all right, Anna. I'm going to lift you up a little and move you off to the side of the litter."

That accomplished, Anna awkwardly managed to get her pants down and relieve herself. Michael held her until she had buttoned up again and then he put her back on the litter. He took off his wool sweater and placed it over her.

He had to stop every fifteen-feet to rest. His shoulders, arms, and thighs felt like they were on fire. His hands and fingers burned like hell, too, so he tried wrapping some gauze around them. It didn't help much. Every time he stumbled, he knew Anna got jostled and was sure that was painful for her, so he tried to ignore his own pain as much as possible.

After another forty-five minutes on the trail, both of Michael's hands were bleeding, and he had a pounding headache that throbbed with every step. The muscles in his legs, arms, and back felt like they were being torn apart. The snow was falling even faster and was still the size of cotton balls.

Every time he glanced at Anna, she looked more uncomfortable, and was shivering harder. Then, just when he thought he was losing the last of his strength, the motorhome came into view. The sight of that tan and brown beast looked like home and it provided him with enough extra strength to climb up the last section of trail and cross the now slippery and snow-covered asphalt.

Chapter Fifteen ~ Oliver and Ruth, Holly and Drew

THERE WAS AN EIGHT-year-old boy named Drew who also lived with the same foster family as Holly. Drew and Holly were becoming good friends and Holly asked if she could bring Drew with her one Saturday.

Drew was tall for his age and loaded with pure adrenaline. When he arrived at Ruth's apartment, Oliver saw his energy level and immediately suggested they head over to a nearby park so he could teach Drew how to throw a football.

Oliver thought that he had kept Drew active enough at the park that he would relax a bit after returning to the apartment. No such luck. As Drew began running in the apartment, Oliver reprimanded him.

The expression on Drew's face said he wasn't sure if he should listen to Oliver or not. At that point, Oliver assured Drew that if he can't follow the rules when visiting, he would immediately be returned to his foster parents' home.

Holly then reprimanded Drew too. "Drew, I asked that they invite you over today, so if you don't do as you're told, you're embarrassing me."

Drew apologized to Holly, who reminded him to apologize to Oliver and Ruth as well. He did that, and somehow managed to calm down.

More and more of the time Ruth and Holly were together, they spoke to each other in Italian or Spanish and Oliver loved hearing it. He felt it brought an added dimension to their relationship.

"That little lady must have a word magnet in her head," he told Ruth.

In fact, the first Italian phrase that Oliver learned was when Holly called him to come for dinner by saying, "*La cena, Signor Oliver.*"

Ruth had started giving Holly homework to do during each weeknight. It consisted of writing exercises in Italian. She warned Holly that her regular school work came first, but Holly always found time to write her Italian sentences each night and proudly showed them to Ruth and Oliver each weekend.

***

Holly's foster parents suggested that Ruth attend Holly's school conference with them and while they were there, Holly's teacher noted that Holly's attitude in class was improving, and she seemed to have more friends. She wanted to know who was teaching Italian to her.

Ruth smiled. "I've been working with Holly for a while now. I'm a language professor at the University. It isn't interfering with her classroom studies, is it?"

"Not at all," Holly's teacher responded. "In fact, she's staying after school every day for an hour to work with one of my newest students. She's from Chile and didn't speak a word of English when she arrived."

She looked from Holly's foster parents back to Ruth. "Holly will certainly follow you into teaching," she said. "You should see the patience she has, even though she is only twelve. Holly has all my other students speaking slowly and enunciating clearly, to give Paula a chance to understand them. Paula is actually writing sentences in English now, and Holly gives her homework every night."

Ruth couldn't have been prouder and she was sure she was beaming with pride.

Holly's teacher continued. "As Paula's English skills developed, more and more of the students befriended her. Her English skills developed so quickly that she fit right in with our class. When Paula's parents called to thank me for working with her, I told them that I was only supervising one of my students who was spending her own time working with Paula. They sent a letter to school with her to give to you."

The teacher handed the letter to Holly's foster parents, who read the letter then handed it to Ruth. "This is really for you."

She read it quietly.

> *To Holly's parents: Thank you so much for allowing your daughter to help Paula with her English studies. We were most concerned that Paula wouldn't be able to make friends and study here due to her lack of English. Your daughter has been most gracious with her time. We can't thank you and Holly enough.*
>
> *Carlo and Berta Niera*

When they returned to the foster parents' home, Ruth asked Holly about working with Paula.

Holly shrugged. "Everyone thinks it's such a big deal, but it really isn't. I'm beginning to think I'm going to be a teacher. Teaching Paula is so much fun, I know I could teach all day long. I mostly do the same things that you did to start teaching me Italian. Instead of the farmers' market, I started by walking with Paula around our classroom and naming things. I did it just like you did, Ruth."

Holly smiled. "Every time I named an object, I had her hold it in her hand while we pronounced the word. It grew from there. I even give her ten sentences to write every night just like you do. My teacher gave me a red pencil to correct her sentences. That was cool. When she gets frustrated, I remind her that learning a language takes time and practice. Just like you tell me, when I get frustrated. After she learns English, she wants to learn Italian. Maybe she could visit some weekend and speak Italian with us."

"That would be wonderful, Holly," Ruth told her. "You are really being a good friend to Paula."

"That's easy, because she's so nice. I do have one problem, though. She still has a heavy accent. I don't know what to do about that."

"Give me her phone number, so I can call her parents," Ruth said. "Next Saturday, I'll reserve the University's Language Lab. We can use it to help her hear what she sounds like, so she can improve her accent."

Holly bounced with excitement. "Can I spend time in the language lab?"

Ruth thought for a while. "I'm not sure how much that would help you. Your pronunciation is fine. You need more vocabulary. I have a student from Italy who is learning Russian. She is an art and language major. I'm going to call her and see if she has time to spend Saturday morning at the art museum with you, while Paula is at the language lab with me. You would be learning the Italian vocabulary of art. Would you like to do that?"

"Oh yes, I would. I'll get Paula's number for you."

***

The following Saturday morning was gray and rainy. "A perfect day to study and learn," Holly declared to Paula after they met at the University's Language Lab.

Holly left for the art museum with Francesca and Ruth's mom, who was ecstatic to be spending a day with Holly. She was especially happy for the opportunity to spend an entire day speaking Italian with her granddaughter.

Then, with the help of the Language Lab and her teaching skills, Ruth could tell Paula started hearing her accent and was markedly improving it. Ruth taught her how to look in a mirror to see if her mouth was forming the English sounds properly, among other exercises. While it was gray outside, Ruth observed nothing but sunshine in the Language Lab for Paula.

At lunchtime, the five met at Pikes Market in Seattle and Paula spoke to Holly, slowly and with good enunciation. "I had a wonderful time learning English pronunciation in the University Language Lab."

"Paula that was great pronunciation," Holly said.

"Your mother is a great teacher, and patient with me, just like you."

In excellent Italian, Holly told them, "Francesca, Ruth's mom, and I had a marvelous time at the art museum."

Paula smiled longingly and told them in English, "Italian sounds so beautiful. I can't wait to learn it."

"English first, young lady," Ruth told her. "I promise I'll teach you Italian when your English skills are up to your grade level."

Paula slowly repeated the phrase under her breath. "Up to your grade level." Her face brightened when she realized what that meant. "Okay. That is a deal."

"Good English, Paula," Ruth complimented her.

After lunch they toured the fascinating sights and sounds of Pikes market. Ruth continued to converse in English with Paula, and Francesca conversed in Italian with Holly and Ruth's mom. When they went to dinner at a small restaurant on the Puget Sound waterfront, they decided to give Paula a break by speaking Spanish. Paula said she was amazed at Ruth's beautiful pronunciation of the Spanish language. She also had quite a bit of fun with Francesca, because Francesca's Spanish was rudimentary, at best.

Ruth noted that Paula spoke to Francesca slowly and with careful enunciation, just like Holly and her mom spoke English to Paula. *A table of past, present and future teachers*, Ruth thought and smiled.

***

As Ruth and Oliver's wedding was approaching in two-months, Holly wanted to know where they would be going on their honeymoon. Ruth and Oliver smiled at each other.

"We're going to visit a car factory." Oliver told her. "What?" Holly looked confused.

"We're visiting a car factory, but it won't be until the end of your school year. You and Drew will be coming with us."

Holly looked really confused now. She shrugged. "You guys are weird sometimes."

Then she suddenly had a bright expression on her face. "Hey, I didn't tell you guys. We have this new kid at school and he threatened to knock my block off. You remember Tom, the kid who tried to hit me the first weekend I met you guys? He and his best friend, Allen, stood right in front of me, looking at the new kid and asked the kid if he had a death wish. The kid immediately walked away and Tom told me, 'No sweat. I've got your back, Holly.' I said thank you and told him that was very nice of him."

Oliver and Ruth turned to each other and smiled. This was the first time they had heard Holly say anything nice about the boys at school.

Drew, in an angry eight-year-old voice, told Holly, "Tell me who he is and I'll kill him for you."

Oliver looked at Drew. In a stern voice he said, "We need to talk about some things, young man, before you get in trouble threatening to kill someone."

"Yes, Mr. Holt," a thoroughly chastened Drew replied.

***

The next Friday evening, Ms. Hollings visited Ruth to talk about Holly's future. She noticed Ruth's engagement ring and congratulated the couple.

"I talked to Holly last night," she said. "When do you think it would be an appropriate time to have her start living with you?"

"It really up to Holly," Ruth told her. "I know I'm ready." "Why don't you call her," suggested Ms. Hollings.

Ruth picked up the phone and called. Holly came to the phone and then Ruth heard her yelling at the other children at the foster home. "Quiet you guys. My mom is on the phone."

As this was the first time Ruth had heard Holly refer to her as Mom, she started to get choked up. She breathed deep and managed to ask, "Holly, when do you think you would like to start living with me?"

Holly replied, "Madre, quanto presto può passare a prendermi?" "Okay, we'll do that." Ruth hung up the phone and began sobbing. She tried to tell Oliver and Ms. Hollings what Holly said, but couldn't talk because she was crying so much.

After taking a minute to calm down, she cleared her throat. "Holly said, in Italian no less, 'Mother, how soon can you pick me up?'"

Oliver walked over to Ruth and embraced her. Even Ms. Hollings, who must have seen many great family moments, was overjoyed at Holly's response.

"There is something that occurred while I was interviewing Holly," Ms. Hollings mentioned. "Drew was acting out. Holly caused him to calm down immediately by telling him, 'If you don't act nice, I'll tell Mr. Holt.' Would you mind telling me what that was about?"

Oliver chuckled. "He's come over with Holly a number of times. He generally spends all day Saturday with us. And, well, I let him know that if he doesn't behave, whether at our place or his foster parents' home, then the visits will end."

"Yes," she agreed, "He does have a lot of energy. We can't seem to place him with a permanent family because of it."

"That's no big deal," Oliver told her. "All you need is a football."

"I beg your pardon?"

"First thing when he visits, we take a football over to the park and throw it around. I run him all over the place and he loves it. Actually, I've been thinking a soccer ball might be more fun for him, so I picked one up on the way home from work yesterday. If he likes it, I'm going to get a net he can practice with. Drew could do that even if I'm not around. He would have a blast being on a soccer team. Also, you should probably let any family that he's placed with know that getting him out for a run every day before school, would be a good idea for him."

"I'll keep that in mind," Ms. Hollings said. "So, after you run him around, what do you do?"

"Unless we have a family type of activity, I've been showing him my civil war maps. I started building a little scale model of the battle of Antietam. Drew and I have been painting the scenery and the little plastic soldiers on the battle ground. I can't be sure, but he may have a real artistic streak in him. You put a paint brush in Drew's hand and that's usually good for a couple-of-hours of concentrated painting. He's a good kid. You put him in the right family and he'll be fine."

"Yes," Ms. Hollings agreed, smiling at Oliver and Ruth, "I'll look for the right kind of home for him." Then she stood and glanced around the room. "Oh, my goodness," she exclaimed. "I've just found the right kind of home for him."

She then put a serious expression on her face and looked over her reading glasses at Ruth and Oliver. "Please, just think about it. He's so big for his age and full of energy, he needs a family that *gets* him." She looked directly at Oliver. "You, sir, *get* him."

***

When Ruth and Oliver drove over to the foster home to pick Holly up, everyone there was happy for Holly, except Drew. He clearly felt that he was losing his best friend, and it showed.

Oliver found Drew alone in the room that he shared with two other foster children.

"Hey buddy, why so sad?" Oliver asked.

"Holly gets to live with you guys, and I won't see her again." "That's funny. I just asked your foster parents if we could get together tomorrow so you could attend soccer camp at that park near my house. It's for kids who've never played soccer before. I'm going to be teaching passing skills. But as sad as you are, maybe you'd rather not attend."

"You mean we're still friends? And I can still visit you guys?" "I'll pick you up at eight o'clock tomorrow morning. Your foster parents said you can stay for the weekend if you like." "Wow. Thanks, Mr. Holt. I'll be ready."

The next day Oliver picked Drew up and drove him to the soccer camp. Children from all the nearby areas were in attendance. Drew was given a bright yellow t-shirt to wear that had the name of the camp, the date, and Drew's name across the back.

The kids were moving constantly the entire day. The only interruption was for lunch. Then, the last couple of hours the kids played a few matches against each other.

Drew nearly kicked a goal, but the ball hit the post instead. Much to the assembled parents delight, he and his little teammates cheered anyway because it was *almost* a goal.

The camp ended at three o'clock. The kids were told that they had worked very hard and had most likely run a full two-miles during all the practice. Ruth and Holly walked over to the park to meet Drew and Oliver.

When Drew saw them, he screamed excitedly, "Ms. Case.

Holly. I ran two-whole-miles today and I almost kicked a goal." "Wonderful," Ruth exclaimed.

"Excellent," Holly added.

As they walked back to Ruth's apartment, it was apparent that Drew was extremely happy, but completely exhausted. Once there, as soon as he sat still for two-minutes on Ruth's couch he fell asleep. Oliver carried him into Ruth's bedroom, put a blanket over him, and quietly closed the door as he left the room. While Drew was sleeping, a real estate agent called and told them that a townhouse in their price range was available and they could see it in a couple of hours. Ruth said that they could go over when Drew woke up.

After a tour of the townhouse Drew was excited. "This place has three bedrooms, so you guys would have space for me—I mean, if you wanted to."

Ruth and Oliver looked at each other.

"Bringing Holly into our home was easy because I'm her birth mom," Ruth said. "I can't promise you anything, but we couldn't even start adoption proceedings until we get married, and that's not for another two-months. Besides, you barely even know us yet."

"Oh," was all a disappointed Drew said.

"If you think you'd really like to live with us, we can talk about that," Oliver assured him.

"Great!"

Later that evening, after Drew and Holly were asleep on the couch in Ruth's living room, Ruth and Oliver were sitting in bed talking. She looked at Oliver. "Have you considered our adopting Drew?"

"I have. I've been thinking about it since the first day he came over, but I'm worried that he'll want to do something with me and I'll have one of my headaches. Drew is such a great kid. I'd hate to disappoint him like that, but when the headaches happen, I feel like a huge vise is compressing my head. It can throb for hours and I can't do anything when that happens."

"Oliver, what does your doctor say about the headaches?"

Oliver looked at the floor for such a long time without saying anything, that Ruth finally asked, "Oliver, did you hear me?"

"My psychiatrist told me that I have to come to terms with what's called survivor's guilt, or I'll keep getting headaches."

"I didn't know you were seeing a psychiatrist. You're experiencing survivor's guilt?" Ruth asked.

"I'm sorry I kept the details from you. I didn't want to burden you with this while you were developing your relationship with Holly. I should have told you a long time ago."

"It's okay, Oliver. At least you're getting some help. Can you tell me what happened?"

"While I was in Iraq I was on patrol with twelve guys. We'd been together since infantry training. It was morning and we were walking back to our base, around three-kilometers away. We were ambushed by about forty enemy soldiers. Two men in our squad were killed immediately. We started shooting back and maneuvering to better shooting positions. We called for artillery to help us and twenty-minutes later the bad guys gave up and left the area. Only four of us were alive when it ended. Two guys were wounded really badly. They both died within a day. The other guy and I weren't hurt at all—so we thought. Instead of sending the two of us back to combat, they sent us to truck repair school. That's how I started learning about fixing trucks."

Ruth touched him on the shoulder. "Oliver, that must have been a terrible experience."

"That's the funny part. It didn't really get to me until I was discharged. The other survivor and I kept in touch at least once a month, but we never talked about what happened. I've learned that not talking about what happened was a mistake. A huge mistake, as it turns out. You and I had been dating about two weeks when I told you that I had to fly to San Diego to see a friend from the army. The other survivor had tried to kill himself. I visited him at a VA hospital. He was so full of medication he could barely talk. He's so bad he may never leave the hospital. As I flew home, I realized I had to get some help, so I've been seeing a psychiatrist at the VA in Tacoma."

"Oliver, I'm so sorry all this happened to you."

He had tears in his eyes. Ruth wrapped her arms around him and then pulled his head onto her shoulder. Oliver held her and began crying.

Through his tears he continued. "They were some great guys. One of them was a brilliant violinist. He could play classical, jazz, and blue grass on his violin. Ruth, he could make that violin cry or laugh. Another of the guys was going to start medical school when he returned home. They had plans for great futures in front of them, and I was just a guy with no plans and no education. Why the hell should I have survived and those guys died?"

A teary-eyed Ruth used her warm hands to remove the tears sliding down each side of Oliver's face. "Oliver Holt, I can't tell you why you survived, but thank God you did. Holly told me that after our first visit she really didn't care if she ever saw me again, but she wanted to spend time with you. Even now, she can't wait to tell you what happened in school every day. Her twelve-year-old mind listened to you and watched you. She knew that you would always be there for her. Holly and I have a wonderful loving relationship now, but it really took many weeks before she started to believe in me. She and I owe you a debt that we can't possibly pay back."

Ruth paused to kiss Oliver. "And the way Drew looks up to you. Remember when I had my professor friend come over to show him how to begin learning to use acrylic paints on canvas. You set up an easel for him at his height and he did a remarkable job putting the image of one of your little civil war soldiers on canvas. When he was finished, who was the first person he yelled for to see the painting?"

Oliver nodded his head.

"Drew liked showing me, but he was positively enthralled when you told him how much you liked it. He's even starting to use expressions like you do. He would be completely happy coming home to our house, even if you couldn't always do what he wanted to do. Oliver you are the center of joy in my life, and those children's lives too. I couldn't be happier that the Lord saw fit to keep you safe and put us together. I have a family now, and you, Oliver, are the glue that got us, and keeps us, together."

Oliver wrapped his arms around Ruth. He was quiet for a long time and then took a deep breath. "If anything has made my life worth living, it's certainly been the time I have spent with you—not to mention the joy I get from Holly and Drew. Even your parents treat me like gold."

"That's because you treat Holly, Drew, and me like gold." "Ruth Case, I love you so much."

"Please, let me make you feel better tonight," she told him. He began kissing her and caressing her beautiful body.

"Anytime I'm with you, makes me feel better, Ruth."

They made love then, and afterwards Oliver wrapped his body around Ruth and thought that having her in his life was, and is, giving him the strength to work out his problems. He thanked the Lord for putting this blessed woman in his life.

***

After they brought Holly over to live with them she immediately started calling Ruth and Oliver, Mom and Dad. The first time she referred to Oliver as Dad, he pointed out to Holly that he wasn't really her dad.

Tears welled up in her eyes. Then with firm conviction in her voice, she assured him, "Yes, you are." She wrapped her arms around Oliver. "You've been my dad since the first time we met. I love you, Dad."

Oliver held his little girl and told her he loved her too. "*Ti amo, la mia piccola figlia.*"

Ruth was shocked. She had never heard Oliver speaking in such lovely Italian.

Oliver looked at Ruth's shocked expression and grinned. "I've been listening to you guys for months now. I had to pick up something."

"*Ti amo,* Oliver. *Ti amo,*" Ruth told him.

Holly looked up at her father with a loving smile. "*Ti amo, mio Padre.*"

Chapter Sixteen ~ Michael and Anna

CAREFULLY SETTING THE LITTER down for the last time, Michael opened the door to the motorhome and carried Anna inside. He rapidly pushed three buttons to start the generator and interior heat. Within seconds, the heater fan could be heard starting up. After carefully setting Anna down on the bed, Michael pulled a sheet over her and helped her get out of her wet clothes.

Then, as gently as possible, he wrapped her in blankets and quickly got out of his own wet, soiled clothing, pulling on a sweatshirt and sweatpants.

"Hey," Anna called. "I'm scared over here." "How about I make some warm soup for you?"

"Look, mister, we have a deal. When I tell you I'm scared, that means you have to hold me."

"Ok, but only for you, sunshine lady."

Smiling, Michael lay down on the bed next to Anna and stretched his arm over her blanket-covered body.

"Uh-uh. Not good enough," she said. "You're too far away."

Michal crawled under the blankets and snuggled up close, making sure there was still a sheet between him and her now-naked body.

"Much better." Anna sighed and relaxed into him.

After a few minutes, Michael noticed that Anna had stopped shivering, but now had tears in her eyes.

"Are you in pain, Anna?"

"My leg is starting to throb. The pain killer must be wearing off, but that's not why I'm crying."

"You don't have to cry. We made it."

"Michael, that's *why* I'm crying. I just kept telling myself—Michael is going to take care of me. I have to hang on, no matter how much I hurt, because I know Michael's going to get me out of here. And you did. I'm crying because I knew I could depend on you."

Anna looked at him with tears running down her cool, red cheeks. She put her hand behind his head and pulled him into a kiss. He was flooded with warm feelings.

He looked into her eyes. "Anna, I've already lost one special lady in my life, and I wasn't about to lose another. I wasn't about to lose you."

When he moved his hand to brush a strand of hair from Anna's face, she reacted to the bloody gauze. "Michael, your hand is bleeding."

He tore his eyes away from Anna's face and looked at his hand. "It's not bad. I just have some blisters."

"Michael, you put something on those hands and wrap them.

If I have to, I'll get out of bed to—"

"Okay, Okay." He raised his hands in mock surrender. "Stay still and I'll take care of them now."

As he left the bedroom, his eyes lingered on Anna's pale face. There she was, in a lot of pain and she insisted he take care of himself. He washed with antiseptic soap, treated the blisters, and wrapped bandages on his hands and fingers.

He went back to the bedroom, gave Anna a couple of pain killers, and within a few minutes she was asleep.

Michael went to the kitchen and took out some of Anna's home-made tomatillo salsa, then he opened two cans of navy bean soup, placing them on the stove to heat. With a little effort because of his bandaged hands, Michael cubed two chicken breasts, chopped some parsley, fresh basil, and onion. Then he melted some butter in a sauté pan, added a little olive oil, and chopped garlic, then sautéed the onion and herbs in the fragrant oil.

He added the fresh ingredients to the soup, and it was nearly heated through when he heard Anna moan. He went to her. "Are you okay?"

"I forgot to keep my leg still. I'll be okay. But hey, something sure smells good out there."

Michael smiled at her. "I'll be right back." He put the soup in bowls, then on trays with toasted French bread, a few Rainier cherries, and a nectarine.

"Oh boy, dinner in bed," Anna exclaimed.

He gently set the tray next to her lap. "The pills I gave you will help take the edge off the pain, but not much else."

"I'm okay, Michael. Besides, with a lovely dinner like this, ending in my favorite fruit, I can hardly complain about a little pain."

He leaned over and kissed her cheek. "Thank you, Michael."

After they ate, he walked back to the front to check on the motorhome's systems. The snow was still coming down quite heavily and was now accompanied by a strong wind. There was probably a good two-feet of snow on the ground. The windows on the left side were completely covered in ice and snow. When he turned on the headlights, he could only see a few yards ahead.

Michael went back and told Anna they should stay the night. He didn't want to take a chance on driving down the steep, snow covered hills in the dark.

***

The next morning, Michael awoke before Anna. It had rained throughout the night and the temperature had warmed significantly. This would help make it an easy drive out of there now.

He went and checked the motorhome's systems to see if there was any damage from the storm. The snow had turned to slush and his boots went down to the asphalt with every step—the motorhome would have good traction going down the hill. Everything looked good.

He noticed the litter he had constructed to carry Anna down the mountain and he stuffed it in one of the storage bays.

Then, while Anna was still sleeping, he decided to fire up the engine and get down to the ranger station. As soon as he could get cell phone service, Michael called 911 and asked that an ambulance meet them at the ranger station.

Anna woke up just as he was pulling into the station's parking lot and the ambulance was pulling in as well. She was surprised to see help was already there.

He watched as the paramedics immobilized Anna's leg, put her on a stretcher, and wheeled her out of the motorhome and into the ambulance. Michael drove over to the emergency center behind the ambulance.

When he got inside he talked to a doctor who told him that Anna needed a specialist who would surgically repair the wound near her knee and she was being flown to Boise within-the-hour.

"How did you learn to suture like that?" the doctor asked him. "I read a book and talked to my doctor at home. She told me to suture some thin-skinned-oranges and then try suturing some cooked pasta," Michael replied.

"Well, your sutures could have been further apart, but you probably saved her leg. As bad as I suppose she was bleeding, you probably saved her life as well," he told Michael. "She's going to be tired for a while with all that blood loss, but after the surgery, she'll be fine. And by the way, Anna told me, she wouldn't fly anywhere until I looked at your hands."

Michael grinned and stuck out his hands. "That's my Anna."

The doctor cut the gauze off and instructed a nurse to clean the wounds and put clean dressings on Michael's hands. He also prescribed an antibiotic.

Afterwards, Michael went to Anna's room to talk to her. He was happy to know that she was going to be okay, even if it meant she had to fly out ahead of him. "You get to ride in a helicopter, lady."

"I know. They're going to have a surgeon work on my leg mid- afternoon. Did the doctor look at your hands?"

He proudly held up his hands to show Anna the new bandages. "He gave me a prescription for an antibiotic as well."

"Good." She wore a relieved-looking smile on her face. "How soon can you get to Boise?"

"I should be there around dinner time. I'll park the motorhome at the house I've rented and get my car out of the trailer to drive over to the hospital. How are you feeling?"

"I mostly feel tired. They've given me a pain killer, so the throbbing ache in my leg is gone for now. They also x-rayed my ankle and said it's just a minor sprain. I can start putting weight on it in a day or so."

"I can wait with you until your flight if you like."

"No, I want you to hurry and get to Boise. I'll probably be scared after the surgery, so I'll need you then. Right now, I just want to sleep."

"Okay. I'll see you in Boise."

Her face turned serious. "Listen carefully to me, Michael. You must drive safely." Her expression turned to a grin. "I don't want anything bad to happen to my furniture."

Michael shook his head with a smile. Anna was in a hospital bed, facing surgery to repair her leg, and still with the jokes. He leaned over her, put his hand on the side of her face, and kissed her.

"Thank you, Michael." Anna closed her eyes.

Michael quietly left the room as soon as Anna was asleep. He got back on the interstate and drove about three hours to Meridian, Idaho, where he had rented a small house. He knew Meridian to be a lovely town. It was adjacent to, and just west of, Boise.

He'd called the rental agent and told her when to meet him there and as he pulled the motorhome in front of the house, he saw the agent arriving too.

She showed Michael around and gave him the keys. After she left he opened the back of the trailer and got his car out, then maneuvered it into the driveway. Next, he disconnected the trailer and pulled the motorhome into the driveway beside it.

"Nice camper," a new neighbor called out to him.

Michael looked over and noticed that the neighbor had a big fifth-wheel trailer in his driveway.

He smiled and waved. "I have to run now, but come by later and I'll be happy to give you a tour."

"I'll look forward to that," the neighbor yelled with a wave of his own.

Michael had heard from his friends, Sean and Trisha McCarthy, that the people in the Boise area were friendly. If his new neighbor was any reflection on that, they had been right.

He'd met Sean and Trisha on a job in Oshkosh, Wisconsin, and after telling them he would be taking a consulting job in Boise, he had to promise them that he'd call when he was settled. The couple had a home in Eagle, Idaho and had grown up in the Midwest just like Michael had. They said they loved the Boise area—Treasure Valley, they called it.

Chapter Seventeen ~ Oliver and Ruth, Holly and Drew

FOUR-WEEKS BEFORE THEIR wedding, Oliver received a letter from a truck manufacturer. He had recently written them a letter complaining about the poor design of their newest truck. The new design made it much more difficult to repair. Oliver didn't just complain, but had suggested changes to alleviate the problems. The letter said the chief of their engineering research division would be in Seattle and would like to take Oliver to dinner.

"That's quite a compliment," Ruth told him.

"I've written to them before. This is the first time I added suggestions. I wonder if that's why they want to talk to me," Oliver said.

Oliver was curious and agreed. He met with Sam Johnson over dinner and learned that Sam loved engineering, especially the unique challenges of truck engineering. With a degree in automotive engineering, he had been hired by a major truck manufacturer and had quickly moved up the ranks to head their R & D division.

He was of medium build and average height with a low voice that he said allowed him to sing the bass line in his church choir or with his friends when they competed in barbershop quartet contests.

Sam had that amazing personality quirk that made someone feel they were his friend as soon as they met him.

After dinner, Sam handed Oliver an envelope. Far from a mere reply to his letter, this envelope had a job offer in it. Oliver was shocked beyond words and went directly over to Ruth's apartment. As soon as he entered, he started right in on the news. "They've offered me a job at their technical center," he told Ruth. "It's in Boise, Idaho and I'd be working with their engineers, making sure their designs were easy to repair. Apparently, there's a big university out there. They'll pay me to get a mechanical engineering degree while

I work for them. They'll also pay to move us out there, Ruth, and it's more money than I earn now. He said we can buy a nice house in Boise for what we're considering paying for the townhouse here in Seattle. They'd like me to start right after Labor Day." A beaming Ruth gave Oliver a huge hug.

"Oliver, this is an incredible offer. Imagine the impact it will have on Drew when he sees you going to university and studying every day."

"What about your job, Ruth?"

She smiled. "Well, I've been thinking, Oliver. I would like to take time off from teaching for a year to be an at-home-mom for our family."

"We can do that easily, if I take this job." "What about all the friends Holly's made?" "We should talk to her and see what she says." Ruth agreed that would be best.

"I'll miss my friends," Holly said when they told her about the potential move. "Especially Paula. But as long as I'm with you, that's what's most important to me. What about Drew?"

"Keep this to yourself," Ruth said, "but Oliver and I have a meeting with Ms. Hollings next week. We're going to appear before the county adoption board. Normally it takes months of visits from Ms. Hollings to determine if a family is suitable for an adoption.

She wants to use the visits she performed while you were visiting us, as a basis for Drew's adoption too. We have letters from your teacher, Drew's teacher, and the foster family, so Ms. Hollings doesn't think it will be a problem. It's not certain yet, which is why we haven't said anything to Drew."

"I can go with you if you like, so I can talk to them."

"We thought about that," Oliver said, "but Ms. Hollings doesn't think it will be necessary."

"Well then, I'll write a note to Ms. Hollings on why Drew should live with us," Holly decided.

At the adoption board appearance, after the interview with Ruth and Oliver, Ms. Hollings presented all her paperwork and then read Holly's letter to the board.

> *"These are the reasons why Drew should live at my house. One. I have amazing parents who love me and value my opinion, even when they get upset with my—only occasional—bad behavior. Two. Drew is an amazing boy and sometimes a brother needs an older sister—me— to talk to. My parents always have been good listeners for me, so I can be a good listener for Drew. Three. I speak English, Spanish and I am learning Italian. I can teach Drew Spanish and Italian because he already knows English. Four. My gym teacher at school said I have two left feet, so I need Drew to teach me how to properly kick a soccer ball. Five. Some of my friends at school have brothers and they are very close. I'm always nice to Drew and he is always nice to me, so he would be a good brother to be close to. Six. This is most important. My parents and I love Drew already, so when he moves in he won't ever be lonely again. Thank you very much. Holly"*

The head of the adoption board smiled. "Well that should certainly cover it. Ms. Hollings, all your paper work is in order, so we just need a couple of signatures, and we're done with this case."

She congratulated a beaming Ruth and Oliver, and then Oliver drove Ruth over to the townhouse to get ready for Drew's arrival. After that, he drove over to the foster parents' home.

After speaking with the foster parents in private, Oliver took Drew aside. "These are your adoption papers," he said. "It's official. You can start living with us today."

Drew's eyes went as wide as they could. "Today?"

"Yes."

Oliver could tell Drew was restraining himself from bouncing up and down.

"Now?"

"I have boxes in the car, if you're ready now."

"I'm ready. I mean, I'm really ready." Drew let loose the self- restraint and began jumping. "Are we going to move into the house I saw before?"

"Yes, but only for a month. At the end of the week, we're all driving out to Boise, Idaho to look for a house to live in. I'm taking a new job out there."

Drew was so excited, he said he could hardly think straight.

Oliver helped him pack all his things.

After thanking his foster parents for taking care of him, Drew helped Oliver carry his boxes down to his SUV. Oliver was astounded at Drew's strength.

***

When they arrived at their new home, Ruth and Holly were waiting for them.

Holly greeted him first. "Hello, brother."

Drew smiled from ear to ear as he replied. "Hello, Sister. Hello, Mother." Then he hugged them both.

"Go and see your new room," Ruth said. "Holly and I fixed it up for you."

Drew started to run, but must have remembered the no-running-in-the-house rule, so as calmly as possible he resumed climbing the stairs to the second floor, with Ruth and Holly close behind.

As he walked down the hallway, he glanced in Holly's room. He stopped and read the pink letters on the wall. "Holly's Hutch," he said.

She smiled. "Just wait."

When he walked into his room he grinned widely as he noticed the letters in large, black gothic type that spelled out Drew's Den. His easel was set up in the corner next to a shelf with his paints on it. The shelf was deep enough that many of his paintings were already stored there. The room also had a desk and a bunk bed.

Holly had put some posters on the walls with soccer themes, plus Drew's favorite comic book character, The Hulk. On another wall, Ruth had framed Drew's first acrylic painting of the toy soldier.

Drew walked over to the bunk bed that was off to the side of his room. He ran his hand along it and turned back to Holly, Oliver, and Ruth, who were standing just inside the doorway smiling at him.

"Thank you guys so much. This is the best room in the world." As he looked at them, his eyes filled with tears.

Ruth immediately walked over, kneeled in front of him, and put her hands on his shoulders. "What's wrong, Drew?"

He shrugged and sniffled. "I don't know. I'm so happy. I don't know why I'm crying."

Ruth hugged him tight. "Sometimes it happens like that, Drew. It happened to me when your sister told me she wanted to live with me. I cried with joy—so much I couldn't even talk."

Oliver stepped in. "Would you like to go out for a walk?"

"No. I mean, no thank you. I just want to stay in my room for a while." Drew smiled, then wiped at his cheek.

He looked around. "This is my room. This is my very own room." Then he plunked down on his bunk bed.

Ruth ruffled his hair. "Okay, you can stay up here, but in an hour dinner will be ready."

He nodded. "Okay. It smells great in here," he said.

Then Holly told him in an excited voice, "To celebrate your homecoming, we made ravioli and *sugo Bolognese*."

Drew exclaimed in Italian, "*Il mio favorito. Grazie, Sorella e Madre.*"

"Oh, my Lord," Oliver proclaimed. "Another one with a head for language. I'm going to have to get serious about learning Italian, just to keep up with your characters. Come on, Drew. Let's get your boxes out of my car and into your room. I'll help you get unpacked. We'll set up your dresser like I have mine set up and you can move things around the way you want later on."

Then after a lovely meal, that included spumoni ice cream for dessert, Oliver started clearing the dishes from the table. He nodded to Drew, who jumped up to help.

When the table had been cleared, Ruth looked at Drew. "When Holly and I are done cleaning the kitchen, Drew, I'll want you to take out the garbage for us."

Drew grinned. "Okay, Mom."

Holly got a pensive look on her face. "Mom," she asked. "When you're doing my, and now Oliver's, laundry, do you get tired of doing that, or everyday things like cooking and cleaning the house?"

"No, Holly, I don't. You help me, and Oliver takes clothing that needs dry cleaning to the cleaners." Ruth smiled. "Besides, every time I look at yours or Oliver's clothing, it makes me happy that I can do something to take care of my family."

"It doesn't seem like work?"

"When you made the ravioli for Drew's dinner tonight, did it seem like work?"

"Not really. I kept thinking how much Drew would enjoy having his favorite meal with us."

"In other words, you were getting happiness from an event that hadn't even happened yet."

"Wow, that's right. Also, when Drew walked in the house and he was so happy to call me sister, I felt happy from his happiness then, too."

"Yes," Ruth continued. "So now I get to take care of my own family, with the help of my daughter and son, and shortly, my husband. That makes anything that I do to help the family a source of joy for me. Sometimes I do get tired, but it's a good tired, because I did something important for the family."

***

An hour before bedtime, Oliver told Drew to get ready for bed.

Drew quickly walked over to his new sister to give her a hug and a thank you for making ravioli for his coming home dinner. He then hugged Ruth, thanking her for making sure he had such a nice room.

When he had washed and was in his pajamas, Drew called to Oliver to let him know he was ready. Oliver went into Drew's room with a book entitled *The Adventures of Huckleberry Finn*. He read to Drew for thirty minutes. Drew was enthralled with the story, but also worn out from the day's excitement.

Drew smiled and rubbed his eyes. "Good night, Dad." Oliver patted Drew on the shoulder. "Good night, Son."

As Drew drifted off to sleep, he thought that being called Son sounded mighty nice.

Chapter Eighteen ~ Anna and Michael

AFTER ARRIVING AT THE rental home, Michael made some phone calls and drove over to the hospital. It was actually located in Meridian and only about fifteen minutes from the house he rented. He arrived at Anna's room about dinnertime. "This food is so bland," she told him. "I'm sure people get better just to get out of here and eat some food they can taste."

Michael smiled at her spunk. She looked better—not as pale as she had previously. She had a big brace on one leg and the ankle on her other leg was wrapped.

"My sprained ankle isn't too bad, but I have to stay off my other leg as much as possible for two weeks. I won't be able to start the job with you."

"Don't worry about that, Anna. I made some calls and we're all set."

"Did you call the apartment complex and tell them that I wouldn't be moving in today?"

"I called them. I told them that you wouldn't need the apartment."

"What?" Anna tried to sit up, but winced in pain and leaned back on the pillows.

"You know how big my rented house is. You can have the master bedroom with the attached bath. That will be easier for you. I'll set up a connection to work, so you can use my laptop to telecommute."

"Michael..."

He reached down and gently took her hands in both of his, lifting one up to kiss the back of it. "Anna Cardozo, you are the most important person in the world to me. I know we come from very different backgrounds and very different life experiences. But, Anna, you and I are going to put together the world's greatest relationship. I know this is going to happen because I love you so much."

Anna's eyes filled with tears. "What about your feelings toward Sharon?"

"Two months after you and I started working together, I visited Sharon's grave. I had a long cry and said good-bye to her. I also thanked her for putting you in my life. Only Sharon could understand how lonely I was and how much I needed you."

Michael brushed away a tear from Anna's cheek.

"As I tore up my hands getting you back to the motorhome, I didn't just do it for you. I did it for my future as well. Anna, you are my future. So yes, you're going to move in with me so I can take care of you. My place—*our* place—even has a fireplace, like you told me you liked. I'll put you in the master bedroom so you'll be close to the bathroom, and I'll sleep in one of the small bedrooms. We are going to work things out between us, Anna. I promise you that." "Thank you, Michael," she told him through her tears, "for making feel me so loved."

A day later he brought Anna over to *their* house and she sat on a chair in the living room cheerfully directing him as to where the furniture should be located.

After lunch, Anna was tired from all the morning's activity, so she wanted to sleep for a while. She asked Michael to place a blanket and pillows in front of the fireplace, then he lay down next to her. "Michael, I want to tell you something. I've been thinking about this for the last couple of days. This is very difficult for me, so please don't say anything until I'm finished."

"All right," he said and kissed the back of her head.

"I've learned that I want you in my life. I've always been the wallflower. I never spoke up on my own behalf because I worried people wouldn't like my thoughts and ideas. I rarely believed in myself, but you seemed to believe in me from the start. Whenever I said something, you wanted to know exactly why I thought that way. That frightened me at first, but I learned that you respected what I thought, whether you agreed or not. You provided a safe environment for me to express my thoughts. No one dares talk to me in a disrespectful manner, because you will be there to take their heads off."

Anna reached up and hugged the arm Michael had draped over her. "When I started my career in Seattle, I was scared every morning. I would wonder if today would be the day when I made some stupid mistake and got fired. Within a few weeks of working with you, my thinking changed. I was still frightened of making a big mistake, but I knew you would help me fix it if I did. You believe in me without reservation. I've never experienced that before. Because of that you taught me to believe in myself."

She turned to look at him. "Michael, wherever Sharon is, she put you in my life because she saw how desperately I needed you. I have always felt alone and often disappointed in myself, finding fault in my accomplishments. But for the rest of my life, instead of worrying about disappointing myself, I am only going to be worried about disappointing you. Every morning when I wake up, I know you are going to be there, and I'm going to thank the Lord every day that you are. I've tried to ignore my feelings for you, but the more time we spend together the more I want—the more I *need*— us to stay together."

Michael brushed the hair away from her eyes and kissed her forehead.

"My life has two parts, Michael," she continued. "Before you came into it and after. Your confidence in me makes me feel more secure. You remind me that I'm a great engineer, and a great person. I feel safe even when you tease me. For the first time in my life, I can laugh at myself. Now I want you to be proud of me in another way—proud that I'm your partner, your forever partner. It doesn't matter where we are, what we are doing, or what happens to us. As long as we're together, we're happy."

"My beloved, Anna," Michael told her as he kissed her cheek. "Four-months-ago I found myself thinking that Sharon must have sent you to me, because when I met you, my life started to have meaning again. Anna, you are truly the sunshine of my life. I love you so much."

"I know, Michael." She rolled over and held his arm tight. "Every moment of every day that we are together, I know."

Then, Anna fell asleep while Michael read in front of the fireplace.

***

By the end of the day, they had everything in their little house. They ordered pizza for dinner, and ate it on the floor in front of the fireplace.

"We still have a deal," Anna reminded Michael. "You still have to hold me if I get scared."

He grinned and made an exaggerated sigh. "You are so difficult to deal with."

Anna laughed. "That means that you have to sleep in the same bed as me, because it might take too long for you to come into my room if I get scared."

Michael chuckled quietly. "Yes, Anna."

Then she stopped eating and became serious. "I'm worried about something, Michael. I know I have an ugly body—"

"What?" He exclaimed in astonishment. "What idiot told you that? Anna, you have a *beautiful* body."

"No, Michael."

"Yes, Anna. Do you remember in the motorhome when you were putting your robe on and you dropped the sheet that was covering your chest? Well, let me just say, it was a beautiful sight, and believe me, I've seen more than a few."

"But I'm so skinny."

"Anna, you're not skinny. You have a body that most women would kill to have. This may not sound nice, but you should know that I got so excited from that one glance at your chest, I nearly exploded in my pants. That has *never* happened to me before. Every time I think about your pretty breasts, my flag goes up."

Anna giggled. "Your flag?"

Michael took her hand and put it on the bulge in his hiking shorts. "That's what you do to me, just thinking about you."

"I don't have any experience with this, Michael. What if I disappoint you?"

"Anna, I love you. There's no way that's going to happen. Even if it doesn't go perfectly the first time, the great thing about this is that we keep on practicing until we get it right. We are going to go slow. You let me know what you like, and I'll let you know what I like. Things we don't like, we won't do. It's that easy, we just practice until we get it right."

Anna felt relieved. Even with sex, Michael was going to help make it easy for her.

He kissed her and they relaxed and read in front of the fireplace for a few hours. They cuddled and enjoyed the nearness and the crackling sounds from the fire. Four weeks later, as the evening turned into night and they were again reading in front of the fireplace, Anna looked at him with a huge smile on her face. "It's almost bed time," she said. "I have no pain from my leg and the doctor said it's healing quickly so I think we should start practicing to get it right tonight."

Michael grinned and then helped her up, handing her the set of crutches from the hospital. They moved into the master bedroom. "It's usually fun to undress each other, but with you on crutches, why don't I get out of my clothes first," Michael suggested, "and you can have a naked guy undressing you."

Anna smiled and nodded yes.

Michael turned off the bedroom lights. The only remaining light came from the flickers of the wood burning fireplace in the living room. As she watched him undress, Anna thought that even though he hadn't touched her yet, just looking at him made her feel warm down there.

Michael unbuttoned Anna's blouse and slid it off her shoulders. He put his hands on either side of her face and kissed her.

Anna felt like his kiss was setting her lips on fire. Michael undid the belt on her slacks. He unzipped them and kneeled in front of her as he slowly lowered them to the ground, leaning forward, kissing her belly.

She saw that his "flag" was up, and it seemed to point straight at her.

Michael reached behind her to undo her bra.

Talk about starting fires, she thought. Then she decided it wasn't just a fire, but would be a multiple-alarm inferno if he kept kissing and caressing her. She luxuriated in the sensation of their bodies touching, the warm feeling of her breasts against his bare chest.

Michael slowly kneeled, placing kisses along her body as he lowered her panties. He helped her into bed, and she pulled a blanket over them, as Michael lay down beside her and began to caress her.

"Michael, I don't know what to do."

"Anna, this body lying next to you, is yours now. You can touch me anywhere, anytime you like. Just see what I feel like and I'll show you what I want you to do. If I'm doing something you don't like, you can tell me or just push me away, and I'll stop doing whatever it is."

Anna started tentatively exploring Michael's body. She was excited to finally be able to run her hands over his muscular form. As she did, Michael continued to kiss her lips and caress her.

Anna pulled back from his kiss. "Michael, I want to do everything tonight."

"Are you sure?"

She nodded. She *was* scared—not just of her first time making love, but also of her injured leg. But the desire in her was stronger than her fears.

"I'll be very careful," he assured her. Then, Michael placed her injured leg on a pillow and gently inserted himself inside her.

Anna could not believe the amazing sensations Michael moving inside her produced. It wasn't long before she felt her first explosion. Shortly after, Michael started his own.

"Thank you. Thank you, Anna. That felt so great. That was fantastic."

Michael remained inside her for a while and then gently withdrew and lay down next to her.

"Michael, I can't believe how beautiful that was," Anna said.

Every inch of Anna's body ached from all the wonderful sensations making love to Michael had produced. "I love you, Michael."

"I love you, Anna. That's what really makes all this so special. You have truly brought sunshine into my heart and into my life."

Anna murmured her thoughts. "I don't care if we never become business partners, as long as we can be together."

"I agree completely, Anna. We will, however, become excellent business partners."

She smiled. "I guess I was thinking louder than I realized."

"Good night, sunshine lady." "Good night, sunshine man."

Years later they would reminisce about that first time and declare it one of the most beautiful events in their lives.

***

Michael had suggested that they make a special meal for the following Saturday evening. She prepared roast rack of lamb, and since the roast was so large, Michael decided to use some of it to make a special dish for Anna.

He filmed a sauté pan with olive oil and added finely chopped onion and garlic. He then ground the leftover lamb and added it to the onion and garlic mixture. When it was cooked, he added chopped parsley, thyme, rosemary, white wine, and chicken stock. Then he cubed an eggplant and sautéed it until it was just tender, mixing it into the lamb.

Michael hollowed out some tomatoes and added the fragrant lamb and eggplant mixture. He dusted the tops of the stuffed tomatoes with bread crumbs and put them under a broiler for a few minutes.

He gestured to the oven. "My dad taught me this recipe," he told her. "I think he got it out of a Julia Child cookbook."

Anna sampled the lamb and eggplant mixture. "Michael, if you can cook like this, I need to get you into the kitchen more often. This is so aromatic and flavorful. What a great accompaniment to the rack of lamb."

Anna had prepared shrimp ceviche for an appetizer and served it in a cup made of butter-crunch lettuce leaves. She'd also boiled fresh carrots in orange juice, honey, Grand Marnier, cinnamon, and nutmeg. She had Michael steam fresh asparagus as well. For dessert Anna had ordered an Apple-Plum streusel from the European bakery in Meridian.

When everything was ready, Michael changed into nice slacks and one of his favorite Jane Bharnes shirts. As it was only practical for Anna to wear shorts, with the big brace on her leg, she put on one of her most colorful patterned tops.

Michael set the table with his autumn-patterned Lenox china and glassware.

Anna admired it. "Michael that is such lovely china. It's perfect for a special dinner."

They sat down to eat. Anna looked as content as Michael felt. "Michael, this is really nice," she said. "We should plan on doing this once a month, just for us." "Hmmm, this isn't quite nice enough."

He reached into his pocket and took out a small velvet-covered box.

Anna's eyes opened wide and she started to tremble.

Michael kneeled in front of her and opened the little box, showing her a beautiful engagement ring. "Anna Cardozo, will you marry me?"

"Yes, Michael, I would love to marry you."

He put the ring on her finger and they engaged in a long embrace.

"I won't be able to see this lovely meal through my tears," Anna said.

***

Throughout the meal, and over the next few days, Anna would look at her ring and wonder how she deserved this sign of Michael's commitment.

As she was unpacking more of the boxes she had moved from Seattle, she found her old drawing supplies. She remembered that one of the smaller bedrooms only had one window and dull, white paint on the walls and ceiling. So, she went to do something about that. From memory, Anna created a mural of the sights of her hometown. She included a scene of her parents' restaurant and home, with a red sky over the Organ Mountains. She laughed and giggled as she included a scene with a glass of lemonade on a table, and an older woman and little girl painting together.

When Michael arrived home, Anna yelled for him to come into the small bedroom.

He entered the room and looked appraisingly around. "Did you do this?"

Anna nodded.

"Anna, I had no idea...this is gorgeous."

"I haven't drawn anything since high school. I woke up feeling pretty well today and when I found my old art supplies, I decided to put them to work."

As Michael admired her work, he started looking at her with immense pride which was followed by a look that Anna would eventually call Michael's let's-do-it-now expression.

"Michael," Anna teased him, "we can't do it in front of my hometown."

"It's okay," Michael told her. "None of those people know me, and the ones that know you won't recognize your beautiful grownup figure."

Anna laughed. "One more room and we've done it in every room in this house, and I've loved doing it in each and every one of them."

Chapter Nineteen ~ Anna and Michael

THE JOB IN BOISE was going well for Michael and Anna. Anna came into work two-days-a-week and worked from home the other days. This allowed her to keep pressure off her still healing leg, as well as attending physical therapy.

Anna's relationship with Michael was growing on a daily basis. Michael repeatedly told her that she brought more joy into his life than he could possible deserve. She was sure she could feel her heart glow every time Michael told her that.

They made plans with their neighbors to drive out to Crater of the Moon National Monument over Labor Day weekend. When Anna told Chela of their plans, Chela said that she and Warren would love to join them.

Their motorhome pulled up in front of Michael and Anna's home on Wednesday around five o'clock in the evening, after a nine-hour cruise on the interstate highways from Seattle. It was a warm evening in Meridian when they arrived. Warren and Chela were wearing matching shorts and short sleeve shirts.

"*Hermana*," Chela screamed as she saw her sister.

"Welcome, Chela, welcome," Anna yelled as she walked out of their house and hugged her sister. "You've been losing weight, Chela," she said. "Your figure is nicer than ever."

"One of the engineers you used to work with showed us how to do some exercises with weights. We do upper body one day and then lower body the next. I hated it at first, but I look forward to it now. I'm down two-dress-sizes in the last-six-months, and it's easier to go on long hikes. I can show you what we do. It's really easy and inexpensive for some simple weights."

"I look forward to that," Anna replied.

As Warren came out of their motorhome, Michael yelled to him. "Nice rig there, buddy."

"Yeah," replied a grinning Warren, "some yokel from the Midwest convinced me to buy it."

As they entered the house, Warren commented on the huge speakers on either side of pre-amplifiers, CD transports, a turntable, and a couple of huge amplifiers. Wires were strung out here and there.

Michael was just installing an audio system and Warren enthusiastically offered to help while Chela and Anna went into the kitchen to prepare dinner.

Michael walked into the kitchen and showed Anna the specially shaped diamond needle which he was about to install in the tone arm of his system. It came in a pretty case, about three inches on a side.

"That's tiny, Michael. What does that cost?" Anna asked.

"A little over four-thousand-dollars—part of it is made from coral," Michael said in a casual voice as he walked back to his audio system.

Chela looked at Anna. "What did he just say?"

"Chela, brace yourself. That needle goes on a machine that does nothing but turn the vinyl records. That machine costs over forty-five-thousand-dollars. Michael hasn't told me what the electronics cost, but the cable he uses to connect the speakers runs ten-dollars-a-foot and his speakers cost over ten thousand each."

Chela just stood there with her mouth open.

"I know. It's hard to believe," Anna told her. "Michael has been working and earning a nice living since high school. He has a lot of investments, so over the years he bought all this audio equipment. He told me that he only buys his audio stuff for cash and would check with me before he buys anything else. Chela, he's had this system in storage since his fiancée, Sharon, died. He's setting it up again—for me. He's going to play Copland's *Appalachian Spring* for us after dinner tonight. He said it would be a religious experience to hear it on his system."

Chela beamed. "Anna, he loves you so much."

"I know, Chela. More than even *you* can imagine. Driving home from work a week ago, I had to get off the road and stop. I was thinking about how he makes me feel so loved. I just started crying thinking about how good he is to me. Chela, I've noticed that Michael says a couple of prayers every morning. In one of them he thanks God for giving him another day to spend with me. He loves me that much."

At dinner, Chela discussed her upcoming wedding. Anna had talked to her the previous weekend, so she knew that the wedding would be on Saturday during Thanksgiving weekend. Anna hadn't been back to see her family since she started her new job in Seattle and looked forward to seeing them again.

Then, after dinner Michael and Warren connected up the last of the cables to Michael's audio system. As thanks for his help, Michael offered to give Warren some extra equipment he had so that Warren could set up his own system.

"I don't think I can afford to maintain a system like this," Warren said. "I'd feel terrible if something broke and I couldn't afford to repair it."

Chela looked relieved to hear Warren say that. Anna knew she liked music, but didn't think she liked it enough to spend that kind of money on it.

As *Appalachian Spring* came wafting out of the speakers, Chela sat up straight in her chair. She mentioned that she and Warren had heard the Seattle symphony play that same piece.

"Warren, can you see them?" she whispered.

"Yes, Chela, I can definitely see the musicians. I know where each of them is sitting."

"Michael," Anna whispered. "This is amazing. I don't believe how real it sounds."

Michael just grinned.

About half way through the piece he saw an adolescent boy near the open front door. Michael walked over. "Can I help you?"

"No," replied the boy. "I play drums in my junior high school band and tympani in the school orchestra. I just wanted to hear the music."

"Come in then." Michael opened the screen door.

Fourteen-year-old Trace Beckham introduced himself to everyone. Michael guided him to a seat, perfectly situated in front of the speakers, that he called the sweet spot.

As the piece ended, Trace remarked, "Wow. That was so real. I felt like I was sitting right in front of the orchestra. Thanks so much, Mr. Levin."

"It's my pleasure, Trace. Come back another time and we'll do some serious listening to some of my other recordings."

"Warren," Chela said, "why don't you reconsider Michael's offer? If something breaks we'll just have to wait until we can afford to fix it."

Warren nodded. "Michael, if the offer still holds, I'd love to utilize your extra equipment."

"Of course it does, Warren. It's an honor to think that the equipment will be creating a great sound for someone instead of sitting in storage gathering dust."

Warren turned to Chela and asked her what had changed her mind about the stereo system.

"Well, I thought that if the system Michael gives us, sounds half as good as his monster system, I'm going to be overjoyed listening to it."

"Chela," Michael added, "I'm certain it will sound *nearly* as good as my system. We're going to set them up tomorrow so we can ensure that everything works before you two take it home."

"Isn't family wonderful?" Chela said.

"I'm so lucky." Warren added. "A few months ago, I was basically alone. Now, I not only have a fiancé, but Michael and Anna are like a brother and sister to me."

Chela took his hand. "Warren, I still find it amazing that the least social member of my family—my sister, Anna—got us together."

Anna smiled at Chela and then turned to Michael. "I was afraid to breathe when we were listening to your music system, Michael. I didn't want to miss a note. It really sounds that good."

"If it brings you joy, then we have one more thing we get to share."

Chapter Twenty ~ Anna and Michael, Trace and Linda, Anna and Michael

TRACE BECKHAM HAD BEEN fascinated by all types of blues music, and drums in particular, since he heard his grandfather playing the drums when he was a toddler. While his eighth-grade contemporaries were listening to rock and roll in all its various guises, Trace loved the blues.

In particular he had a near-obsession with Chicago Blues. He had received a vinyl album from his grandfather at age fourteen. It was an old recording of a Chicago blues musician named Muddy Waters. As no one in Trace's family had a record player, he had never had a chance to hear the album.

One Saturday morning, Trace went to see his friend from band, Linda Schulman. Linda played guitar, plus clarinet, in the school band. She and Trace got together sometimes to create blues sounds of their own, but today they decided to take the recording over to Michael's house to see if Michael would play it on his system.

When Trace handed the album to Michael, the look on his face was one of absolute shock. He was quiet for so long, that Trace thought Michael was upset.

Finally Michael spoke. "Trace, this is an absolute treasure. Ignoring the fact that I love the blues, it would be an honor of very large magnitude to play this on my system. Please come in and let's get to some serious listening."

Trace and Linda watched in fascination as Michael carefully removed the record from its jacket. He was holding it like it was made of gold or something.

"Trace, after we're done, I'm going to give you a new inner liner to protect the record better than the original. Keep the original liner in a safe place. This recording is worth a lot of money, and even more with the original liner. Now, first we're going to clean the record on a special machine."

They saw Michael place the record on something that looked similar to a record player. When he turned on the machine, he put cleaning solution on the record which was then vacuumed off, leaving it clean and dust free.

As they walked into Michael's living room, Michael called to Anna. "You have to hear this. It's an old recording by one of the best musicians that created the Chicago Blues sound."

Trace insisted that Linda sit in the sweet spot so she could hear the most accurate sound. He sat in a chair just in back of her in the next best listening position. Michael had his system warming up, giving the tubes time to stabilize before he played the recording. Trace and Linda were astounded to see vacuum tubes glowing on the main amplifier. They learned that many audiophiles prefer the sound of analog audio equipment, compared to the sound of digital audio equipment.

While the four of them listened, Trace and Linda seemed entranced. Anna and Michael had fun watching the two of them enjoy the music, along with their own joy at hearing Muddy Waters.

Anna smiled when it was time to turn the record over to play the second side. Her smile was caused by Linda telling Trace that he should have the best seat during the second side of the recording.

Trace politely thanked her and they exchanged places.

When the recording ended, Michael removed the disc from his turntable and placed it in its new liner and jacket. Linda and Trace had millions of questions about his audio system, which of course, Michael was more than happy to answer.

Anna invited them to stay for lunch, and as they ate, the two-eighth-graders explained to Anna and Michael that they were saving up money to attend music camp the following summer.

"It takes place at the university here in Boise. Our parents are putting up half the money and we have to earn the rest," Linda told them.

"We've been doing everything from shoveling snow to washing RVs," Trace added. "Even so, we only have part of the money we need."

"Three weeks from tonight, I have a project for you," Anna told them. "Michael and I are having a progressive dinner party with our friends. The last location will be this house. Desserts and after- dinner-drinks will be served, followed by a selection of jazz and blues recordings. I think it might be nice to have some live music. What do you think, Michael?"

Michael laughed. "Live Chicago Blues, by any chance? What do you say guys?"

Trace and Linda looked at each other in surprise. "We don't have anything prepared," Linda told them.

"I'll call your parents to make sure it's okay," Anna said. "Write something and play it for us. This is going to be a fundraiser for diabetes research. We'll pay each of you fifty-dollars for twenty-minutes worth of music. What do you say?"

Trace just sat there with his mouth open, so Linda answered for both of them. "We'd love to."

All Trace could manage was to nod in agreement.

Anna called up Linda and Trace's parents to make sure it was okay for them to perform at the fundraiser. The Beckhams were already invited to the progressive dinner, so Anna invited Linda's parents as well. Mrs. Schulman told Anna that they would love to attend. She also said that she had recently completed a course in Italian cooking, and practically begged Anna to let her make a few Italian desserts for the fundraiser. Anna was delighted to have someone else help make desserts.

The progressive dinner turned out to be a successful evening.

Everyone had a wonderful time and plenty of money was raised.

Trace and Linda had a great time performing together, and looked great doing it. He wore a dark suit, electric-blue shirt, and a yellow tie, while Linda, who was about a head taller than Trace, wore a long, black dress.

***

Trace's parents, Wilson and Dell Beckham, were accompanying Michael and Anna on their weekend camping trip to the Craters of the Moon National Monument, as well as Michael's friends, Sean and Trisha. Anna had met them at dinner once and she thought they would be a great addition to the group trip.

The Beckhams owned a spacious fifth-wheel trailer which provided plenty of room for them and their two children, although the children were staying with cousins that week, so they didn't accompany them.

Sean and Trisha still had their lovely Airstream travel coach, but instead of Sean's old pickup, they were towing their coach with a new full-size, four-door pickup truck that had a monster diesel engine.

Anna thought their pickup was so big, it almost made their twenty-five-foot Airstream look small.

Anna and Michael filled their motorhome with food and supplies for the four-day trip. Their caravan of two motorhomes and two travel trailers left early Friday morning and arrived at a campground around noon.

It was decided that they would have a group lunch, so Anna reheated some pulled pork that she had barbequed earlier in the week. Chela prepared a spring mix green salad, Dell and Wilson prepared warm German-style potato salad, and Trisha prepared an old Irish farm recipe, apple-barley pudding, for dessert.

They all gathered at a picnic table and Sean brought out a couple bottles of wine for the group to share.

Anna noticed immediately that Trisha didn't take any. "Trisha," Anna said, "I noticed the bigger pickup...and you're not having wine."

Trisha grinned. "Yep, and we're going to have to buy a bigger coach for camping."

Everyone congratulated the happy couple and Wilson proposed a toast for a healthy baby.

"And an easy delivery," Dell added.

Sean offered a toast too. He raised his glass. "To friends, family, and neighbors."

The four women laughed and enjoyed watching the four men as they began falling all over each other to make sure that Trisha didn't have to lift or carry anything heavier than a sweatshirt. Warren even offered to carry her binoculars for her.

Trisha finally told the men, "Look guys, six-months from now I'll need all kinds of help but seeing as I'm only two-months pregnant, I can manage everything as long as there's a place to pee nearby."

Everyone laughed at Trisha's remark. The guys did slow down trying to help her—but not by much.

***

After lunch they headed out in Warren's and Michael's Jeeps to begin their exploration of the appropriately named Crater of the Moon Monument. They found the park, its caves, and its lava flows fascinating.

It was quite hot, but some of the caves still had icicles inside them due to the insulating properties of the lava. The terrain was certainly desolate, but everyone was amazed by the myriad of shapes, textures, and colors of the lava flows.

They went on a number of hikes around the park. Anna was quite aware that Michael and Sean were keeping a close eye on her and Trisha to make sure they weren't getting carried away with all the hiking. Anna's leg was nearly healed, but occasionally felt sore if she walked too much. Michael continually reminded her to stay on the trail and look where she was going, as they were all entranced by the strange landscape.

Warren was taking quite a few photographs of the bird life, while Chela was keeping a log of the birds they were seeing. They found Turkey Vultures, Northern Harriers, Northern Flickers, and Rufous Hummingbirds, among many other species—and Warren photographed them all.

They all made sure to stay on the trails, as the fragile lava was also quite sharp and could easily harm someone if they tripped or fell on it.

"The northern edge of the lava flow is one of the areas that the wagon trains followed coming west," Michael told them. "I can't imagine what a hardship it must have been for those brave folks to come across this desolate area. They were some really strong people to head west along here."

Everyone agreed.

Along one of the trails Michael stopped and whispered to Anna. "Warren seems more outgoing. Chela's helped him find his voice in group settings. He sure exhibits a keen sense of humor. I'd never seen that in him previously."

"Some partners have that effect." She squeezed Michael's hand tighter than usual.

Anna was getting quite skilled at cooking Texas-style barbeque, thanks to Dell, who grew up in Texas. Anna and Dell were about the same age and Anna eagerly learned about very slow cooking at low temperatures from her new friend.

Dell had her own recipes for dry rubs, and instructed Anna in the preparation and cooking of Texas-style barbecue. The best part was that Michael loved Anna's efforts at barbeque as much as he adored her other cooking.

Dell told everyone her father belonged to a Texas religion that regularly made slow-cooked offerings meant for the gods. "Of course, the gods never showed up," she said, "so out of respect for them, we ended up eating those slow-cooked offerings ourselves."

While they were cooking, Dell mentioned to Anna that her husband, Wilson, owned a construction company and was a native Idahoan. They had met when Dell attended college at Boise State and aside from all the common interests they shared, Wilson practiced the same religion as she did, which made her parents very approving of their relationship too.

That comment made Anna think about one thing that still bothered her. Although Michael never brought the subject of religion up, it was obvious that one of the reasons he had felt close to Sharon was because she was Jewish. Anna had been to church, but never felt a close connection to a religion. She wondered if this would ever be a problem for their relationship.

***

The next day, the group gathered around a picnic table for breakfast. There was an older couple walking around the campground. Anna pointed out that the woman was wearing a rather silly-looking wide-brimmed hat and Trisha commented that it somehow looked familiar.

The older couple turned toward the group eating at the picnic table.

"Oh, my goodness," Trisha said. "I can't believe it." "You know these people?" Anna asked.

Just then the older man spoke to his wife in a loud enough voice for everyone to hear. "Oh, no. Edna, pull up the tent-stakes." Then he looked right at Trisha. "We're leaving. We are not tying up your boat again. And watch out for those guys." Ralph pointed at Michael and Anna. "You can see in their eyes that they're already planning a nap.

Although maybe we should try and keep her awake until she cooks us one of those incredible northwest-style meals."

It was the Gersons. They were immediately invited to join the group. They had already eaten breakfast so they sat down and had coffee. They discussed what a coincidence it was, as Michael and Anna explained to the others how they had met the Gersons.

Then, Sean and Trisha described how they had encountered the Gersons on a boating excursion.

"You two were on your first date, if memory serves," Edna said. "I see you followed my advice, Trisha, and stayed with him."

Trisha grinned. "Edna, you were absolutely right. I was basically a cripple the first few months of our relationship and Sean just kept thanking me for taking such good care of him."

"I am so happy you found each other so young," Edna said. "And you too," she turned to Michael and Anna. "Ralph and I didn't find each other until our late-fifties. Our previous marriages were nightmares. All that wasted time..."

The older couple had many funny stories to tell of their adventures touring the northwest. After the meal, Ralph and Edna joined the group on a three-hour hike near the campground. They fell in with Warren and Chela, because the Gersons were fellow bird lovers.

Before they left, Trisha asked for their email address. "We live in Eagle, Idaho—north of Boise—so if you're out this way again, let us know and you can come by our home."

"We have room to park an RV as well," Sean added.

Ralph chuckled. "I don't know if we want to see you guys again, but if you're offering free RV parking, we may just take you up on that."

As everyone laughed, Ralph and Edna started saying good-bye to the group. They were heading over to Jackson Hole, Wyoming that afternoon to meet friends from the Midwest who were joining them to visit Yellowstone National Park.

Edna gave a big hug to everyone, but when she got to Trisha, she patted her belly. "You stay healthy and happy. We'll be out next summer for sure. We're planning on exploring more of the Oregon Trail plus northern Washington State, so you'll be on our route west. Take care of yourself and your new little one."

"Thanks, Edna. You have a safe trip and we'll look forward to seeing you next summer."

"We live in Seattle and know some of the best birding sites from shore birds around the Puget Sound to the alpine valleys of the Cascades," Warren told Ralph. "So if you're in town, let us know. We also like to go birding and fly fishing around Lake Chelan in north central Washington State, so we could meet you there as well."

"Thanks, Warren. We'll let you know for sure when we're out your way."

Chapter Twenty-One ~ Trace and Linda

TWO WEEKS AFTER A wonderful time at music camp, Linda Schulman was walking to a friend's house along a trail that cut through a heavily wooded area and opened into a lovely park. Linda always loved the path through the tall trees, and today the wind in the leaves made a pleasant rustling sound.

Linda was thinking how much she looked forward to starting high school when she felt a blow to the back of her head, and then things mostly went blank.

Two-days later, she was released from the hospital. Linda had been attacked and raped. She had talked to the hospital's rape counselor, and together they had explored her vague memories of having a huge weight on her body, pain between her legs, and someone repeatedly calling her dirty names.

The tremendous ache in her head had subsided for the most part, and the counselor reviewed the various emotions she would probably be experiencing in the next days, weeks, and months.

On a logical level, Linda knew that the rape wasn't her fault. Even so, she kept thinking that somehow she had done something wrong. Why did this awful man choose her? The counselor told her that most victims felt that way and she needed to continue to talk about her feelings to come to terms with them.

Linda's parents were devastated. Her father felt particular pain, knowing his little girl had been hurt this way. He was supposed to protect his family. What happened to his daughter made him feel like a failure—at least in that respect. The parents did their best to be upbeat when they talked to Linda and her brothers and sisters. They knew from the rape counselor that Linda would want to withdraw and may not want to leave the house. She probably wouldn't want to see any of her friends and relationships with men could become a problem for her.

As the whole community had learned of the rape, Linda dreaded meeting anyone who knew her. The look in their face made her feel like she had become a different person. She no longer looked forward to high school.

According to news reports a few weeks later, after his successful attack on Linda, the rapist felt emboldened and followed a pretty college coed back to her apartment. As she opened the door, he shoved her inside, and closed it behind him.

She screamed and he hit her in the face to shut her up. Apparently, he didn't see much else—unknown to him the girl's boyfriend was in the apartment too.

According to neighborhood gossip, upon hearing her scream, the boyfriend came roaring out of the kitchen like a Burlington Northern freight train, yelling in a voice that rattled the windows. He said, "Wrong house, dip shit!" And, the gossipers were happy to add, he proceeded to beat the hell out of the would-be rapist while his girlfriend "talked" to her attacker by way of a cast iron skillet.

Apparently, by the time the police arrived, the rapist was curled up on the floor begging for mercy. The community felt a sense of relief that the police were able to trace this person to other rapes, including Linda's.

Unfortunately, Linda's relief was short-lived, as she still needed to live with the horrible memories and the emotional scars.

***

Trace's parents talked to him about the awful attack that Linda had endured. Like everyone else who knew Linda, Trace wished he could remove his friend's pain.

"This is not something we can just have erased from Linda's memory, even though we all wish we could," his mother told him. "She has to come to terms with what happened on her own. We can't treat it as if it's the only thing that's happened in her life. We also can't ignore what happened."

So, Trace gave her some time to heal. After his initial calls to check on her, he waited two-months before he called Linda again. He wanted to see if she wanted to get together to perform some blues music he had written. She politely answered no, thanked him for calling, and hung up.

"I know you were one of Linda's best friends, but it takes time for something like this to heal," Trace's mom told him. "It may be a long time before she feels comfortable even leaving her own home. Do try to stay in touch with her. Just don't put any pressure on her." Trace occasionally talked to Linda at school, mostly during band rehearsal, but the cheeriness that had always surrounded her before the attack was gone. Still, every once in a while, he tried to get her to play music with him outside of school. She always turned him down.

Linda didn't attend band camp with Trace the following summer. He missed her presence, but still had an incredible time. His reputation as an accomplished percussionist was growing. He even received a medal for Most Improved Drummer. In the back of his mind he wished that Linda had been there to share that moment with him.

Upon his return he called her to tell her about band camp and his award. Linda mostly listened. Then, just when Trace thought he had run out of things to talk about, Linda said something that surprised him.

"How about we get together at your house to play some of that music you've written."

Shocked, Trace happily replied, "I'd love to."

"I'll walk over. I'll be there in ten-minutes," she told him.

Linda lived three-blocks from Trace's home. In the time it probably took for Linda to run a comb through her hair, check her makeup, and pick up her guitar, a joyous Trace had run full speed the entire three blocks.

When she opened the door, he stood on the stoop, slightly out of breath, waiting for her.

"Are you here to protect me?" she asked him.

"Don't be silly. I'm here to carry your guitar for you. I'm here to make sure nothing bad happens to your *guitar*."

Linda laughed. "In that case, my guitar thanks you."

***

They started playing music together again on a regular basis after that. Although Linda didn't realize it then, her willingness to engage in those musical sessions is what began her healing.

Just after school started that year, she asked Trace to accompany her while she walked back through the area where she had been attacked.

It was a bright, sunny, and warm Saturday morning, not unlike that awful day. Linda was nervous as they approached the entrance to the trail, her body on alert for signs of danger. What she saw surprised her in a most unexpected way—a crowd was standing there. The entire marching drumline had shown up to escort her. The drummers' girlfriends or boyfriends showed up, too. Nearly all of them were in band and had known Linda since grade school.

Stopped dead in her tracks by the outpouring of support, the only words Linda could manage through teary eyes were to say, "You guys," and then wipe at her cheeks with her shirt sleeve.

One of the girls spoke up. "When we heard you were going for a nice walk with your boyfriend, we certainly didn't want to miss out on that."

Linda hadn't really thought of Trace as her boyfriend, but when he held out his hand to her, she reached out with her own. The group progressed along the trail and about half way down the trail, Linda stopped.

Her heart in her throat and her pulse beating wildly, she fought back the tears and shame, unwilling to let her attacker own another moment of her life. "This is where that asshole attacked me," she told her friends.

One of the boys spoke in a most aggressive tone. "Let some jerk try something now."

Some of her friends said, "Yeah," while others nodded their heads in agreement.

Her good friend, Kelly, reminded her, "Linda, no matter what happens, please remember, you've got friends. If you ever need a ride, or just someone to talk to, please don't forget us."

"I won't forget you. I won't ever forget all of you coming out to walk with me today." Linda looked around at everyone. "I love all of you."

They completed their walk down the trail which opened up to a nice park with picnic tables. They had arranged a lovely picnic party for Linda.

One of the girls asked her boyfriend to get the food on the tables and a few older boys ran off to their cars, returning with coolers. They all started putting out the food after three picnic tables had been lined up together.

As soon as the meal ended and cleanup began, some of the drummers brought out various Latin rhythm instruments. From congas to claves, timbales to maracas, and cowbells to bongos, they began playing. As they experimented with various beats, some of the guys and girls started dancing. The better dancers started teaching salsa steps to the others.

As the Caribbean and African rhythms began echoing across the park, many people came out of their homes to see what was going on.

Soon a crowd had gathered. Little children and adults started moving to the Afro-Cuban rhythms.

The drummers kept changing places so they could dance with their partners, and Trace left the timbales to one of the other drummers so he could take Linda's hand. He helped her off the picnic table so they could dance.

Linda was nervous, but now she was nervous in the sense that she didn't want Trace to think she was a bad dancer. The music and dancing went on until three o'clock when the marching band had to leave. They would be performing at that night's football game, and they had to get ready for the pregame and halftime performances.

Kelly and her boyfriend, James, came up to Linda. "Remember," Kelly said, "you've got friends."

"I know," Linda replied. She then turned to the group and shouted to them once again. "I love all of you."

As Trace, Linda, and two other couples who lived in their neighborhood, walked home together, Linda asked Trace if he had set everything up.

"I initiated it," he admitted. "But once James mentioned it to Kelly, it kind of snowballed from there."

Chapter Twenty-Two ~ Anna and Michael, Steven and Jackie, Kelly and the Drumline

ON A GRAY, CLOUDY, and cool Friday in mid-October, Anna was telecommuting at home when she received an early morning phone call from her mother.

"I don't want you to worry," her mother said. "Grandma is still healthy and strong these days, but she's been asking for you. I know you have your own life up there and we'll see you next month at Chela's wedding, but is there any way you can come down here and visit us for a few days? Grandma would really appreciate it if you could spend some time with her."

"I'll let you know, Mama," Anna said. "It might take me a couple of days or so to get everything arranged to get down to New Mexico. I'll call you and let you know what I can work out."

Then, Anna called Michael at work to tell him that she wanted to go home to see her grandmother as soon as possible. She said she would start shopping for airline flights. Then she mentioned to him that she was worried that it would take a couple days to get tickets and interconnecting flights from Boise down to her small town in New Mexico.

Michael called her back five minutes after they hung up and had news for her. "Pack your bags, Anna. I have a flight ready—and I'll be right home to start packing clothes for myself."

"You're coming with me?" Anna asked.

"The airline we're taking has a two-for-one special."

This sounded strange, but Anna was mostly thinking of seeing her beloved grandmother, so she just hurried and started packing.

Once they were packed and ready to go, Michael drove them to the airport. Instead of parking on the commercial side, he parked in front of a small, low building on the back side of the airport.

As they entered, a woman called out to Michael. "Mr. Levin?"

"Yes."

"This way," the woman replied.

Confused, Anna followed Michael and the woman out the back of the building where a small private jet was waiting.

She caught on then. "Michael—"

"Don't worry, Anna. I wrote a check on my investment fund. We'll be there in a little over two hours."

Anna felt so happy—Michael was taking good care of her as usual. She couldn't help but be concerned about the cost, however. So, after they belted themselves into their seats, Anna asked Michael about that.

He squeezed her hand. "Anna, I wanted to. You know that I never spend my investment money on anything. It's been sitting and growing since my high school years. The investments had a good run last year and I earned quite a bit of money. This flight and a return flight will cost us less than five percent of that."

"But Michael, this is your investment money."

"Anna," Michael smiled, "this is *our* investment money, and this is certainly a more than appropriate use of those funds."

Anna wrapped her arms around Michael's arm, and putting her head on his shoulder, promptly fell asleep.

Two-hours-later they were landing at a small airport just outside of Anna's home town.

The flight attendant approached them. "Your rental car will be on the ramp for you, Mr. Levin."

He thanked her and they stepped out into the warm, dry air and brilliant sunshine of southern New Mexico. There was a cobalt blue sky overhead—it was quite a contrast to the cool damp weather they had left behind in Boise.

Anna directed Michael as he drove across town to her family's home. As he parked the car in front of the house, she pointed to the building next to the house. "That's the restaurant next door."

They entered and found Anna's grandmother sitting on a couch in the living room. She stood up immediately.

"Anna. You're here. You're here," Anna's grandma said as she walked over to Anna and Michael.

"Hi, Grandma." Anna hugged her grandmother. "This is Michael."

"Hello," Michael said. "Nice to meet you."

"Michael, it's a pleasure to meet you. I've heard a lot about you."

"Believe me," Michael grinned, "none of its true." Anna and her grandmother laughed.

"Anna, I didn't expect you so soon. I thought your mother just called you a few hours ago."

Anna looked at Michael and felt so proud to have him in her life. "Michael arranged for a plane," she told her grandmother. "It only took a couple of hours to get here after Mom called."

"So you're the one," a beaming grandma said to Michael.

Michael smiled at her. "Yes, ma'am."

She looked back to Anna. "Does your mother know you're here?"

Anna shook her head. "No. We came over to the house first."

"She's with your father at the restaurant." Anna's grandmother gestured to the door. "Go over and see her. She'll be thrilled that you're here. We'll talk later."

"Look at you two," Anna's grandma said as she watched Michael and Anna walk hand in hand to the door. "You look as full of joy for each other as I remember my parents being. Remind me later—I must remember to tell you about my parents."

Michael and Anna waved and headed over to the tan, stucco, southwest-styled restaurant.

Michael gazed around. "The southwest style of the buildings around town fits incredibly well against the background of those magnificent mountains," he said.

"I really didn't notice it growing up," Anna looked around, appreciating the surroundings as if through Michael's eyes, "but I can see now it's true."

***

Carmen Cardozo had just finished taking an order. She had started walking toward the kitchen when she noticed a nicely dressed, professional-looking young couple walking across the restaurant's parking lot.

When she recognized it was her daughter, she yelled into the kitchen. "Arturo! Come out here."

"Carmen, what's wrong?" Her husband ran out of the kitchen, wiping his hands on his apron.

"Look at those two walking hand-in-hand." She pointed out the window.

After a long pause, a huge smile started spreading across his face. "Oh, my Lord, it's Anna. That must be Michael with her."

They quickly walked outside to greet their daughter and meet her fiancée.

After introductions, Carmen asked them if they'd eaten lunch yet.

"No," Anna said. "We just ran out to the airport and flew down here."

Arturo looked at his watch. "It's not even noon yet. How did you get here so quickly?"

"I told Michael that I wanted to come as soon as I could, so he arranged for a jet to fly us. It only took a-couple-of-hours flying time."

Arturo grinned at Michael, pointing a playful finger at him. "I've heard stories about you."

"They're not true, believe me. Anna exaggerates a lot," Michael said.

Anna laughed. "Exaggerate. Right."

"Kids," Arturo told them, "come over and I'll fix you something to eat."

"Papa, go easy," Anna warned. "We don't eat so much."

"Watch and see," she said to Michael, "he'll bring out enough food for an army."

As Arturo disappeared into the kitchen, Carmen agreed. "Of course he will bring out enough food for an army. His Anna is home."

"Where's Steven?" Anna asked about her younger brother.

"He doesn't start working until late afternoon on Fridays," Carmen told them as she seated them at a table on the patio. "He's really taken over the restaurant. He took many courses at the university on restaurant management. Your father takes off three- days-a-week now and has cut his hours way back. Steven is brilliant at managing the restaurant and the staff. Everyone loves working for him."

Carmen gestured that they go over to a table.

"You remember that Mr. Mayer and his wife that own the RV Park next door? They're going to build an RV Park in Arizona next spring with a restaurant on that property, and they have asked Steven to manage it for them. They're giving him half the ownership."

Carmen prattled on proudly. "Steven's already managing a restaurant in Texas for them. Every day he has meetings with his staff and he's constantly on the computer seeing what's going on. He is so good with the money. Wait until your father tells you about Steven.

He's positively glowing when he talks about what he's done for the restaurant."

"Is Steven seeing someone?" Anna asked.

"He hired an office assistant three-months-ago. Someone he met at school. The minute I saw the way she looks at him I thought, this is going to be trouble—or it's going to be great. It turns out it's great. She is the shyest, quietest, and kindest young lady a mother could ever want for a son like Steven. He's going to give her an engagement ring next week at dinner. I know because I helped him pick it out. You remember how Steven was always overweight and always worried about every little thing? How he was so short tempered? Here comes this skinny, little girl named Jackie..."

Carmen paused for a moment looking at Anna. "Anna, you're not so thin like before—when I gave you a hug—"

Then she glanced at her daughter's chest. "Is that all you in there?"

In a slightly exasperated voice, a grinning Anna said, "Yes, Mother."

"I can personally verify that, Mrs. Cardozo." Michael jumped in. "In fact, I already have. It's all Anna in there."

"Michael." Anna gave him a playful push. "Not in front of my mom, please."

Michael chuckled. "You skinny girls are so sensitive." Anna laughed even harder upon hearing that.

After they all stopped laughing, Carmen continued. "Anyway, when Steven starts to get nervous and anxious, Jackie puts her hand on his arm and talks quietly to him. He's fine after that. Not only that, but she has him out before work every day and they run together. Your brother hasn't been this healthy his entire life. The two of them always look like they're ready to run a marathon. They really work hard at taking care of themselves, although to tell the truth, it's really Jackie. She watches what your brother eats. Jackie also notices, before any of the rest of us, when he's getting stressed."

"Here you are." Arturo set a large number of dishes in front of Anna and Michael.

Anna raised her eyebrows and smiled at Michael as if to say. "See, I told you."

Arturo sat next to Carmen and they commenced eating lunch. They ate and talked, everyone enjoying the food and the company. Then, as they began dessert, Arturo glanced out the window.

"Here they come. My son and his *office assistant*." Arturo pointed out a young couple just getting out of their car.

Carmen smiled. "They don't know you're here. Your brother will be so surprised."

Steven and Jackie entered the restaurant. They both were wearing colorful polo shirts and matching denim shorts. The colors really complimented Jackie's short dark hair, dark eyes, and tan skin. One of the staff members guided them over to the outdoor table where everyone was sitting. When they arrived at the table, Arturo stood and spoke to Steven. "These northerners don't like our food."

Steven looked at the two pale northerners. First at Michael and then at Anna, who both maintained straight faces. "What? Anna! It's you. This must be ah...ah..."

"Fred," Michael told him, looking completely serious as he stood up and held out his hand.

Steven shook Michael's hand, but now wore an even more surprised look on his face.

Anna and her parents laughed at him.

"Michael, stop it," Anna told him through her laughter. "Steven, this is Michael."

Anna and Michael were then introduced to Jackie. She behaved just as shy as Carmen had told her daughter she would, hardly looking Michael in the eye when she shook hands with him.

Anna immediately asked Jackie how she had managed to get Steven to lose weight.

Jackie opened up a bit at the question. She looked toward Steven, then back at Anna. "It was easy. I pointed out to Steven that we could spend more time together if he got up earlier and came running with me. He was very in favor of that. The first few weeks he ran so slow that it was barely exercise for me, but after a couple of months, he had lost a lot of weight. We gradually worked up to running three-miles every day. Toward the end of the semester, we even started adding weights to our routine. We still run three-miles every day before we come to work and we work out with weights three-times-a-week."

Steven and Jackie joined them for lunch, and between them all they managed to eat almost everything Arturo had brought to the table. Everyone seemed full and satisfied. Arturo and Carmen rose to clean up from their meal.

Once they were in the kitchen, Carmen smiled at her husband. "Did you notice Michael making fun of Anna? She just laughed. Before, no one could ever make fun of her like that without her getting furious. This Michael is really special." After a pause she continued. "Arturo, he even made a joke about her body in front of me."

"What? I don't believe it. She was always so sensitive about that."

"Apparently she's not sensitive about that any longer. Arturo, I'm telling you, she just laughed."

"Did you see how much they both laughed?" Arturo said. "They keep saying things to entertain each other. She seems so happy. Chela's right about those two. They were made for each other. I really thought Anna would never find someone because she always seemed unhappy and angry as a child. I think I noticed a change a month or so after she took that job in Seattle. She started telling me funny stories about things that happened at her job. I didn't think much about it at the time but they were mostly about Michael doing something silly. I don't know who I'm happier for, Anna or Chela."

"They both seem to have such wonderful partners," Carmen concluded as they returned the table where the others were just getting up.

Anna informed them that they had decided to return to the house so that Michael could connect his laptop to the internet to display some examples of his and Anna's work so Steven and Jackie could have a better idea of what Michael and Anna did for a living. "But first," Anna said to Jackie, "I want you to take a walk with me. I want to hear all about how you and Steven met."

***

The two women went for a walk and Michael and Steven went inside to get to know each other.

"All right, Jackie, tell me how you got mixed up with my crazy brother," Anna encouraged.

"We were assigned to a team to create a project for a restaurant management class at school. I was amazed how Steven was admired by the other members of our team. He helped everyone and we all got great grades on the project. He was, without a doubt, the nicest guy I had ever met. So I did everything I could think of to get him to notice me."

Jackie smiled and Anna could see in her face how much love she had for Steven.

"Whenever my circle of friends got together, I always had them invite Steven too. But conversation was not my strong point, and honestly, Anna, I didn't really feel as though I had a pretty figure to attract a guy."

Anna understood that. "I can relate, Jackie, I always felt the same. Michael showed me that he liked my figure and he helped me be more comfortable with my body."

"Yes," Jackie agreed. "I feel much better about myself now too, but at the time, Steven didn't seem to show the least bit of interest in me. I was sure it was because he didn't find me attractive. Then, one of my friends told me that I might have to drop a stove on Steven's head to get his attention. I was starting to think it was hopeless."

"So, how did you get through to him?"

"Well, when Steven and I were at the school cafeteria with some friends one day, someone started to tease him about having a body like a marshmallow. Steven was getting angry and had started to clench his fists. I thought he was going to take his tormentor's head right off, which would get him thrown out of school. So I put my hand on his arm and I told him to calm down. I said that they were our friends and they were just kidding."

"And that worked?"

"Yes, Anna. To my absolute amazement, Steven completely calmed down and told me, 'If you say so, Jackie.' Then he walked me back to my dorm that evening. He said good-bye, turned and took a few steps away—then he just stopped."

Jackie stopped walking then too. "He looked at me very seriously and he said, 'I know I'm kind of a funny-looking guy, but I really en-joy spending time with you.' Then he asked me if we could get to-gether sometime, just to talk."

Her face lit up in a smile as Jackie continued. "Well, I walked over to him, threw my arms around his neck, stood on my tiptoes, and...well, I gave him the kiss of the century. He looked so shocked—I always wished I had a picture of that face."

Jackie shrugged and looked wistfully at the sky. "We went out the next day and we started spending every moment we could to-gether after that."

"That's a great story," Anna said. "I am so happy you found each other."

"Not only that," Jackie said, "but my family loves Steven as well. My mother told me I get the award for bringing home the nicest guy in the family. My father is in heaven with the way Steven takes care of me. Anna, we are so blessed to have such great partners."

"I know," Anna replied to her future sister-in-law.

"Thank you so much for talking to me about all this, Anna. I don't have a sister, so it's really great talking to you. I hope we can stay in touch."

"We will, Jackie. I guarantee we will stay in touch."

They strolled back to her parents' house to join Michael and Steven. Anna was very happy for her brother. She smiled to herself as she thought that all three of the Cardozo children had found great partners.

***

Late the following spring, the drummers and their partners verified again that they were indeed the best of friends when Kelly was diagnosed with a tiny tumor in her brain.

She was out of school for a number of weeks and the powerful treatment she endured caused all her hair to fall out.

Her mother bought her a wig that looked reasonably like her own hair. The Saturday before she was going to start back to school James called to tell her that the drumline was going to throw another Afro-Cuban musical picnic session at the same park as the previous fall.

Kelly didn't feel like doing anything, but her mother insisted that it would be good for her to get out and have something to do besides sit at home and think about how weak she felt and how awful she looked without hair.

Five minutes before her boyfriend was supposed to pick her up, he called and said he had a flat tire so she should get a ride to the park and he would meet her later. Kelly's mom had been right by the phone, so she volunteered to drive Kelly over to the park.

Her mom was unusually quiet as she drove, and when she stopped the car Kelly saw that her mother was crying.

"Mom, what's wrong?"

"Nothing is wrong." She pointed to the assembled group of Kelly's drumline friends who were standing in front of their car. "Look."

Kelly turned to look at her friends. They were all grinning like mad, wearing matching wide brimmed floppy hats.

As she got out of the car, James walked up and held out a floppy hat for Kelly too. "Here's your hat," he told her.

As he spoke those words everyone removed their own hats—they had all shaved their heads.

Inspired, Kelly slowly took the wig off her head and dropped it back in the car.

Everyone cheered, including Kelly's mom. Kelly looked at her mother. "You knew?"

With tears streaming down her face, her mother just nodded. Linda walked up to Kelly with a huge smile, giving her a hug.

"Remember, you've got friends."

Next James hugged Kelly, and then everyone else in the group took their turns too.

"We need some music for this girl," a teary-eyed Linda proclaimed.

Kelly looked back at her mom and she was waving her forward, to go with her friends.

From then on, Kelly was so busy helping make music with her friends, that she barely had time to think about how she felt, or looked.

James stayed close to her, knowing that she was still weak from the treatment. He only let her dance one fast dance, but of course many slow ones.

During one of those slow songs, Kelly asked James if it was his idea.

He nodded toward Linda and Trace. "I told those two that you had lost your hair, so they got the drumline together, and this is what we decided to do."

"I will never forget this," Kelly said, looking at her friends.

Someone took a picture of the bald-headed group and Kelly hung a copy of it in her room. She posted a sign above it that read Kelly's drumline friends give meaning to the word friendship.

Chapter Twenty-Three ~ Sam and Carrie, Anna and Michael

LATER THAT EVENING, ANNA'S grandmother invited Anna and Michael to sit outside with her. She wanted to tell them the story about her parents from a journal her mother had written and left her when she'd passed away.

Anna and Michael learned about Anna's great grandparents that evening—Sam and Carrie.

***

Carrie Yoselovitch was a wonderful person. Intelligent and kind. Unfortunately, she had a curved spine and a less-than pleasing face, with one eyebrow higher than the other and a nose that seemed to have been intended for someone else's face, pointing slightly to the right.

The person that could get past those defects could see that she had bright eyes and an incredibly warm smile, but men never seemed to have an interest in her. She realized from early in her life that she would have to take care of her own financial needs, feeling it was unlikely that she would ever marry.

She took bookkeeping courses in school, and when she had completed them, she started looking for a job. One interview after another went by. It seemed as soon as the various interviewers saw how she looked they didn't want her.

One day she interviewed with a very nervous-looking Mr. Rosen. It was the longest interview she'd had and he asked her a million questions. Then, he'd hired her on the spot.

When she arrived to work the next day, Mr. Rosen began pulling paper out of his desk to give to Carrie to organize. It was a jumbled mess.

She asked Mr. Rosen if he had more papers that she would need, and he replied that his desk was full of receipts, invoices, and other documents that a bookkeeper would need. She suggested that they exchange desks.

Mr. Rosen said he thought that was a great idea and quickly agreed. It took many weeks, but Carrie found that Mr. Rosen's clothing business was losing money like water down a drain. No one was watching receivables and invoices weren't being handled in a timely fashion.

Carrie made a list of companies that owed Mr. Rosen a lot of money. He started going around to those companies and getting checks for what he was owed. It took three months, but with all the money Mr. Rosen was collecting, he finally had a slightly positive bank account. He was a brilliant salesman and understood clothing, but didn't have a clue about the financial side of a business.

Some of his bigger accounts owed him quite a bit of money and didn't seem to want to pay him. Carrie learned that Mr. Rosen's brother was an attorney. She called him to help with the accounts that didn't want to pay up. At first he appeared reluctant to be of much assistance, stating that he was a criminal attorney.

"Good," Carrie told him, "if we have to go to court you'll be ready to put these people in jail."

"Miss Yoselovitch, I'll see what I can do, but this could take a lot of time that I need to spend on other cases."

"Fine, I'll walk into your brother's office now and tell him you don't have time to help him. By the way, please remind me, who paid for your law school education?"

"Okay, okay. I'll be there in a few hours."

"Excuse me, when will you be here to help your brother that put you through law school?"

"I'm on my way right now, Miss Yoselovitch."

"He's a good brother," Carrie concluded. "He just needed a little reminding."

Needless to say, when a criminal attorney showed up to collect a bill, it made a great impression on those business owners who owed Mr. Rosen money.

Mr. Rosen realized what a treasure he had in Carrie Yoselovitch. He spent more time working in sales and his business grew. Carrie got regular raises and made a nice income for herself.

One day carpenters came and started converting some open space into an office. It was lovely, with windows on two sides. Carrie didn't think much about it until the office was complete. A painter put the name of the person who would be occupying the office on its door.

It read Carrie Yoselovitch—Finance Officer

A grinning Mr. Rosen, and one of the men from the factory, moved her desk and file cabinets into the new office.

As she was moving, she heard one of the secretaries saying, "The witch got lucky."

No matter how nice I am or how hard I work, it always comes back to my appearance, Carrie thought.

Unfortunately for the individual involved, and the person who laughed at the inappropriate remark, Mr. Rosen had heard everything. He invited them into his office. After closing the door he started yelling.

Carrie had never heard Mr. Rosen yell before. The individual who made the remark was fired, and the person who thought the remark was funny was suspended for two weeks without pay.

A red faced and trembling Mr. Rosen came to her office. "Miss Yoselovitch, I apologize for the unkind remark from one of your fellow employees. I assure you that will *not* happen again."

Carrie thanked him. She never did hear another unkind remark as long as she worked for Mr. Rosen and Carrie continued working for him into her mid-thirties.

***

A short, middle aged man with broad shoulders and a wide body had opened a leather goods and shoe repair store in town. He was introduced to Carrie when he was making a delivery of fine, handcrafted leather belts to Mr. Rosen's factory.

Carrie lived alone in a small, one-bedroom home about two blocks from work. Around ten o'clock on one warm Sunday morning, there was loud knocking on her front door.

Not expecting anyone, she shouted, "Who is it?" from the back of her little house.

"It's Sam Shulman, the shoe repairman, Miss Yoselovitch."

"What does he want from me?" Carrie said to herself.

She opened the front door just the tiniest crack and quite abruptly announced, "My shoes are fine, Mr. Shulman."

"That's not why I'm here, Miss Yoselovitch." "What do you have? A delivery or something?"

Sam looked down at his hands. "Actually, I do have a delivery."

Carrie opened the door farther, to find Mr. Schulman wearing a lovely suit and tie, a bouquet of flowers in his hand, with his hair slicked over and his shoes shined to brilliance.

"These are for you," he said to her, a smile stretched across his face.

"Now you're making flower deliveries?" she asked him, still confused.

He laughed. "I had hoped these lovely flowers might brighten your day."

Then it hit her—he was here to see *her*. She wondered if he was crazy. "Since when do single men come to see me?" she mumbled under her breath.

Only, Mr. Schulman had heard this. He smiled warmly. "Since at least this morning, I would think." He extended the bouquet toward her.

Carrie looked again at the flowers, then with a shaky hand, she took them, smiling nervously. She couldn't believe it. Here she was in her mid-thirties and a man was calling on her. She thought her knees were getting weak. She felt like a schoolgirl.

"I was wondering if you would like to go for a walk with me," Mr. Schulman asked.

"Thank you, Mr. Schulman. I really don't take walks. My back, you know. Why don't you sit on the swing here on my front porch, and I'll get us some lemonade."

Upon reentering her house, she quickly ran a brush through her hair. She looked in the mirror and said to her reflection, "What in the world could he see in this face, such that he would want to spend time with me?"

Upon returning to the porch with lemonade for the two of them, Carrie and Sam engaged in a long discussion of how they each ended up living in Albuquerque.

"I had a store north of here," Sam told her, "but I thought I would get more business if I set up a store in town. So far, that seems to be the case."

Carrie told him, "When my parents, of blessed memory, were coming west and arrived in this town, my father told my mother, 'This is it. We're going to make a living in this town. I'm not spending one more day in this God-forsaken wagon.' Fortunately it's been a nice town. They had a small farm not far from here. They had cattle and grew chili peppers and peanuts."

A-few-hours-later, a man on a buckboard pulled up in front of Carrie's house and yelled to Sam. "Are you the leather repairman?"

"Yes, but I'm closed today."

"I'm sorry to interrupt you on a Sunday, sir, but one of your neighbors told me you were visiting over here. We've got three families threshing out north of town and the belt on our big thresher just tore itself to shreds. My father said he was sure you could put together a new one or fix the old one. My brothers are down at your store with the old belt right now. We'd sure be in your debt if you can fix that belt for us, so we can keep working before it rains again."

"It will take at least three hours to repair. Maybe more..." "I'll have one of my brothers wait for it, and he can help you as well, sir."

Sam looked at Carrie. "I'm needed," he said. He stood and put out his hand to assist her while she stood up.

"Thank you for stopping by to see me," she told him. "May I see you again sometime?"

"I think that would be very nice, Mr. Schulman."

He quickly walked over to the buckboard and climbed on.

Instead of walking back into her house, Carrie felt as if she were floating back in.

"This is silly," she said, to no one in particular. "I'm not a little girl. Why should I wait for him to call on me again? Besides, that nice man will be working the next few hours and won't have time to make himself a lunch. I better make a little lunch for him and take it down to his store."

So, Carrie prepared a lovely lunch and changed into one of her nicest dresses.

When she arrived at Sam's store, the door was open and she saw Sam and a young man wrestling with a huge leather belt. Sweat was pouring down both their faces and arms.

"Hello," she called into the store.

Without looking up Sam yelled, "I'm closed. I'll be open tomorrow at—"

He looked up then and saw Carrie standing in the doorway.

"But for you, of course, I'm open. Please come in."

"I thought that you and this young man were working so hard that you might need a little lunch."

She started clearing off space on a table and began spreading out the food she had carried over in a lovely woven basket.

She had prepared oregano garlic chicken, potatoes au gratin, steamed fresh green beans, and refried beans that her Mexican neighbor had taught her how to prepare.

"I didn't have time to make a proper dessert for you, so I have a cinnamon ginger apple strudel that I bought at the bakery yesterday. I think mine is better, but this will have to do."

The two men looked as if they couldn't believe their luck. They were both wide-eyed in amazement at the food she had set out.

As the scent of the oregano chicken permeated the store, Sam told the young man, "We should stop for a while I think. My hand is getting sore from all the sewing. It would be good to wash up and have some lunch."

"I couldn't agree more, sir," the young man excitedly told Sam.

They disappeared into the back of the shop to wash, as Carrie put out plates and silverware for them.

When they returned, she told the young man, "I hope you like lemonade because that's all I brought for you to drink."

He politely told her lemonade would be fine.

As she ate, she couldn't help notice Sam smiling at her. Then, when they had finished, the young man kept thanking her for the lunch.

"You're welcome, you're welcome," she said. "Now hurry and finish the repair so you can get this belt back to your father."

"Yes, ma'am," he replied with a huge grin on his face.

He and Sam started working again, while Carrie packed her basket. She was very pleased to see that there was very little food left over.

"Mr. Schulman," Carrie asked, "would you mind if I waited here until you are done? My shoulder is sore from carrying the basket down here. I was wondering if you might have time to walk me home and carry the basket for me."

"It will be my pleasure, Miss Yoselovitch," he told her with a huge smile on his face.

Carrie watched Sam. He was a very hard worker. He gave clear instructions to the young man, so there was little wasted motion while they completed the repair. When the belt was finished, Sam and the young man stuffed it onto a freight wagon.

"My father will be in next week to settle with you for the work on this belt."

"Tell your father to see me after harvest is complete. We'll settle up then."

Sam returned to his store and told Carrie, "I'm going to wash up and put some clean clothes on."

On the walk home, Carrie mentioned, "He didn't pay you for the work you did today."

"I'm not worried. I have very few needs, so I don't spend much money. I'm able to save quite a bit. Besides, that boy's father is as honest as the day is long. He was one of my customers when I had my store north of here, closer to their farm. Two-years-ago, in the spring, I made work shoes for him and all his sons. He paid for them with money he had saved from the previous year's harvest.

"Two weeks after that next year's harvest was complete, Larry the local butcher, stopped by my shop. He asked how I want my side-of-beef cut up before he put it in the icehouse. I told him that I didn't buy a side-of-beef. He told me that this farmer left it there for me with a note that read, 'Mr. Schulman, the shoes you made for us lasted from planting through harvest. We've always planned on buying new shoes after planting to get us through to fall harvest. The shoes you made for us were still in good condition so I didn't have to buy additional shoes before harvest. You saved me a lot of time and money plus your fine shoes saved our feet from a lot of wear and tear. I hope you will consider this side-of-beef as adequate payment for the extra wear we are getting from your shoes. We'll see you in the spring for new shoes again.'"

"That's quite a compliment," Carrie told him.

"I always try to work in a way that reflects well on me."

They talked, laughed, and joked, all the way back to Carrie's house. Carrie was pleased to see how many people warmly greeted Sam by name. When they arrived at Carrie's house, they sat on her porch swing. It was a lovely afternoon, with a cool breeze replacing the midday's warm air.

"Mr. Schulman, I think we need to talk about some things," she said. "I'm not a young woman. I've never had a man in my life and I'm a bit unsure of how to do this. I've very much enjoyed our time together today and would look forward to seeing you again. I hope I'm not being too forward."

Sam smiled at her. "First of all, if you think I'm a spring chicken, we need to get you some new glasses. I got married when I was eighteen, so I have had a woman in my life. Unfortunately for me, it didn't last long. After ten-months she left me for some other man and I haven't seen her since."

"Mr. Schulman, that's terrible."

"It was twenty-years-ago. It was quite painful then. I thought she was pregnant when she left as well. But that was a long time ago. As far as you never having a man in your life before, it's easy to start a relationship. All we have to do is spend enough time with each other to see if we can be friends first. After that it's easy—and please—call me Sam."

"Thank you, Sam. Please call me Carrie."

As they sat on the swing, they were soaking in the lovely weather and watching the birds and butterflies that flew around them.

"Sam, will you please stay for dinner with me?"

"Carrie, I would love to, but what will your neighbors say?"

Carrie smiled at him. "They will say, Carrie, you are certainly lucky to be dining with one of the nicest men in town. And they will be right."

Sam laughed and they continued talking until dinnertime.

And so it went, until two-months-later, when Sam and Carrie were married. Then, one year after that, Carrie endured a very difficult delivery, finally giving birth to a daughter. After the baby was born, Carrie and Sam were advised against having more children.

Carrie was disappointed at the doctor's advice, of course, but Sam was strong and helped her look at it through different eyes. He held her hand and told her, "Instead of dividing all our love between many children, we will give our new daughter *all* of it. Our little Perla will be the luckiest, most-loved little girl."

And that's what they did. They gave their daughter the most loving home to live in that you can imagine. They insisted that she learn everything from table manners to proper speech. They set an example of a loving relationship in front of her every day of her life.

When they had disagreements, they didn't last long, and one of them always gave in, just to keep harmony in their home. Then, once a disagreement was over, it never came up again. They always took such good care of each other.

When their dear daughter was but twelve-years-old, Sam passed away. His small body had just worn out from all the years of hard physical labor. Carrie was devastated at the loss of her Sam, and she was never the same after he died. Carrie lived another-four- years after his passing, then joined her beloved Sam.

***

When she finished telling the story, Anna's grandmother wore a sad smile on her face. "I'm telling you all this, Anna, because of all my grandchildren you are the most like my mother. When Chela first told me about someone named Michael, who was taking such good care of my brilliant granddaughter, I started wondering if you had inherited my mother's ability to have a great relationship. My marriage to your grandfather was good, but it was not great like my mother and father's. I am certain, too, that you have my mother's intelligence."

She turned to Michael. "When I see how Anna looks at you, Michael, it warms my heart. Anna looks at you the way my mother looked at my father. And when I hear the two of you discussing things, I also hear what an amazing relationship you have."

She stood, walking toward the back of the house. "My mother gave me a box of things that she received from her mother, who had brought them from Europe. I think you should have them. I'm not sure what they all are, but I suspect Michael will know.

Her grandmother returned with a box. As Anna opened it, she found a number of items and each had been carefully wrapped in cloth. The first item was an odd candle that looked like a number of small thin candles had been woven together, providing multiple wicks. The next item was a tarnished little silver cup.

Following that was a peculiar metal object about ten-inches-high. It consisted of a square-shaped metal container that looked like an intricately decorated box. It stood on a pedestal with an ornate top that came to a point.

As Anna carefully unwrapped the items, she noticed that the cloths surrounding them had some kind of lettering on them. Following the ornate little box, came two candleholders—one with space for two-candles and the other with space for nine-candles.

Eight of the candles were on one level and one branch was raised above the others.

The last item was a ceramic plate with a central depression and six surrounding depressions. Each of the depressions had the same type of lettering as the cloth used to wrap the items. The plate itself was wrapped in a beautiful hand embroidered tablecloth.

"Oh, my Lord, I have to sit down," Michael said, looking at the items and collapsing onto a chair. "I'm absolutely overwhelmed."

It was nearly impossible to overwhelm Michael, and Anna looked at him, thoroughly surprised.

"Michael," Anna held up one of the cloths, "is this Hebrew lettering?"

"Anna, those are all Jewish religious ritual objects. You are holding up a *challah* cover used to cover the *Shabbat* meal's bread. The other cloth is a *matzo* cover, used during Passover. The plate is a special plate used during the Passover *Seder* to hold ritual foods." He pointed to the other objects. "Those are a *Shabbat* candleholder and a *Hanukiah*—a candleholder for the Jewish festival of *Hanukah*. The odd-looking candle is a *Havdala* candle, that is a *Kiddush* cup, and the ornate box is a spice box. Your great- grandmother was Jewish, Anna. According to Jewish custom, that makes her daughter—your grandmother—Jewish, which makes your mother Jewish, which makes *you* Jewish."

From his seated position on the couch Michael covered his face with his hands and started quietly crying.

Anna turned to her grandmother. "Grandma, you knew."

"Yes, Anna, I've always known, but it didn't seem important until now. I've saved these things for a long time, and now I know why. They were waiting for you and Michael to start using them again."

Anna sat down next to Michael and put her arm around him. "Do you know what this means?" Anna asked him.

Regaining his composure, Michael said, "This means that Linda's family isn't the only Jewish family on our block. It most assuredly explains one of the greatest mysteries in our relationship. Something I've never understood about you, Anna. With all your sophisticated cooking and tastes, with all the choices of food venders around Pikes Market in Seattle, you always want to go to the New York Deli and order a simple pastrami on rye sandwich, with a cup of chicken soup."

Later that afternoon, Steven and Michael polished the candle-holders and *Kiddush* cup. Then at dinner that night, Anna lit her first *Shabbat* candles, and with her grandmother, recited the blessing for the candles. Next came the blessing for the wine, and after chanting the *Kiddush*, Michael pronounced the blessing for the lovely *challah* Anna's mother had baked. They also recited the *Shehechianu*, as this was the first *Shabbat* Anna and Michael were celebrating together.

Anna's grandmother smiled and told the family, "I remember my parents reciting those prayers when I was very young. That is a very joyful memory for me."

***

Chela and Warren's wedding was a marvelous affair. All their family was in town. Michael's parents even flew down to join them at the wedding and to meet Anna's parents.

Then, a couple of months later, in the warm sunshine of southern New Mexico on a delightful December day, Anna and Michael were married. As they were comfortable financially, they paid for almost everything themselves, and donated a similar amount to charities in New Mexico and Idaho in honor of the occasion.

A Rabbi from Las Cruces performed the ceremony. Once Anna's father and brother knew they were having a Jewish wedding, they prepared an absolute feast of Jewish and southwest dishes for the wedding dinner and the parties that accompanied that glorious weekend.

Sean and Trisha, the Shulmans, and the Beckhams flew down for the wedding, as well as Lydia and Bill Nelson, who came from Seattle with their little one. Everyone who attended, commented on what a joyous wedding it was.

A few months later, another joyous announcement was made—Anna was pregnant.

Chapter Twenty-Four ~ David and Linda, Trace and Tina

LINDA AND HER FRIENDS, James, Kelly, and Trace, attended band camp together the following summer. Just after arriving and storing things in their dorm rooms, the campers were slowly gathering in front of the football field where they would be rehearsing.

As they greeted new and old friends, Kelly, pointed at a couple of boys—identical twin boys. "See those gorgeous identical twins, Linda. They're from Seattle and they were here last summer. They're juniors too. Their names are David and Ethan. The one with the longer hair is David. From what I remember, they have had identical-twin girlfriends since sixth-grade. C'mon I'll introduce you. They're really fun guys and incredibly nice."

They approached the twins and as soon as Ethan noticed them he yelled, "Hey, it's the Meridian Mob." The band-camp friends greeted each other with handshakes and hugs.

Kelly made the introductions. "Ethan and David, I want you to meet my good friend, Linda Shulman. She's from Meridian as well."

They both shook hands with her, but David couldn't seem to take his eyes off Linda. With a crafty expression on his face, he said to her, "*Shalom. Mah Shlomcha?*"

Linda's heart skipped a beat at hearing David talking to her in Hebrew. She immediately replied, "*Tov, Todah. V'Aht?*"

David replied in a joy-filled voice, "*Tov. Tov Ma'Od.*"

"Wow, Jews in Idaho. Who knew?" Ethan laughed. "So, I see you two are part of the floppy-hat brigade. We heard about that. Some of the guys in our band kept in touch with some drummers in your band and we heard what happened here in Idaho."

David spoke up. "That's one of the greatest things I've ever heard of high school kids doing for someone. That was an incredible sacrifice for a friend. That was real *Menchlekiet*."

"I'll say it was," Ethan added.

Linda told Kelly, "*Menchlekiet* means it was a very appropriate and grown up thing to do."

"You can't imagine what it did for the girl who had lost her hair," Kelly proudly told them. "Once she saw what her friends had done, her emotional healing started immediately—even now I can get teary-eyed thinking about what they did for me."

"It was you?" Ethan inquired.

"Yes, they did that for me. The drumline and their partners, all did that for me."

"And you're okay now?" David wanted to know. "Yes," Kelly told him. "Both physically and mentally."

A whistle blew indicating that it was time to separate into different groups and begin rehearsing by sections. Linda went with the woodwinds while Kelly, James, and Trace rehearsed with the percussionists. David and Ethan went over to practice with the brass section.

***

In the cafeteria at dinner that night, Linda spotted Ethan and David in the food line, looking around for somewhere to sit. She watched as David's eyes scanned the room for a table. They stopped when they looked toward her, and then David made a beeline for the empty seat next her.

"Is someone sitting here?" he asked Linda.

"No," she replied, as casually as she could manage. "Please, sit down."

They talked for a while about what a fun but grueling day it was, marching and rehearsing in the sun.

"We get a couple hours off after dinner, then there's a dance tonight," David reminded Linda. "Last year my brother and I, and a couple of other guys, played 'Holiday for Trumpet' at the end-of- the-week talent show. I've gotten into fifties' jazz during the last year and I want to put a small group together to play 'Fly me to the Moon.' We had a girl lined up to sing the vocal, but she didn't make it to camp. Do you sing?"

"Only in the shower," Linda replied, laughing. "Bring your clarinet over and join us."

Trace interrupted them, telling David, "What you need to do is ask Linda to bring her guitar over. She is one mean blues player on a guitar."

"Is that true?" David asked.

"Trace and I have been friends since grade school and we've gotten together many times to play blues, so I guess it's true...but I'm really not that good. Besides, I didn't bring my guitar."

"There's a guitar in the rehearsal hall. Why don't you come over with us and let's see what we can put together."

Linda didn't really want to do anything that would put her in front of an audience, unless she could hide herself in the one- hundred-ten-member marching band. But there was something about this guy—he wasn't like Trace, who was more like a buddy.

Someone sat down at the table next to David. When David moved toward Linda to make room for the new arrival, his shoulder pressed against hers and his thigh was touching hers for a brief moment. Linda's body reacted to the brief touch with more excitement than all the times she had kissed Trace.

"Do you have enough room?" David asked Linda.

Linda moved her chair a small distance from David and nodded.

Linda looked across the table at Kelly, who grinned at her and silently mouthed, "You're blushing."

Embarrassed, Linda smiled and mouthed back to her friend, "I know."

The group walked over to the rehearsal hall and Linda checked out the electric guitar. With Trace on drums, a base player from Pocatello, a rhythm guitar player from Pendleton, Linda on lead guitar, and David playing trumpet, they started rehearsing.

The first time through the song David sang the vocal, had a trumpet solo in the middle, followed by a solo by the bass player, and then David sang the refrain of the vocal to the end of the song. The second time through David, who was standing next to Linda, moved the mike over toward her and asked Linda to sing with him. She did and it was fun. Not too musical, she thought, but fun.

One of the camp counselors was listening to them.

"Do the last vocal again, but Linda, start singing a lot lower." "That was just for fun," Linda insisted. "I'm not going to sing for the show."

"This is band camp," the counselor told her in a cheery voice. "Just for fun, try it again."

They repeated the song and a chorus of cheers erupted— everyone was amazed at the difference.

"Okay," the counselor continued. "From the beginning, but just the base line, and let Linda do the first vocal alone. Percussion, play a simple hi-hat-only beat with the base to back up Linda, and then come in completely at the trumpet and base solos in the middle. Then David and Linda together for the final vocal."

Linda was nervous, but figured it was just for fun, so why not. They ran through the song again, as suggested. When Linda's vocal ended, Trace and David were supposed to start playing, but they just stood there staring at her.

"What's with you guys?" Linda asked them.

David replied quietly to Linda, "That was fantastic. I mean, your phrasing was astounding, and you didn't miss a note. You have one lucky shower at your house."

"I think we have a budding Diana Krall here," the counselor said.

As Diana Krall was one of her favorite artists, Linda enjoyed the comparison, but was certain she didn't sound like Ms. Krall.

"I have a recording of Diana singing that song in my dorm," the counselor told them. "Keep rehearsing and I'll be back with the recording in ten minutes."

Upon her return, she played the CD on the sound system in the rehearsal hall. Everyone listened carefully, and sure enough, they all said Linda's singing voice sounded an amazing amount like Diana Krall.

"It's not that close," Linda insisted, but both Trace and David vowed, just as strongly, that it was that close.

"Linda, put down the guitar," the counselor told her. "I'll accompany the group on piano. First I'm going to set up the audio system in here to record us on this next take."

Having just heard Diana's phrasing on the recording, Linda did her best to imitate it. Upon listening to the playback, she was surprised to hear that she really did have a nice sounding singing voice—and yes, to her absolute astonishment, she did sound somewhat like Diana Krall.

"I hate to break this up, but there is a dance tonight for you guys," the counselor reminded them.

"Are you going to the dance?" David asked Linda. "Yes, but I'm going back to the dorm to change first."

"Don't take too long," David told her, with a serious look on his face. "I don't want to miss any chances to dance with you."

Linda smiled at him. "Thank you, David. I'll see you shortly."

It was a lovely dance that lasted two hours. David danced with a number of the girls but mostly with Linda, except for the slow songs—she didn't dance to any of those.

***

Trace was starting to feel sad—Linda seemed to be ignoring him once she met David. He was off to the side of the group, feeling alone and trying to figure out what to say to her, when someone grabbed his hand.

"Hey. Drummers shouldn't be sad," a female voice said.

He turned to look. On the end of his arm was a short, slim girl with pink-streaked, shoulder-length, blond hair. She was wearing a maroon beret and a paisley-patterned blouse with a matching maroon vest. Her cutoff shorts went down to her knees and she wore black loafers on her feet.

Trace looked into deep, dark eyes set below heavy eyebrows. He remembered seeing her playing flute during rehearsals earlier in the day. She wasn't pretty exactly, but she had a smile that radiated happiness.

She pulled Trace toward the dance floor. "I'm Tina," she yelled over the sound of the music.

"I'm Trace," he replied.

When the music stopped, she leaned in and told him she lived on a farm outside Nampa.

"I live in Meridian," Trace replied. "That means you only live about a-half-hour away from me."

She mentioned that she had noticed some of the guys and girls from Meridian had real short hair.

Trace related the story of Kelly's illness and the group decision to shave their heads.

"I heard about that," Tina exclaimed. "Your drumline is so cool. The pastor at our church did a whole sermon on the meaning of friendship, based on your incredibly unselfish act."

Tina beamed with admiration, and then she put her hands on Trace's shoulders, stood on her tiptoes, and kissed his cheek. "That's for being so cool that you would do that for someone."

Tina slid her hands off Trace's shoulders and grasped his hand. "I'm a sophomore," she said. "I think we should get to know each other."

"Sound's good to me," Trace told her with excitement, as they started dancing again.

Trace spent the rest of the evening dancing and laughing with Tina. He'd forgotten to be sad about Linda, and he was amazed that he could find so much to talk and joke about with someone he had just met. After the dance, he walked Tina back to her dorm and they engaged in a hug and a long kiss.

Trace decided that band camp was fun for a whole new reason this year, and that reason was named Tina.

***

David walked Linda back to her dorm after the dance too, and she mentioned she had heard that he had a longtime girlfriend.

He told her that he broke up with Megan when he realized that he didn't miss her while he was here at camp. "It's a long story," he said, "but I would be glad to tell you sometime."

The following day after lunch, all the band camp members were given a break from rehearsing. They were offered numerous choices of activities around the Boise area, one of which was visiting the beautiful Idaho Botanic Gardens.

It was located at the old, now-empty prison in Boise and had originally been built by the prisoners incarcerated there. The gardens had since been taken over by a local group and when they were discussing which activity to get involved in, Linda spoke up.

"I love visiting that place, David. Its beauty brings such a sense of peace to me."

David smiled. "If you enjoy it, then I'm looking forward to seeing it, too."

So they joined the group heading out to the gardens, and as they walked among the beautiful flowers, David told Linda the story of his break up with Megan.

Chapter Twenty-Five ~ David and Megan

ON THE THIRD DAY of band camp last summer, David noted that his brother, Ethan, called his longtime girlfriend, Sheryl—Megan's twin sister—every day to tell her how things were going. David hadn't thought to call Megan at all and then he came to the realization that he didn't miss her in the way Ethan missed Sheryl. The two had been close since they'd met at a Jewish overnight camp when they were twelve. There was lots of talk of *Bashert* at that time, but by David's sophomore year of high school, it seemed that they were spending a lot of time arguing, while Ethan and Sheryl hardly ever argued.

So, when he got home from camp, David decided that he needed to talk to someone about how he felt. They went to his Uncle Meyer's home for a Sunday brunch the following weekend, and all his family and many friends, including Megan's family were there. David decided to confide in his uncle.

His uncle told him to be sure, because it was better to break up now, than three-kids-from-now. He also warned David that a lot of the people in the family just assumed that he would marry Megan, so there was the potential that many family members would be upset with him and not understand.

Sometime after everyone had eaten, David took Megan out to the garage where his uncle kept his antique cars, and told her how he felt.

She was shocked, started crying, and then became quite angry. She even started swearing at David and calling him names. Then, Megan ran out of the garage and went home, while David walked back into the house.

Sheryl asked him where her sister was, so David told her that he had just broken up with Megan. And, as Uncle Meyer had predicted, David had a roomful of angry faces looking at him.

"Nice, David," Sheryl told him in a huff. "I better go home and make sure she's okay."

As Sheryl left, David looked around at the shocked and angry faces. He shrugged, raising his hands in defeat. "I don't love her. What else should I have done?"

His cousin, Ari, looked right at him. "Better telling her now how you feel, than getting a divorce years from now."

Ari's wife, Leah, added, "Ari's right. I'm sad that it didn't work out, but it's certainly better that you and she found out now."

David's younger brother walked home with him and David talked a little about what happened, but Jonah was mostly quiet. David thought he simply wasn't interested—Jonah was eight-years-younger than David was, and his life was still about kid stuff.

At home, David went to his room and started studying. Soon, he heard his parents come in, and they marched directly upstairs, and into his room to talk to him.

His mom informed him that Megan's mom had called her. "Megan said that you called her terrible names and were swearing at her. David, I'm shocked that you would do such a thing."

He couldn't believe Megan had said *he* did those things. "Mom, I didn't swear at her, or call her any names. She swore at *me* and called *me* filthy names."

"David, don't lie!" his father shouted.

David defended himself. "You weren't there, so you don't know what happened, and I'm telling you, she's the one with the filthy mouth."

His mother shook her head. "I'm sad that you would say such terrible things to Megan."

He looked at his mother. "And I'm sad that you don't believe me."

In a stern voice, his father spoke again. "We've seen the two of you for many years, and I know who gets angry, and what you sound like when you get angry. Denying what happened doesn't mean this is over, young man."

"If you're not going to believe me, then yes, it is."

His father's face starting turning red and David thought he might get slugged, but he was saved by a knock on his bedroom door.

"Go away! This is a private matter," his father raged. Jonah opened the door anyway and walked into the room. "Didn't you hear me?" his father screamed at Jonah.

"David's not lying," he said. "I heard the whole thing. I was in the attic of the garage, cleaning up an old drum set, and I heard them."

Their mother turned to Jonah. "I appreciate you trying to stick up for your brother, but this has nothing to do with you, so please leave the room."

Little Jonah got an expression on his face that David knew he would never forget. It reminded him of the supremely confident and angry look on Neo's face at the end of the movie *The Matrix*, when Neo realized that he was "the one."

Jonah spoke in a slow, confident, and measured tone that neither David nor his parents had ever heard before from Jonah. "Someone is telling a lie about my brother, and I know it is a lie, so it has *everything* to do with me."

Both their parents looked dumbfounded.

Jonah placed his hands on his hips. "Call Uncle Meyer. He was with me."

Their shocked gazes turned from Jonah, to each other. Then their mother immediately called their Uncle Meyer, who confirmed what Jonah and David had told them.

As she got off the phone, she turned to their father and told him in a rather subdued voice, "David and Jonah are correct. Meyer heard the whole thing. Meyer was with Jonah helping him repair the old drum set in the attic of the garage. He said that David's speech was nothing but polite the entire time."

David's father's eyes began filling with tears. "I apologize to the both of you. Apparently I have acted like a complete fool. I am thoroughly ashamed of my behavior."

He slowly walked out of the room, and then the door to his father's bedroom closed and they could hear him quietly crying.

"I'll call Megan's mom, then I'll talk to your father. I'm completely ashamed of how we acted toward you two." Their mother hugged them both and left the room.

"Thanks, Jonah." David gave him a soft pat on the arm. "That's what little brothers are for." Jonah beamed at David.

David hugged his brother. "You know, sometimes you're not as little as you look, Jonah."

Chapter Twenty-Six ~ David and Linda, Trace and Tina

WOW, YOUR LITTLE BROTHER is something special," Linda told David.

"He really is. I'll tell you another story about him. Every Sunday morning, my Uncle Meyer and Jonah go for a ride in one of Uncle Meyer's antique cars, and a few years ago they drove onto the interstate just in time to witness a multicar accident."

Linda gasped. "Oh, my. How horrible."

"They went over to the wreck with a first aid kit and found a man with a fairly blue skin tone. He had a sucking chest wound, which means his lung had a hole in it from an external puncture."

Linda shuddered and covered her mouth with her hand.

"The man was trying desperately to breath, but the hole prevented his lungs from functioning properly. His chest was moving at a rapid rate, but his face was still blue. Uncle Meyer is a Vietnam veteran, and he knew to put the proper bandage on it and hold it in place so the man could breathe. Uncle Meyer realized that six-year-old Jonah wasn't bothered by the bloody scene, so he asked Jonah to put on some latex gloves. Then Jonah held the bandage in place so the man could continue breathing, and my Uncle Meyer started taping the bandage to the man's body."

"He was so brave. And only six-years-old. Wow."

"I know. After that, Uncle Meyer had Jonah tell the man a story—about himself and Uncle Meyer's car—so he could start checking on other people. He kept an eye on Jonah, and every time he glanced in Jonah's direction, he said Jonah appeared calm and was smiling at the injured man—talking to him while occasionally checking the bandage. Ten-minutes-later the paramedics arrived.

One of them saw what Jonah was doing and told him, "Good job, big fella. I'll take it from here."

Jonah was in heaven when he heard that, and I guess he ran to Uncle Meyer and told him that the paramedic called him big fella.

Uncle Meyer told Jonah that he helped save that man's life, so when they buckled themselves in Uncle Meyer's antique car, apparently Jonah shouted, "A-two-two—we are the Tigers!"

"What?" Linda asked.

"I'll tell you about A-two-two another time." David chuckled. "Now, how about having someone take a photo of you and me standing here in the picturesque English flower garden?"

Tina and Trace were nearby, so they took photos of David and Linda, and then they switched places and David took some photos of Tina and Trace.

As they continued walking, Linda turned to David and asked him a very direct question. "So David, do you have someone special in your life now?"

David shrugged. "No. It's been a pretty lonely year." He grinned at Linda. "Until now, that is."

Linda smiled back and then they walked quietly along the garden's walkways. A slight breeze had picked up, stirring the trees and bushes on this otherwise bright and sunny day. As they strolled, Linda watched the trees and bushes swaying in the wind, and David watched Linda, as a peaceful expression filled her face.

He studied her as the serene aura changed to a more pensive one. David wondered what she might be thinking, and he hoped she knew that she could trust him with her feelings.

Linda continued to watch the flowers and plants bending in the breeze, then suddenly she stopped walking and stared right into David's eyes. She bit her bottom lip and then took a deep breath. "I'm damaged goods, David."

"What?" That had caught him off-guard.

Her eyes looked to the ground now. "David…I was raped two years ago and I'm still getting over it. That's why I don't dance close with anyone. I get an awful reminder of what happened—it's kind of a nightmarish flashback."

For a fraction-of-a-second, David felt like he wanted to go find the guy that would do such a thing and teach him a lesson. He looked at her, realizing that she did trust him. He would be careful not to take that trust for granted.

"I'll have to take your word for what you're going through, because I can't imagine what that's like." He shook his head. "But you're not damaged, Linda—the monster that did this to you is. What you are, well, you seem like an awfully special lady to me."

"Thank you for saying that, David. I think you're special too. I was afraid to tell you—it wasn't easy and I appreciate you being kind."

David turned to face Linda and smiled broadly at her. "I promise I'll never hurt you, Linda. Would it be all right if I kissed you? Just on the cheek, I promise."

She smiled sweetly at him and raised her cheek.

David took hold of Linda's hand, and he slowly bent down and lightly kissed her on her warm soft cheek.

"I'm really happy we met, David. I almost didn't come to camp this summer because it's so difficult for me to be around strangers. If Trace, Kelly, and the others from our band weren't here, I don't think I'd have come. I guess someone had plans that we should meet."

"I can't imagine how much trauma it would take to feel damaged two years after something occurred. Linda, if I ever do or say something that makes you feel uncomfortable, you have to tell me immediately."

"Thank you, David. I know that I can trust you with my feelings." Linda looked up at him as he walked next to her, holding her hand.

"I know I've only known you for a few days, but I feel so...I don't know...complete with you. I feel secure whenever you are around."

Linda squeezed David's hand and stopped walking. "Secure enough to do this," she said as she stepped in front of him, placed her free hand behind David's head, and gently pulled his face down to hers. She kissed him once, briefly, on the lips.

"David you make me feel absolutely wonderful, ever since you first talked to me."

David smiled. He knew it must have taken a lot for her to kiss him. "I feel the same way, Linda."

"Was it this way for you, with Megan?"

"This is different—very different. Megan and I were in love with the idea of being in love. I think that's why our relationship fell apart. With you, I have this warm feeling inside me whenever I'm with you. That's completely new for me."

A huge smile swept across Linda's face when David told her that, and they resumed walking through the lovely gardens, admiring the flowers and various birds that visited there.

"Linda, do you know what *Bashert* is?"

"David," Linda exclaimed, her cheeks flushing with embarrassment. "We just met three-days-ago."

"I know. It's just that I feel so...so at peace when I'm with you. I don't know how else to explain it. I really didn't care about seeing a bunch of flowers, but when you said you wanted to come here, I knew I had to be here with you."

She looked up at him with apprehension in her eyes. "David, this is kind of going too fast for me."

"Linda, tell me that you don't feel the same way."

Linda looked away, toward the ground again, and she shrugged. "I could tell you that I don't feel the same way, but it would be a lie. My heart skipped a beat when I first heard you speaking in Hebrew and I've loved every moment we've spent together. Whether we're seeing these beautiful gardens, playing music together, or sharing a meal—I feel great that you're with me."

David stopped walking and pointed at a trumpet vine covered in red tubular flowers, snaking through a trellis nearby. "Linda, look. A Rufous Hummingbird is feeding over there."

"Oh, David, it's beautiful—and look, it's hovering and staring right at us." Linda turned to Tina and Trace. "Come and see this. It's flashing its iridescent red neck feathers at us. What a beautiful display."

Tina and Trace came over to observe the little hummingbird as well.

"I'm always amazed at the angry-bee sound those tiny little birds make," Trace told them.

"We get Rufous and also Calliope Hummingbirds at our ranch," Tina added. "I just love them."

As the two couples started walking together, a Northern Flicker flew by and entertained them for a while. It had discovered a European Starling on the suet feeder it wanted to feed from. The Flicker wasted no time in chasing the Starling away and then positioned itself to eat at the suet feeder.

"That Flicker sure let the Starling know who the boss is." Tina giggled. "We get them out at our ranch all the time, too, but I never get tired of watching them."

As the group was ending their exploration of the garden, the girls wanted to visit the gift shop. David and Trace groaned, as if on cue, but accompanied them in exploring the unique items on display.

After a few minutes in the gift shop Trace came over to David and whispered to him. "David, come with me, I want to show you something."

The girls continued looking through some colorful, glass garden ornaments, while Trace took David over to the earrings on display.

He looked around as if making sure the girls were not watching. "Look at the second and fifth rows, David."

"Perfect." David gave Trace a quick pat on the back.

As they were walking back to the bus to return to campus, Linda asked David what he had purchased in the gift shop.

He grinned. "I got something special for my brother. I'll show it to you when we're on the bus."

After they sat down, David opened the package, showing Linda two earrings in the shape and color of a Rufous Hummingbird.

"David," Linda questioned, "your brother wears earrings?"

David put a confused look on his face. "Well gee... I must have made a mistake. I guess these must be for you."

Her face lit up in a smile. "David, they're beautiful. Thank you so much."

As Linda was putting on the earrings, they heard Tina yell, "Trace Beckham, you didn't."

Linda looked at David and laughed. "Did Trace buy something for your brother, too?"

"Northern Flicker earrings, I believe."

"You guys are the greatest," Linda told David as she linked her arms around his for the ride back to campus.

***

On Friday afternoon, one of the counselors announced that any students who wished to celebrate the beginning of *Shabbat* should come over to her apartment at five-thirty. This was early for a summertime *Shabbat* celebration, but she said she thought this would be nice for the students who lit candles each week at home.

David and Linda arrived with Kelly and James, and about twenty other students showed up as well. James and a few of the other students had never been to a *Shabbat* celebration before, and they had many thoughtful questions, which the others were most pleased to answer.

Kelly said she had attended *Shabbat* at Linda's house many times, so she knew what to expect. As each girl lit a candle, the room began to take on the glow of the golden-colored light of the *Shabbat* candles.

After the last candle was lit, the counselor asked, "How about our own version of Diana Krall leading us in the blessing for the candles?"

Linda smiled and walked up to the row of candles. She covered her eyes and chanted the blessing in the most perfect tones.

As she started to chant the blessing, David felt a growing closeness to Linda while he listened to her sing the ancient melody. He had never felt like this about anyone—Linda made him feel as if she was almost a part of him.

"Thank you, Linda," The counselor said. "That was beautiful. Everyone please pick up a little cup of wine. Which of the boys knows the blessing for the wine?"

Almost all of the Jewish boys knew the short version, but the counselor wanted someone to sing the full *Shabbat* version.

"I know it," David volunteered.

David held up his cup of wine and closed his eyes as he began chanting the melodic ancient prayer. After the first few lines, he opened his eyes and looked directly at Linda as he continued singing the lengthy blessing.

Afterwards, a teary-eyed Linda walked over to stand next to David. "That was beautiful, David. You sounded just like my dad." Feeling most proud, David smiled and thanked her. Then everyone joined hands and recited the blessing for the *challah*. Then they each took a piece of the lovely homemade *challah* to enjoy.

David then turned to the group. "As this is the first *Shabbat* celebration that Linda and I are observing together, I would appreciate everyone singing the *Shehechianu* with us."

Linda's face reflected deep appreciation, as she slipped her hand into David's and joined everyone in the blessing that is sung at the time of significant beginnings.

The counselor clapped her hands. "I hate to break this up, but you guys have a talent contest to attend tonight."

Kelly, James, David, and Linda volunteered to help with cleanup duties but the counselor sent them out. "It's an honor that all of you joined with me to celebrate the start of *Shabbat*. I'll take care of putting these few things away."

***

Linda was quiet as she and David walked hand in hand back to the campus—she had many thoughts running through her mind. She abruptly stopped walking.

David turned to face her. "What's wrong?"

Linda started to speak, but the words got stuck in her throat. She threw her arms around David, holding him as tight as she could.

"Linda, I thought..." "Be quiet and hold me."

David wrapped his arms around her. His body felt tense at first, but then she felt his warmth as he relaxed into her. Linda buried her face in David's chest and quietly cried.

After a few minutes, David pulled back to look at her. "Are you okay?"

"No, I'm not okay—and it's your fault that I feel like this. You and your *Bashert*. It's not enough that you were so kind and considerate to me every moment we were together this week, but you had to sing the *Shehechianu* tonight. I'm just a crazy high school girl who wants to go to med school. You've turned my whole world upside down, David, and I love it. I just love it."

"Linda, you don't mind me holding you like this?"

"After singing the *Shehechianu* together, do you think I was going to let that jerk come between us? I guess *not,* David Kaplan."

"Linda, you are so special."

"If I am special, it's because of the way you treat me." She looked up at him and they engaged in a long kiss.

When they started walking again, David asked Linda, "Did my brother talk to you about my intended major in college."

"No, he didn't. Why do you ask?"

"Because I plan on going to med school, too—to become an obstetrician. I plan to practice for a few years and then get a PhD to do research. I've even watched some videos to make sure any goriness doesn't bother me."

"David, I've always dreamed of becoming a pediatrician."

"Perfect! I'll birth them and you'll make sure they're healthy as they grow to adulthood."

"David, you are crazy."

"I'm crazy enough to care about you and envision a future for us."

Chapter Twenty-Seven ~ David and Linda, plus the Neighbors

THE LAST DAY OF band camp dawned bright and sunny. The students were going to put on their final performance and receive awards. As it was a Saturday morning, most of the parents of the band members were in attendance. All one-hundred- fifty campers were on a football field getting ready for their final performances.

The parents gathered in the stands overlooking the field, their faces searching for their children.

Jonah turned to his parents and Sheryl. "I think I see David. He's over there to the right, holding hands with that pretty girl in the bright yellow top."

From the row behind them, a man spoke. "I think we should introduce ourselves, as your son is holding hands with our daughter."

The two families started laughing and got acquainted with each other.

Linda's father, Alex Schulman, gestured to the people seated next to him. "These are our neighbors, Anna and Michael Levin. This is Dell and Wilson Beckham—their son, Trace, is also attending band camp."

After greetings all around, they all quietly listened to the students put on a wonderful performance.

"We're now going to announce the awards for this year's camp," they heard over the loudspeaker system. "Most improved since last band camp goes to the same winner of this award during last year's camp, someone who is obviously a very hard worker—our top snare drummer, Trace Beckham."

Tina screamed and clapped louder than anyone.

"Award for the best instrumental duet on talent night goes to Marvin Kalispell and Ethan Kaplan."

"Yay, Ethan," a young female voice screamed from the stands. Ethan looked over his shoulder at David and said something.

Jonah grinned. "I guess Ethan just realized Sheryl is here."

"Award for the best vocal duet on talent night goes to Linda Shulman and David Kaplan."

Linda's father looked amazed. "I didn't know Linda could sing," he said.

After receiving their award, Linda and David walked back to stand with the other students. They engaged in a tight embrace.

Linda's mother said in a surprised voice, "Oh my God. They just hugged—Alex did you see that? Linda threw her arms around him, and she let him hold her."

"The award for the best comedy act at talent night goes to a couple who performed a skit from the old radio show, 'The Bickersons.' Tina Wagoner and Trace Beckham."

They accepted the award amidst cheers and laughter, but the man handing out the awards stopped the couple before they exited the stage.

"This year we have a special award to give out. As I'm sure many of you parents are aware, countless friendships start here at band camp. This year we decided we needed to have an award for the cutest couple. The winners are—Tina Wagoner and Trace Beckham."

"The next award is for the happiest person at band camp, and this year, there is a tie for that award. It goes to Kelly Kelsey and James Callahan."

A mighty cheer went up from the Meridian contingent.

When the program ended, the group from the stands met with their children and they started walking to the parking lot together.

Mrs. Schulman turned to Anna with excitement. "I met the nice couple who bought the Williams's old house, Anna. They're from Seattle. He's going to be doing engineering for a truck manufacturer out here and they have two of the nicest children. Their son is the same age as Andrew and they're already friends. While the parents were going over paperwork with the real estate agent, Andrew and their son, Drew, were throwing a football up and down the street. And their twelve-year-old daughter is just the sweetest—she speaks English, Italian, *and* Spanish. They're moving out here in two weeks. I told them about the neighborhood block party on Labor Day. They immediately wanted to know what committee they could join and what food would be needed. They're going to fit right in."

Then, as Michelle Kaplan was walking next to Linda, she smiled at her and asked, "So, you and David had a nice week together?"

Linda responded enthusiastically. "We did so many things to-gether—it was like many weeks rolled into one. David was fun to be with the whole week, but Friday night he did something really special. We had a welcome *Shabbat* ceremony at the apartment of one of the counselors. David said everyone should sing *Shehechianu* because this was the first *Shabbat* the two of us were celebrating together."

Michelle Kaplan smiled at her husband, giving him a gentle nudge with her elbow. "You hear that, Morris?"

"David's father did that for me on our first *Shabbat* together," she told Linda. "To this day, I smile when I think about that."

Anna asked Michael if that was the same song they sang on their first *Shabbat* celebration.

"Yes, it certainly is," Michael replied, as he kissed Anna's cheek and squeezed her hand.

"We're having an after-camp lunch at my home in Meridian," Sherry Schulman announced. "We would love to have all of you over. We live just across town from here. It takes around fifteen- minutes to drive there." She turned to the Kaplans and added, "We're two-minutes from an interchange for I-84, so it's near to the beginning of your drive home."

Michelle told them, "We'll be glad to join you for lunch. Actual-ly we're not going home until tomorrow. David told us about some lovely gardens near the old prison that we'd like to see this afternoon. I've become a garden crazy person, so I can't wait to see the place."

"You'll love it. I adore what they've done over there. We haven't been there yet this summer. Why don't we make it a group outing?"

Michelle turned to Linda and David. "Do you two think you can stand to spend a few more hours together this afternoon?"

"It will be very difficult, but for the sake of the families, we'll have to manage," Linda told them with a joy-filled expression.

Sherry called out, "Hey, Levins, how about going over to the Idaho Botanic Garden this afternoon after lunch at our place?"

They all agreed, and as they were approaching their cars, Sherry said, "David and Linda should ride with the Kaplans, so Linda can direct them back to our house if we get separated. Ethan and Sheryl can ride with us so they can tell us Kaplan family secrets."

Everyone laughed and Michelle beamed with pride. "It's just like David to find a nice girl from a nice family and create a great relationship in only one week at band camp."

***

During a lovely lunch of a salad of mixed greens with blue cheese dressing and melt-in-your-mouth cooked overnight brisket, Anna mentioned her grandmother to the Schulmans. "My grandmother's maiden name was Schulman, too."

"That's quite a coincidence," Alex told her. "I've started working on a family tree. I'll show it to you after lunch."

As Alex explained what he had discovered about his family, he told Anna that he'd had a real problem finding a birth certificate for his grandfather. "He was born to a woman who must have remarried when he was very young."

Anna was astonished. "Was his father named Sam?"

"How did you know that?" Alex, too, wore a look of surprise. "My grandmother told me about her parents. His name was Sam

Schulman and there is a family story about his losing track of a pregnant wife. Is your grandfather still alive?"

"No. He died a while ago."

"Please, see if you can find out if Sam Schulman is shown as having married Carrie Yoselovitch. They're my great-grandparents. My grandmother is still alive."

"Let's go check," Alex said.

He and Anna walked into his office and Alex began digging through a pile of papers on his desk. "Sam Schulman, Sam Schulman," he kept repeating.

"Here it is. He married a second wife—named Carrie Yoselovitch."

Anna and Alex stared at each other in silence. At last Anna smiled and said, "Hello, cousin."

Alex laughed. "Hello to you too, cousin."

They walked back out to join the group. "My grandmother is going to be in heaven when she finds out," Anna said. "She'll be out in late October to stay with me, when I bring our baby home. I'll tell her then and she can meet all you Schulmans."

"Tell her what?" Michael asked Anna.

Alex and Anna both grinned. "We're cousins," they announced.

***

As the day was ending, David and Linda started making plans on how they were going to stay in touch.

Jonah overheard them and mentioned that he, his Uncle Meyer, Aunt Joan, plus Ari and Leah were coming out to the Labor Day car show in Boise. "They're bringing two or three cars to enter in the show," he said. "Maybe David can come with us then and he can see you again."

"Great idea," David said and as soon as he returned to his home in Seattle he called his Uncle Meyer to see if he could join them on their trip to Boise. Immediately after, he called Linda to tell her the news.

"He said it would be fantastic if I came with them. He told me there's a parade and tour and that he's always wanted to bring three cars to this event, but he never had a driver for the third car."

"That sounds great," Linda said.

"Yeah. He told me that he, or my cousin, Ari, would teach me to drive the old Auburn roadster—well actually, he teased that Jonah can teach me to drive the old Auburn. Anyway, he asked if you would be joining us."

"Of course, David. I wouldn't miss a chance to see you." "Well, he told me to tell my cousin, Leah, if you were coming.

He said she'll want to talk to you."

***

Two days later Linda received a phone call.

"Hi, Linda, I'm Leah Minkowski. I'm David's cousin and I'll be coming out on Labor Day, so I'll get to meet you in person. I'm sure David told you that he will be driving one of our antique cars in the parade on Sunday morning and with the tour on Sunday afternoon. He said you will be riding with him."

"I'm really looking forward to it," Linda told her. "Also, my mom wanted to know if you would join us for *Shabbat* dinner on Friday night."

"Tell your mom we'd love to. Also, I may have some things for you. I need your shoe size and dress size."

Linda thought that was a strange request from someone she had only met over the telephone, but gave her the information.

"See you in a few weeks," Leah cheerily told her.

Linda agreed and hung up the phone, feeling happy that she was making new friends—friends related to David.

Something else was occurring in Linda's life that she was starting to really enjoy, too. As she'd matured she realized that she was becoming good friends with Anna Levin.

The Levins and the Schulmans would often go to each other's homes for *Shabbat* dinners. Linda's mom was an average cook and had little interest in preparing special dishes. Anna was always happy to teach Linda new recipes, how to shop for fresh produce, and various cooking techniques.

Linda's father was in heaven with every new dish Linda prepared, and Linda's mother was quite proud of her daughter's culinary efforts, thanking Anna for having so much patience in teaching her daughter cooking skills.

Jewish Holidays at the Levins' were epicurean feasts. Anna quickly learned Jewish style cooking from borscht to bagels and even had her own recipes for making corned beef, pastrami, and gefilte fish. She made a Russian brisket that took all night to cook and simply melted in one's mouth. Anna's raisin-and-coconut-filled strudel was to die for. Every time Linda helped Anna prepare something, there was always enough to take home for Linda's family too.

As Labor Day weekend approached, Linda convinced her mom to let her do all the cooking for the *Shabbat* dinner. Over the phone, she and David reviewed that evening's *Parsha* so they could do the bible reading and present a discussion on its significance for the assembled families.

*****

Linda was nervous and excited on the Friday before Labor Day. Every time she'd looked at the clock on that afternoon, she smiled, because it was only a handful of hours before David would be arriving from Seattle. She was glad to be the cook, though, because it gave her something to concentrate on besides the idea of meeting more of David's family.

David, Jonah, and their relatives arrived around five-thirty in the afternoon. David introduced his uncle, Meyer Minkowski, Meyer's wife, Joan, plus their son, Ari, and his wife, Leah.

Twelve-year-old Jonah reintroduced himself and reminded everyone that he was a car guy and a drummer.

At dinner, Linda informed everyone that Anna had taught her all the recipes she'd used that evening. David was quite proud that "his girl" could turn out such an amazing meal and Michael said he was proud that "his girl" could teach a teenager to cook so well.

"Linda, you made the gefilte fish from scratch? I absolutely love it," an enthusiastic Jonah told her.

The families enjoyed, and were impressed with, the *Parsha* reading and discussion that Linda and David had put together. Then, after dinner, Leah presented David and Linda with a box of clothes and asked them to try them on.

They both walked upstairs to change and David followed Linda into her bedroom. "Oops, maybe I should use the bathroom," he said.

"I don't care if you don't." Linda was so happy to have a minute alone with David that she threw her arms around him.

After a long kiss, David stepped back. "We ought to get changed, or they'll wonder what we're doing up here."

Linda smiled. "The way your cousin, Leah, looks at Ari, I guarantee *she* knows what we're doing up here."

They changed into the nineteen-twenties-era clothing and stood in front of the full-length mirror in Linda's room. "This is great," she exclaimed. "I'll bet we wear this stuff while we're in the car."

"Yeah," David agreed. "I can't wait."

Then they headed downstairs, greeted by applause from the family as they modeled their period attire.

"Wait until you guys see *my* outfit," Jonah told them. "I look like an actor from the 'Our Gang' comedies."

"It's going to be great fun," Linda said. "I'm really looking forward to it. Thank you so much for inviting me, Mr. Minkowski." "You're very welcome, Linda. Thank you again for the wonderful meal, too."

***

Joan squeezed Meyer's hand and smiled.

He leaned in and spoke to her. "This Linda is something special," he said. "I'm going to have to get to know her."

Joan gazed across at David. "Did you notice how happy David seems? The way they look at each other, I'm sure we will have plenty of chances to get to know her better."

Then she got serious. "But you know what else I noticed, Meyer? Sherry's smile seemed quite forced today. Even the compliments on her daughter's beautiful *challah* didn't seem to spark a real smile on her face. And when I tried to talk to her, she seemed distant. I mean, she was pleasant enough, but she seemed otherwise occupied."

Meyer agreed. "I noticed that, too. Even when Sherry announced that her daughter had done all the cooking, she didn't seem too excited," he said.

Joan stood up, walked over, and extended her hand in invitation. "Sherry, you and I need to go for a walk—so I can get to know you."

Sherry looked surprised that Joan would single her out, but she also seemed relieved that she could get out of the house for a while.

The two women walked in silence to the end of the block. It's a lovely day, isn't it?" Sherry said.

"It is," Joan agreed. "Sherry, I hope you don't mind me saying this, but—"

"Yes?"

"Well, I realized that you seem preoccupied with something, and I think I know why." Joan felt she recognized the look in Sherry's eyes. "Do you know the results of the mammogram yet?" Joan asked.

A thoroughly surprised-looking Sherry nodded yes. "Have you told your husband yet?"

Tears started forming in Sherry's eyes, as she shook her head. "No—but how did you know?"

Joan put her hand on her right breast and compressed it between her fingers. "It's just foam," she said. "I had a radical mastectomy some years ago. It was before Meyer and I were married, but he still finds me sexy, and he still makes love to me like crazy. Most importantly, Meyer still loves me for the person I am."

Sherry broke down. She covered her face with her hands and began sobbing hysterically.

Joan wrapped an arm around Sherry's shoulder. "Sherry, you have a wonderful husband and family. I know you'll get through this."

Joan sat quietly for a few moments, giving Sherry time to compose herself, then she continued. "Listen, I won't leave town until I find a support group for you and your husband to attend. It really makes a difference if you both attend together."

"I don't know what to say." Sherry wiped at her cheeks. "Thank you so much."

"I know it's difficult, but let's go back to the house and find a room where we can tell Alex. Meyer and I will help you, if you like."

When they arrived back, a solemn-faced Sherry told Alex that she needed to talk to him in his office. Joan nodded to Meyer, indicating that he should join them. She then leaned over and whispered to Anna and Leah, who were sitting next to each other, to keep everyone else away from the office for a while.

When they were in the office, Sherry confessed to her husband. "Alex, you remember my checkup awhile back?"

He nodded and a worried expression came over his face. He reached out and took her hand.

"Well, the doctor called this morning about my mammogram results. I am going in for a biopsy early next week to confirm, but she feels certain I have breast cancer." Sherry began to sob. "I might lose it, Alex—my breast."

Sherry crossed her arms across her chest in a protective gesture, as Alex wrapped her in an embrace and began quietly crying with her.

"I love you and we'll get through this," Alex said.

Alex looked at Joan and Meyer. "But why are you here?"

"We've been through this some years ago," Joan said. "I recognized Sherry seemed upset about something and she reminded me of myself back then. I took a chance and asked her about it on our walk. I knew she must need to talk to someone."

"Thank you," Alex said to Joan. "Thank you for caring." His eyes darted to Joan's chest.

"See that Sherry? He can't even tell which one I lost." "I'm sorry, I didn't mean to—"

Joan smiled. "It's okay. Sherry needs to know that unless she tells people, they won't know."

Meyer had been listening quietly, but now he spoke up. "Why don't we get your kids in here or they're going to imagine the worst." "And the worst," Joan assured them, "is not what's going to happen to you. You did the most important thing already, Sherry.

You had a mammogram. You caught this early."

Meyer and Joan walked back into the dining room and sent Andrew and Linda in to talk to their parents.

They could immediately hear Linda crying as her mother told her children the news.

Everyone else in the room looked on with curiosity, so Meyer told them what was happening.

Ari turned to David. "I know you guys had a great weekend planned, but Linda may want to spend all her time with her mom now."

"I know you'll want to take her pain away," Leah added, "but the most you can do is hold her when she asks you. She may not even want you to do that for a while."

David just nodded that he understood.

Jonah stood up angrily. "This is a bunch of crap," he said. "When the heck is someone going to start curing all this cancer shit?"

Meyer got an angry look on his face, leaned toward Jonah, and in a most stern voice told him, "That will happen when capable people get off their asses and start studying hard so they can learn enough to cure that cancer shit."

Jonah looked down. "Yes, Uncle Meyer."

Anna wore a concerned look. "I'm glad I was here to find out. We're close to our neighbors around here—we'll make sure she gets whatever help she needs."

"That kind of support will be a Godsend," Joan told her.

When the Schulmans came back into the dining room, Sherry's eyes were red from crying, but she smiled at everyone. "Well, we had planned to view *Fantasia* at Michael and Anna's home after dinner tonight. He has a huge video screen and he will play the sound through his magnificent audio system for us."

She looked to her daughter. "Linda has baked a lovely dessert that will be served at intermission...so, I think that's exactly what we should do."

"Great," Joan told everyone in a cheery voice. "Let's go."

***

They all started walking the couple of blocks to Michael and Anna's home. Sure enough, as Ari had predicted, Linda ignored David and walked next to her mother, holding her hand—Andrew walked with his dad.

"Linda, you're allowed to be sad for two more minutes and then that's it," her mom told her.

"Mom—"

"Listen to me, Linda. If you let my illness ruin your weekend with David, then I'll feel even worse that my sickness prevented you from enjoying your time with him."

"I love you, Mom."

"I know, Linda. I'm a lucky woman. Not many moms have a daughter who is so compassionate, and such a strong leader, that she could tell her friends to shave their heads so they could provide support for an ill member of their group. I know I'm not supposed to know that it was your idea, and you told everyone to say that it was a group decision, but that just shows what a wonderful daughter I have. I want you to be strong for your brother. He's going to need his big sister to help him through this. I know your father will support me, so please keep an eye on Andrew. Boys don't show their emotions very well, but I think he'll be willing to tell you how he feels, and that will be good for him."

"Who's going to be here for me when you're recovering?" "You know the answer to that. Who helped you become willing to embrace people again? Linda, your face lights up like a sunny spring morning when you look at him. Go over and walk with David. I'll be fine."

Linda stopped walking and waited for David to catch up to her.

He was walking at the end of the group with Jonah.

David took her hand. "Linda, I'm so sorry."

"Just hold me," she said. "That's what I need."

As David hugged her, Linda thought that with him as her partner, she would get through this.

Chapter Twenty-Eight ~ Jonah and Holly

AS THEY ENTERED MICHAEL and Anna's home, Jonah screamed, "Are those Maggie twenty-point-ones? Wow! You even have Maggie CCRs and Maggie surround speakers. Is everything bi-amplified? Oh baby. McIntosh tube preamps and amps—I must have died and gone to audio heaven."

"Do you know what he's talking about?" Linda asked David. "No, but I'm not surprised. Jonah's head is a sponge for technology, plus he seems to know about the finest in any category." Everyone stared at Jonah, except Michael, who immediately started giving Jonah a highly-technical tour of his system while the tube components warmed up.

The listening room had four couches arranged in two shallow Vs. The second set was on a raised platform, and in between the couches were two single chairs, one positioned behind the other.

Just as everyone got comfortable, the doorbell rang. Anna went to open the door and she came back to the room with another couple and two children.

"Everyone, I want you to meet our new neighbors." She gestured to each in turn. "This is Oliver, Ruth, Holly, and Drew. They've just moved here from Seattle."

As everyone introduced themselves, Holly sat down with her parents. Jonah was the only one her age, but he seemed too busy studying Michael's audio-video system to be bothered talking to someone, so Linda suggested Holly come sit with them.

Holly smiled and came to sit on the floor next to David and Linda. She and Linda talked about the local schools, band, and things to do in the Boise area. When they got around to discussing cooking,

Holly's face light up, and the two girls immediately started comparing recipes, ingredients, and cooking techniques.

The movie was about to start so Jonah looked around for a place to sit. Holly was laughing at something David had said to Linda—as if drawn by a magnet, Jonah walked over and sat down next to her.

"That's quite an audio system," he told Holly.

"I love music," she said, "but I don't know what makes one system better than another."

Jonah grinned proudly and proceeded to tell Holly about Magnepan (Maggie) planar speakers, tube amplifiers, preamplifiers, and class-c-amplifiers—likely more than Holly really wanted to know. Still, Holly seemed to glow with a beaming smile having all of Jonah's attention focused on her.

Linda nudged David with her elbow, then gestured with a subtle nod of her head for him to look at Jonah and Holly.

He grinned at the sight. Then, as Michael dimmed the lights, David leaned forward and kissed Linda on the neck.

As the movie began, Linda observed that Holly had repositioned herself for a better view and she was leaning slightly against Jonah. Linda expected him to move away, but he didn't. She decided that maybe now he had discovered something more interesting than Michael's sound system.

Halfway through, Michael paused the movie and the group took a break to move into the dining room.

Holly followed Jonah and she was looking around, as if wondering where to sit, when Jonah pulled out a chair for her, just like David had done for Linda.

"Thank you, Jonah." She smiled and sat down.

Linda and David watched as his Uncle Meyer and Aunt Joan looked delighted at seeing Jonah's newfound interest in girls.

"Have we burned down the cabin yet?" Joan asked Meyer, who burst out laughing.

Linda whispered to David. "What are they talking about?"

David shrugged. "I don't know exactly. It must be an inside joke, because they always say that to each other."

Everyone was seated as Anna and Linda served Linda's warm apple pies. They offered generous slices with either shaved, sharp cheddar cheese, or a particularly rich vanilla ice cream on the side. They all dug in and seemed to be savoring the delicious flavors.

"The filling is different than any other apple pie I've eaten," Holly commented to Linda.

"We add a touch of ginger," Linda proudly told her. "Whatever you did, it's delicious," Jonah said between bites.

"You are a great cook."

"I love to cook, too," Holly told Jonah. "Especially Italian dishes."

"Italian's my favorite," Jonah replied.

David whispered to Linda, "The only thing Jonah doesn't like is hunger."

Linda giggled and watched Jonah and Holly. "I'd say Jonah is finding delight of a non-technical nature for the first time in his life," she whispered back.

She could see that Oliver and Ruth were delighted by the attention Jonah and Holly lavished on each other.

Anna asked Oliver about their move to Meridian.

He explained how his career had taken a sudden turn for the better, which is what brought them here. "I've noticed a lot of diesel pickups and a diesel motorhome in the neighborhood," he said. "I love that. On the way out here, Ruth and I were thinking that we'd like to get a camper."

Linda's father perked up upon hearing that. "Sherry and I have just decided that we're not going to let another summer go by without an RV. We're sick of hearing about all the fun our rotten neighbors are having with their RVs. We've even decided that we'll look for a used one and just fix it up as we have time. What type of rig were you thinking of, Oliver?"

"We own a full-size diesel pickup," Oliver stated, "so we've been thinking of a fifth-wheel unit."

"The Beckhams up the street have a fifth-wheel and they love it," Michael told him.

"Traveling without suitcases and staying in our own home-on-wheels is just heaven for me," Anna added. "Next summer Michael has promised me we're taking our camper to Yellowstone. With all the space and storage in our RV, it will be easy to take our baby, who will be eight-months-old then."

"There's also a neighborhood plan that you are certainly invited to take part in," Linda's mom said. "A bunch of us—the Beckhams, the Levins and our friends, the McCarthys—are going to try to arrange vacation time so we can wagon train down to Bryce the following summer to see those glorious sights with our families."

"My brother and his wife just bought an Airstream trailer," Anna said. "They may come up from New Mexico to meet us in Bryce, too."

"I think we've come to the right neighborhood, Ruth." Oliver announced.

"You know, last weekend we were up in Sun Valley with my motorhome," Michael said. "When I got home, I noticed that the engine oil level hadn't dropped and usually it would be down about a quart."

"Oh shit," Jonah said, then covered his mouth as if he suddenly remembered that Holly was sitting next to him. "Sorry, I didn't mean to swear," Jonah told her.

Everyone looked at him. "I'm sorry, but that's a real bad situation."

Oliver smiled at him. "Okay, expert, what's wrong with the engine?"

"Well," Jonah replied, "he didn't say he saw smoke, so that rules out a coolant leak. He must have an injector leaking diesel fuel into the oil pan."

Oliver smiled even broader. "Should he drive it to a repair shop to get it fixed?"

Jonah thought for a moment. "No. He might burn a crankshaft, piston, or rod bearing."

"He's right, Michael." Oliver laughed. "Absolutely, positively, don't even start the engine until a qualified garage looks at it. Also you need to get the oil analyzed to look for metal shavings."

Oliver turned back to Jonah. "If you're free next summer, I could use some help. I have an old Jumo diesel aircraft engine that I brought from Seattle. I'm accumulating the specialized tools I'll need and building some special structures to hold the engine while I rebuild it. I could use some help, any time you're available."

Jonah just sat still with his mouth open.

"Do you know about that engine?" Meyer asked Jonah. "Twelve-piston, opposed, six-cylinder, two-cycle diesel. I've read about it, but I didn't know any still existed."

"Wow," Holly said. "I can't believe you know about that. Dad has told lots of people about that old engine and only a few antique aircraft enthusiasts knew about it."

Jonah beamed.

"I'd love to see it," Meyer told Oliver.

"We're spending the day out of the house tomorrow as a painting crew just finished putting new wall coatings on all the rooms. We want to let the house air out for the day. I'll be glad to show it to you later in the afternoon, if you're around."

"We're planning on visiting the Raptor Center in Boise tomorrow morning," Joan stated. "Why don't we make it a group outing?"

"What a great idea," Alex said. "The Shulmans would like to go."

"We'd love to go, too," Michael said. "We've never seen the place, but we've heard many great things about it."

"The Holts will be there," Ruth announced and Holly's face lit up.

"Cool," Drew said. "I'll bring my sketchbook."

"That's a great idea, Drew," Anna said. "I heard you enjoy painting."

"It's one of my favorite things to do," he replied.

"Why don't you come into our future nursery with me, so I can show you something."

They got up and went into the room. David, Linda, and Holly followed along. Drew walked in and saw the wall-sized mural, and his eyes went huge. "Can you teach me how to do this?" Drew asked Anna.

"It would be an honor," she said. "It takes some planning, but we can do that together if you like."

Drew called for his parents, and Ruth and Oliver joined them in admiring the lovely mural.

Anna explained that it represented different memories and scenes from her hometown.

"Look at the excitement in Drew's face," Ruth said to Oliver, before turning to Anna. "Anna, we barely know you, and yet you are willing to find time to teach our son how to paint a mural."

"It's my pleasure, Ruth." Anna smiled.

"We can set up a wall in your room to do that, Drew," Oliver told him.

Drew was positively beaming. "Thanks, Dad."

After the conclusion of the movie, as the evening ended, everyone arranged to meet the next morning for their trip to the Raptor Center.

***

As they walked around the amazing Birds of Prey Raptor Center the following day, Leah was astounded as she watched Jonah and Holly together, talking like they had known each other for years.

She asked Ruth if Holly could join them on Sunday and ride in one of the antique cars with Jonah, Linda, and David.

"I'm sure she'd enjoy that," Ruth said. "Let's ask her." They approached Holly and asked.

"That would be fun," Holly told them.

"Great," Leah said.

They needed to find Holly some period clothes, so that afternoon they headed over to a store near the university where they found enough small pieces to create an appropriate look.

Holly tried on the various pieces, and she and Jonah were constantly discussing which pieces looked best. So, when the two of them finally decided on the right combination, Ruth and Leah could only smile and agree.

"Holly really has an eye for shape and style," Leah told Ruth. "You must have a wonderful time shopping with her."

"Oh, yes," Ruth said. "Holly and I love shopping together. Did you see the way she and Jonah debated over what looked best? You would think they've known each other for years, the way they talk to each other."

Leah smiled at Ruth. "That sort of thing runs in our family. I'll have to tell you about me and Ari sometime."

***

David and Linda returned to the Levins' home, where David started helping Michael assemble new furniture for the nursery. Linda and Anna started preparing dry rubs and marinades for the meats that they would be smoking and barbequing for the block party on Labor Day.

Then, later in the afternoon, Michael and Anna had to do some shopping. Linda and David decided to watch a movie in the media room. Before they left the house, Michael teased them a little. "Anna, do you think it's all right to leave them alone like that?"

Anna smiled at the two of them. "My beloved Michael, David looks at her like you look at me. I know in my heart he wouldn't hurt her, even if you held a gun to his head."

David and Linda knew that was Michael and Anna's way of telling them to make sure they behaved themselves. They smiled politely and thanked the Levins for allowing them to use the media room.

After they were alone, they sat together at the end of one of the couches, and turned on the movie and sound system. Ten-minutes into the movie, Linda turned and lay across David's lap with her head on the arm of the overstuffed couch. She was still pleasantly amazed at how comfortable she felt being close to David. After what she had gone through, she had thought that she would never be this relaxed and happy around a boy.

She breathed in deep, just as David leaned down and kissed her—a long passionate kiss.

"Is this okay?" he asked, as his lips slid softly along her neck and cheek, leaving little kisses as he moved back to her mouth.

She mumbled, "Yes," and they continued to kiss like that for a while.

After a few more moments of passion that warmed Linda's body and heart, David stopped and looked at her with questioning eyes.

"Go ahead," she said.

David unbuttoned his shirt and then hers. He reached behind and unhooked her bra, pushing it up, then he slowly bent over to kiss her lips. He looked up once, as if to check if she was still okay with it.

As Linda luxuriated in the sensation of her breasts pressing against David's chest, she whispered, "This feels so wonderful, David—finally."

She sat up and positioned herself on David's lap, facing him, sliding his shirt off his shoulders, and then removing her shirt and bra. She felt only a little bit nervous as they explored each other with their hands and lips.

In between kisses, David whispered sweet things to her. "You are so beautiful, Linda," he said. "I love the way you touch me."

A wave of pleasure moved through her body and Linda sighed. "Oh, David, you can't imagine how great that feels. I never thought I would feel this way."

He smiled and held her tightly against him.

"That is the most beautiful thing that's ever happened to me." Linda told him.

She leaned away from him and reached down. "Can I please do something for you?"

"More than you can imagine, I'd like you to," a grinning David told her, "but I think we've gotten away with enough for one day. I'd hate to get caught and have the Levins feel like they shouldn't have trusted us to be alone."

"Okay, but my body owes you."

"Linda, you are the most wonderful person I've ever known. I really didn't imagine that being together like this would be so amazing. I absolutely love and adore you, Linda Shulman."

"I love you, David Kaplan."

They helped each other get dressed, then David rewound the movie so they would know what happened if someone asked. They watched the rest of it wrapped as tightly around each other as they could.

When the movie ended, Linda grinned at David. "Dare I mention the word *Bashert*?"

He smiled at her. "It fits us. It really does. For the first time in my life, I know what Ethan and Sheryl have."

***

David drove Linda, Jonah, and Holly over to the hotel on Sunday to help take the antique cars off the transporters, which were about three blocks away from the marshaling area of the parade.

Meyer and Ari had their antique cars in place for the start of the parade, and they were waiting for David and Linda to bring the other car over. David suddenly needed a bathroom break, so he took off in search of a nearby restroom.

While Linda, Holly, and Jonah waited for David's return, a parade official walked up to them. "If you don't move this car to the marshaling area, you won't make it," he said. "We're about to designate this as a parking area and you won't get out of here until the parade's over."

Linda was worried. "David's not back yet. I don't know what to do."

"Why don't you wait here for David?" Holly said in a casual voice. "Jonah and I will get the car to the marshaling area and you and David can meet us there."

Linda hesitated for a moment. "Well, I can't drive this thing, so if Jonah can, maybe he should. Just don't tear it up."

Linda got out of the car, while Jonah and Holly climbed into the front seats.

"Who do you think taught David to drive the Auburn?" Holly proudly informed Linda as they drove away.

***

David and Linda ran over to the start of the parade from across the park.

"Where's the car?" Meyer shouted. "I see it coming," Ari said.

"But who's driving the Auburn?" Joan asked.

Meyer grinned. "Who else? Look." He pointed to the approaching car.

As the Auburn drove up the street in a stately manner, they saw Holly in the passenger seat proudly holding up her cloth covered sunshade. Jonah was driving, wearing his period shirt, bow tie, and leather driving hat—turned around backwards, of course. They were the epitome of a Twenties' couple out for a Sunday drive.

A breathless Leah recorded their arrival on a video camera.

Then, Oliver, Ruth, and Drew arrived at the marshaling area of the parade to take pictures of everyone in their antique clothing. One of the pictures they took was of Holly and Jonah standing up in the rumble seat of the Auburn roadster. They posed, leaning against each other and putting an arm around each other's waist— a photo that would one day be prominently displayed over a fireplace which belonged to a certain genetics mathematician/car guy and his beloved, multi-lingual wife.

***

On Wednesday afternoon, about two-weeks-later, Joan received a phone call from Sherry Schulman.

"They just removed the lump and it had clean edges," she joyfully told Joan.

"I'm thrilled that you didn't need a mastectomy," Joan said.

The two women had a wonderful conversation, and Sherry thanked Joan for all her support and encouragement.

Later that day, Joan told Meyer, and he called David to let him know.

"Linda already called him," he told Joan. "I like that girl." "When I see the two of them together and how they interact,

Meyer, I think of *Bashert*."

"What about Holly and Jonah?" he asked.

Joan shook her head. "They're so young—and she's not Jewish. That could be a difficult problem for them."

Chapter Twenty-Nine ~ Trace and Tina

AT SIX O'CLOCK ON a cold Saturday morning in late October, Trace was driving out to see Tina. As night became day, he saw very dark clouds in the western sky.

"Those look like snow clouds," he muttered.

Trace liked to get out to the ranch early on weekends, so he could help Tina with her chores, and then the two of them could have the rest of the day to themselves. Chores at the ranch were primarily of the physical kind, but Trace didn't mind and always felt like he had accomplished something when all the tasks were complete.

As he pulled into the ranch, he saw Tina running over to greet him. As he got out of his car, he realized she was upset.

"Golden got out of the barn last night, and she's due to have her foal any day now," Tina said, out of breath. "We have to find her and get her back to the barn."

They ran into the barn where Tina had already saddled Feather and Mama. Feather was a golden-colored Palomino. She was Tina's own horse.

Mama was a Percheron—a large horse, bred for pulling strength, generally known as a docile breed—Trace felt a connection to her and he loved riding her. She was a secure and sure-footed mount.

Tina took out a rifle and scabbard, and attached it to Trace's saddle. "If Golden has the foal away from the ranch, mountain lions could try to kill it."

"Are you sure you want me to carry the rifle? I'm not much of a shot," Trace told her.

"You're better at shooting than I am, Trace Beckham, so you get the rifle."

As they rode out, watching for Golden's tracks, Tina told Trace that she was certain she had secured the barn the night before. "If my father finds out, he's going to be furious. Especially if something happens to that foal."

As they left the barnyard, the family's Australian sheep dog, Luke, came running up to accompany them. The salt and pepper colored pooch was always ready for an outdoor adventure.

Trace took a deep breath of the cool, late October air, certain he smelled snow. Looking to the west, the dark clouds were nearly upon them. He was glad his parents had bought him some wool clothing to wear for his days at the ranch. His Filson wool jacket was keeping the cool breeze away from his skin. Tina had her shearling- lined jacket on and they both wore cowboy boots and Stetson hats. Trace was most proud of his Stetson—it was a birthday gift from Tina.

The snow started falling just as they found Golden's tracks. She had entered a national forest that adjoined the ranch.

"If it snows much more, we won't be able to follow the tracks," Tina shouted, worry filling her voice.

Sure enough, within the next-half-hour, Golden's tracks had completely disappeared from sight, but they continued riding along the same trail. Tina knew that Golden would leave the trail and move to a more secluded area if she decided it was time to deliver the foal.

Luke kept running ahead of them, and then racing back. At one point he just stopped next to them and didn't race ahead. As they continued on the trail he started barking at Tina and Trace.

"What's wrong, Luke?" Trace yelled.

"I think he wants us to go into the woods back there," Tina said.

As soon as they turned their horses around, Luke ran into the trees and brush next to the trail. They followed him and about seventy-five yards into the woods, he started barking.

As they approached, they saw Golden lying on her side. Tina jumped off Feather, tied his reigns to a branch, and ran over to Golden.

Trace secured Mama and followed Tina.

A disheartened and anxious-looking Tina told Trace, "She's having a problem delivering the foal. We have to help her."

"Help a horse deliver a foal? You're kidding right? I hope you know how to do that, because I sure don't."

"Trace, I'll tell you what to do. My arms aren't long enough, and you're stronger than I am. We have to help her. Golden looks absolutely worn out. If we can't help her, they both might die."

Trace heard the frightened and anxious quality in Tina's trembling voice.

"Take off your jacket," she told him.

Trace thought that was an odd request and he wondered why having longer arms than Tina would make any difference. It's not like he would be reaching into Golden to get her foal out. Or would he?

"You have to be kidding." He shook off his jacket.

Tina removed a rolled piece of plastic from her saddlebag. "Here, put this on your arm."

Trace slid a clear plastic sleeve with fingers at the end over his right arm.

"Reach in there and see if you can feel the foal's front hooves."

Trace shuddered as he slid his arm into Golden—his hand went from cold to warm and glided along a moist birth canal. Trace was starting to feel nauseous.

"Tina, I feel...wait...I feel a hoof. Just one hoof, though. Shouldn't I feel another one?"

"Slide your hand along her leg and see if you can find the other one."

Trace did as he was told. "I feel the foal's head, but...wait. I found the other leg, but not a hoof. It might be a knee."

"That's why she's having trouble. The foal's leg is bent backwards. You need to gently pull on the knee to help her the next time she pushes."

Any thought of nausea was now gone from Trace's mind, as he concentrated on helping the little foal. When Golden started pushing, he gently but firmly pulled.

Suddenly a hoof and a head appeared, surrounded by the semi-opaque birth sac. On the next push, Trace pulled and suddenly half a foal was sitting in his lap. The birth sac tore at that point, and the little foal started breathing and moving around. Trace stood up and within another minute the entire foal was out.

Tina was overjoyed. "Yes! Yes! You did it, Trace. It's a colt."

Tina grabbed a towel she had brought along and started wiping off the colt. "We need to get him dry and out of this weather or he'll freeze," she said.

Within minutes the little colt was struggling to his feet. Golden was an experienced mother, and she stood in a way that gave the new-born the opportunity to lean against her, as he learned to steady himself on his spindly and unsure legs.

Even though the snow was coming down like cotton balls, Tina said they had to wait until the colt was secure on his feet, before they could guide them back to the barn.

Trace wiped Golden off as soon as she stood up and he put a horse blanket over her.

Then, as soon as the colt seemed reasonably steady, Tina wiped him off one more time, quickly put a colt-sized blanket over him, and secured it across his chest and under his belly.

"We'll give him a few more minutes and then start back to the barn," Tina said.

"Do we have a bridle and lead for the colt?"

"We have something better than that—his mom. He'll stay close to her all the way into her stall."

Tina attached a lead to Golden's bridle. "Secure this to Mama's saddle and she'll walk right out with us," Tina told Trace. "As powerful as Mama is, Golden will come with us, if only to be near her head."

They mounted up. Sure enough, with Mama's encouragement, Golden started walking back to the trail with her little colt walking next to her. Luke trotted about twenty-yards-ahead of them.

Trace was sure glad he had his Stetson. It was doing a great job of keeping the snow off his neck and face. He smiled as he realized that he was beginning to feel like a real cowboy for the first time in his life. "Does this qualify me as a cowboy?" he asked Tina as he rode next to her.

"It definitely qualifies you as my cowboy."

They rode along, the big snowflakes falling all around them. "I felt weird with my arm in the horse at first," Trace told Tina.

"I started to feel nauseous, but then I was so busy helping the mare deliver her colt, I didn't think about anything else."

"Trace Beckham, you are so cool."

After another mile, Luke came running back and stood about ten feet off to the side of the trail, between the colt and the woods.

"Luke, what's wrong?" Tina asked.

Luke growled—a low and angry sound that Trace had never heard before.

Tina sat up straighter. "Something must be out there."

As they looked around, Trace saw a mountain lion on some boulders, about fifty-yards-away. It was definitely eyeing the colt. He slid the rifle out of its scabbard. "I'll put a stop to this shit."

He fired one round.

It hit close enough to the mountain lion that it decided it wasn't a good idea to wait and see if Trace's marksmanship would improve on his next shot. With all the strength of his feline frame, he rapidly bounded away in the opposite direction.

The other horses were startled at the sound of the shot, but Mama was surprisingly calm.

"Dad used to take her hunting," Tina explained.

As they started moving again, Trace reached down and patted his horse. "Way to go, Mama." One of Mama's ears turned upon hearing that. He laughed. "She knows I'm talking about her," he said. "Did you see how Luke stood between the colt and the mountain lion?"

"Luke is one fine dog, Tina."

As they turned from the forest to the trail that led to the barn, they saw Tina's dad quickly riding out to meet them.

"Are you two okay? I heard a gunshot."

"Trace shot at a mountain lion. We're fine, and so is Golden's colt," Tina said. "I'm sorry, Dad, but I didn't secure the barn properly last night."

"You never mind that, Tina. If you look at the hasp on the lock, it was torn loose. She must have just pushed her way through the door. It looks like you two did a fine job. Come on. Let's get these horses inside the barn."

Tina's dad led Golden and her colt inside a stall that had a thick layer of sawdust covering the floor. Tina called over to the house to let her mother and grandparents know that they were okay, and that Golden had a colt.

As Tina related their adventure to her father, he kept smiling at Trace while he checked over Golden and her colt. The colt started nursing.

"He's fine," Tina's dad declared. "Go ahead and get Mama and Feather out of their saddles and into their stalls. Maple-Leaf and I have a few more things to take care of in the north pasture. You two get over to the house after you've taken care of the horses and get some dry clothes on."

He turned to Trace. "Trace, I've been watching you around the ranch and you have an amazing way with the horses and cattle. You ever think about becoming a large animal veterinarian?"

"No, sir, I never thought of that as a career for myself."

"Did Tina tell you that Mama won't let anyone ride her but me? That is, until you showed up."

"No, sir, she didn't."

Tina beamed with pride. "Mama won't even let me ride her. As soon as she hears your voice, or my dad's, she comes across the coral, or sticks her head out of her stall to greet you guys."

Her dad nodded. "We were all shocked the first day you came out here and walked right up to her. I was sure she'd move away from you—like she does with everyone else. You were talking to her and she liked you immediately. Think about becoming a vet, son. You've got the touch, and the animals know it."

"Thank you, Mr. Wagoner. I'll consider that, sir."

Tina's dad smiled proudly at his daughter and her boyfriend. "I never imagined my Tina would find a boyfriend like you, Trace. Whether you're unloading big bales of hay from a truck, or cleaning out stalls, you sure know how to work hard. The way Tina smiles when you're around, it's like you put joy into her heart as soon as she hears your car pull up."

As her dad rode out into the snowstorm again, Tina threw her arms around Trace. "I love you, Trace Beckham."

"Thank you, Tina. You make me feel good every moment we're together."

As he held his arms around her, Trace realized Tina was shivering. "We need to get over to the house and get out of these wet clothes," he told her.

"Get out of our clothes? I could go for that."

Trace laughed, and they forged through the snowstorm to the house. Tina's mom gave Trace some of her dad's clothing to wear. He and Tina stood in front of the living room's gray stone fireplace to enjoy its warmth.

A-few-minutes-later, Tina's dad came into the house. "This is a terrible storm. Maple-Leaf and I decided it's going to get too deep to be out there. I haven't seen a storm this bad, this early in the year, in a long time. Looks like it's heading straight at Boise. You might want to consider staying overnight, Trace." After a brief pause he continued. "On second thought, I don't like the look on Tina's face now that I've said that."

Everyone laughed, as a smiling Tina blushed. Trace called his parents to let them know that he would be staying overnight at the ranch.

They sat down to lunch. After Tina's grandfather recited grace, her dad asked if anyone had thought of a name for the new colt. After many snow-related names were suggested, Tina's grandmother said, "We should name him TNT, for Tina and Trace."

Tina and Trace smiled at each other.

"That's perfect, Mom," Tina's mother declared.

The lights in the house began to flicker and they heard the ranch's emergency generator come to life.

"This storm is bad. We hardly every lose power out here," Tina's grandfather informed Trace.

Around mid-afternoon, Tina's dad announced that he was going out to the barn to check on the colt.

"We'll go, Dad," Tina called out in a joyful voice.

She and Trace got into their heavy jackets and sweaters. They headed back through the storm to the barn.

The wind had picked up and the snow was blowing nearly horizontal. The snow crystals brushed against their faces. Trace likened the feeling to the burning sensation of putting on shaving lotion, after shaving with a sharp razor.

When they got to the barn, Tina looked back. "Wow. I can barely see the house, just one-hundred-yards away, because the snow is falling so heavily."

They checked on the horses. Golden was busy eating, and TNT was curled up on the stall floor, fast asleep.

"I want to show you something, Trace."

Tina climbed a ladder into the hayloft. Trace followed, and Tina walked over to the far side of the loft and started digging into the hay. With an impish grin, she pulled out a huge Pendleton blanket. She walked back to Trace.

As she got close to him, she took two fast steps and pushed him into the pile of loose hay, giggling as she jumped on top of him. After a long kiss, they took off their jackets and wrapped themselves in the soft warm blanket. It was so big, it wrapped twice around them.

Trace rolled on top of Tina. "Is this called a roll in the hay?"

Tina laughed. "It's not an official roll in the hay, until you hold me for at least an hour."

"An hour, huh?" Trace laughed, kissed her, then tightened his arms around her.

"Tina, my beloved cowgirl, I don't know why the Lord saw fit to put us together, but our being together certainly gives me more joy than I deserve."

He rolled over onto his back, as Tina lay against his side. They fell asleep, wrapped in the warm blanket, the snow falling outside and a brand new life lying in the barn below.

Chapter Thirty ~ David and Linda, plus Anna

ON THE SAME SATURDAY morning that Tina and Trace had delivered the colt, Linda and David were visiting Anna. David had taken a Friday evening flight to come for the three-day weekend. Anna was showing Linda how to make crepes. David loved watching Linda's culinary efforts, and he especially liked eating the results. He also helped more than usual, as Anna was in the final weeks of her pregnancy. As they were just cleaning up, Anna received a phone call.

"The two matching Pendleton blankets I ordered have arrived at a store, out near the airport," she told them. "It is a short drive, so we can take my new pickup truck, but we should go now—the weather forecast is for light snow around noon today."

David and Linda agreed.

"David, I want you to drive, please. My stomach is getting so big I can't get close enough to the steering wheel."

"Sure, Anna. I'd be happy to help," he said.

They went out and Linda climbed into the co-pilot's seat as David helped Anna into the back seat.

"This truck is a monster," Linda said.

"Yes, it is," Anna agreed. "Michael bought this four-wheel- drive tank for me. It has a lift-kit, some suspension stuff, and those big tires that make it hard for me to get up into it. He said he doesn't want me to get stuck in the snow."

She laughed. "I told him this monster is so ugly, it could scare its way through a blizzard."

Linda and David laughed, too.

As soon as David drove onto the interstate, it started snowing. He looked in his side mirror and saw very dark clouds to the west— the direction storms usually came from.

In spite of the gentle snowfall, they made it to the store without any problems—traffic was light, it being a snowy Saturday.

They entered the store and the clerk told Anna that they had received the blankets she ordered, but had also received the same design in other colors. He placed a selection of them on the counter.

Linda ran her hand over the thick, natural wool fiber. "I didn't know wool existed that wasn't scratchy."

"Remind me when we get home, Linda," Anna said, "and I'll show you some of my Pendleton sweaters that are so soft I can wear them against my skin like a cotton garment."

Anna had chosen matching baby-sized and queen-sized Chief Joseph blankets in ivory, but when the clerk showed her the other colors, it made the decision more difficult. "Linda, you have to help me decide."

As the great blanket debate went on, David noticed that the light snow was turning into a serious snowfall. It looked like giant cotton balls were falling from the sky, and it was coming down so fast now that it was no longer melting as it hit the ground. It was getting difficult to see to the other side of the outlet mall.

"We need to get going, troops," he said. "This storm is starting to look serious."

"It's only twenty-minutes home," Anna stated. "We should be okay."

Anna and Linda made a decision and the ivory color won the debate. The blankets were boxed up, and David carried them out, as Linda held Anna's arm walking to the truck.

David started the truck, turned on the heat, and then went out to clean off the windows. He shivered at the rapidly dropping temperature, and hopped up into the vehicle.

"I think we need to get home soon," Anna told them. "I was having some abdominal cramps early this morning, and I think they're coming back."

Linda looked worried. "I know a shortcut around the back of the airport, David. I'll guide you. That way we can avoid the slow traffic on the interstate—I'm sure it is getting heavily backed up already. It always does when we get these storms."

David agreed and followed Linda's directions, while Anna tried to relax in the back seat.

After they'd followed the side road for a good half-hour, David began to get concerned. The snow was heavy now and visibility was almost zero. "Linda, are we still on the right road?" he asked.

She shook her head. "I'm not sure anymore, David. None of this looks familiar, and I don't remember going over the last hill we just came down."

"I don't see any house lights," Anna said. "We must be out in the countryside."

"I have a bad feeling—I'm going to turn around," David said. "I could sure use Jonah now. As long as this truck is, it's going to be a bear to safely turn it around. He knows how to do a one-eighty in slippery stuff like this."

"Your twelve-year-old brother has experience doing one- eighties?" Linda inquired.

"My crazy Uncle Meyer found out Jonah got an A in math, so he took him out in one of his sports cars and let Jonah make one- eighties and three-sixties in a snow-covered parking lot near the stadium. I'll have to do an old fashioned three-point turn."

As David began executing the turn, he lost track of the edge of the road. With little warning, the truck embedded itself in mud and snow, and came to a rough stop. David revved the engine, to no avail.

"We are good and stuck." He looked at his cell phone. "And my cell can't find a signal. Lucky me, we seem to be closest to the one tower without a working backup system."

"Oh-oh," Anna shouted. "My pants are wet."

"What? Why?" David asked.

"David, she means her water broke," Linda told him, in an exasperated voice.

"Water broke—nothing. It feels like the Snake River just ran down my legs," Anna said. "Wow that hurts. Am I birthing a kid, or a bowling ball?"

"You don't want to have the baby now," David advised.

"Tell that to this kid. It's got other ideas."

Anna started to pant. "There are some sterile wipes in the emergency kit in the glove compartment. You guys are going to have to help me 'cause this kid is coming."

David stared at Anna. "You're kidding, right?"

"David, this is what you want to do with your life," Linda reminded him. "Just pretend it is one of the videos you've watched."

David sucked in a breath and nodded his head. She was right. He could do this. If he couldn't, then he had no business thinking of this career path.

Linda found the sterile wipes and she and David used them on their hands and forearms.

Now that David had faced what he had to do, his confidence grew. He thought of all the doctors in the videos. "Okay, Anna, Mrs. Levin, you need to lie down and I need to check how far along you are."

"Just do what you need to do." Anna continued to pant.

Linda and David removed the clothing from the lower half of Anna's body as she reclined across the long bench seat of the pickup.

David pulled on latex gloves from the emergency kit. "I'm sorry, Anna, I need to put my hand—"

"David, just do it," Anna told him in a stern voice.

David proceeded to do exactly what he had seen in the videos. He slipped his hand inside to check. "Wow. Oh, my gosh, Anna you must be ten centimeters dilated. I can feel the baby's head."

As each contraction came on, Linda supported Anna behind her shoulders, encouraging her to breathe. The contractions started coming harder and longer, with less time in between.

Linda tried to lighten the mood. "So, Anna, do you want a boy or a girl?"

"This close to Halloween, Linda," Anna panted, "I'll be happy as long as it's not a pumpkin."

David and Linda couldn't help but laugh.

Then, David calmly told Anna how well she was doing. "A few more pushes and I think the head will be out," he said.

Suddenly the head presented itself. "Oh! There it is," David exclaimed. He reached to rotate the baby. "I think I have to move the cord—"

"What?" Anna asked. "I have to push, David. I have to push, now!"

Before David could say anything further, he had a tiny baby in his hands. "It's a boy! Oh, my gosh, Anna. It's a boy!"

He held him upside down like he'd seen the doctors do, and the tiny newborn coughed and started crying. David placed him on Anna's belly and she opened her blouse to lay her son on her bare chest. The baby immediately began rooting around, looking for her breast.

Linda wrapped both Anna and her newborn in the warm wool blankets. "Oh, Anna, he's absolutely beautiful."

Anna held her new son, tears of joy streaming down her cheeks.

"My little baby," she said. "Welcome to the world, little one."

"Are you warm enough?" Linda asked.

Anna nodded. "How can I ever thank you guys?"

"Thank us when this is over," David said. "You still need to deliver the placenta, and I still need to get us out of here, or head out into this blackness to get help. So, Linda, you stay back there with Anna in case she needs help. I'll get out and see if there is any chance of getting out of here."

David started putting his jacket on when his phone rang. Surprised, he quickly answered. "Hello," David said. "Hello? Is someone there?"

"David? David, can you hear me? It's Jonah. I heard the power was out all over Boise. My friend, Mark, and I thought we'd try to boink your cell phone from a satellite."

"I didn't know you could do that."

"How do you think", Jonah replied, "they listened to Bin Ladin's cell phone."

"You did it. You have no idea how great your timing is, Jonah. Now, listen to me—Linda and I just delivered Anna's baby in the back of her truck. We are trapped in snow and mud, somewhere near the airport. We need help."

"Maybe I can talk you out of there. David, what are you driving?"

"A four-wheel-drive pickup with a lift-kit and huge tires, but we're still stuck. I tried, but I couldn't get out. Jonah, we need to get somebody to—"

"David, did you lock the differentials?"

"What?"

"David, you clod! I can't believe you're my brother. Look for a button or switch that says differential lock."

David looked frantically around. "I found one—it says *Diff Lock* on it."

"Okay. Now, lock the differentials, go easy, then drive the hell out of there. When you get home, brother, we need to talk."

David did as Jonah told him. He put the truck in gear and eased it through the muck. Anna and Linda cheered as the truck made slow but sure progress back onto the narrow road. David thanked Jonah and hung up the phone once he was sure they were going to be okay. He headed back the way they had come and found his way to the interstate highway.

"Well, I guess I'll have to apologize to Michael when I get home," Anna said. "I told him I didn't need this big truck, but he was right. Thank God he didn't listen to me when I told him to return it."

She turned to her little baby. "See that? You have a father who will take good care of you, even when he's not around."

Twenty-five-minutes-later, David pulled into the emergency entrance of the hospital.

A nurse was just on her way inside and she rushed up to the truck. "Do you need help?" she asked.

David opened his window. "We just delivered her baby half- an-hour-ago. We were stuck in a ditch. I think she just delivered the placenta."

"All right," the nurse said. "Let's get her inside. You get her ready, and I'll get a couple of orderlies."

The nurse scurried inside and David rushed around to the back seat to help Anna and the baby.

Linda followed them inside.

David parked the truck, and then went to call Michael. After he hung up, David waited by the door, and a short while later, a pale and frightened Michael came running into the hospital.

"David. Where are they?" Michael panted, out of breath.

"They're both fine," David immediately told him. "The doctors have checked them both out and they're doing great. Come on. I'll introduce you to your son."

***

Michael was still shaking as he walked down the corridor of the ER and saw Anna in a bed, holding their son.

He kissed her, then wrapped his arms around them both. "Thank God, you're safe."

"I know," Anna said, "you told me so. I guess we needed that big monster of a truck after all."

Michael chuckled. "Typical Anna," he said to David and Linda as he walked toward them, shaking his head. "She delivers our baby on the side of the road, in a snowstorm, and still she's making jokes." He hugged each of them. "And you two—I owe you guys more than I can say. If I can ever do something for you, please let me know."

Linda smiled. "You should also know it was David's brother, Jonah, who called us and told David what to do to get the pickup unstuck."

Michael smiled. "Activating the diff-lock?"

David grinned sheepishly and nodded in the affirmative.

The head of obstetrics at the hospital stopped by then. He shook Michael's hand and turned to David. "Mr. Kaplan, I presume?"

David nodded.

"I understand you are the one that performed this little miracle delivery."

"Yes, sir," David replied.

"You've got the stuff, kid. Mrs. Levin told me she never panicked because of your calm manner." He handed David a card. "When you become Dr. Kaplan and need a position for your obstetrics residency, you call me. We can always use a good man who can stay calm during an obstetric emergency."

David beamed. "Thank you, Doctor. I'll be calling you."

"You're going to make a great doctor someday, David," Anna added.

"David, I'm really proud of what you did today." Linda gave him a hug.

"I'm really proud of what *we* did today. We make a good team, Linda."

"Well, great team, you two have earned a break," Michael said. "Why don't you drive the pickup home. I'll be staying here until they kick me out." He leaned in and gave his new son a kiss on the head.

***

Across town, Holly looked shocked to hear her cell phone ringing. She answered it with a huge grin on her face.

"It must be Jonah," Oliver told Ruth. "He's the only one who makes her smile like that over the phone." He looked at his own cell phone. "Huh. I still have no service on my cell. How in the world did he manage to call her?"

Ruth grinned at Oliver. "Well, 'Love Will Find a Way' is the title of that oldies song you like, right? Look at your daughter's face—I do believe love just found a way."

Holly got off the phone and bounced over to her family. "Wow! David and Linda just helped Anna deliver her baby—in a pickup truck, in a snowstorm, stuck some place—it's a boy, by the way. And Jonah was the one who told David what to do to get the truck unstuck."

Ruth couldn't believe her ears. "What did you say? Anna had her baby in a truck? It's a boy? Is she okay? Is the baby okay?"

In an exasperated teenage voice, Holly replied, "Of course, they're okay, Mom. I told you—Jonah told David how to get unstuck. Isn't he amazing?"

Oliver stood up. "C'mon, Drew. Put some heavy clothes on and we'll cross-country ski over to the Schulman's house to let them know that David and Linda are okay...and that Anna gave birth to a son."

As they left their yard, Ruth took some photos of her men, on a snowy night, heading over to the Schulmans' to spread the word that David and Linda were not only safe, but had helped Anna have a safe delivery, too.

Chapter Thirty-One ~ Jonah and his Father

JONAH HUNG UP THE phone and laughed as he walked downstairs from his bedroom. "Wow. I can't believe he didn't know that."

"Jonah, what are you yelling about?" his father, Morris, asked.

"It's nothing, Dad. I just helped David with a car problem."

"You talked to him in Boise?"

"Yeah. My buddy helped me boink a satellite to send a signal to his cell phone. I called Holly, too."

"What did you help David with?"

"Well, they were trapped in a snowbound four-wheel-drive pick-up truck, right, and David and Linda helped this lady, Anna, the one from Boise, deliver her baby. But then, David didn't know he could lock the differentials to get the truck out of the ditch they were stuck in—I can't believe my own brother wouldn't know that! I had to call Holly to tell her. She couldn't believe it either."

"Jonah, what did you say your brother did?"

"He got a pickup truck stuck in some mud and snow and he didn't even know to lock the differentials." Jonah chuckled some more. "I'm going to need to sit down with—"

"Jonah, please stop rambling. Focus and tell me about the baby."

"Oh, that. Okay. Well, David and Linda helped deliver a baby."

His father looked shocked. "Jonah, are you sure? Your brother helped deliver a baby?"

"Dad," Jonah said in a matter-of-fact tone, "he *is* planning on going into obstetrics and he's been reading all those books and watching all those hideous videos. It's not a big deal."

"Not a big—oh, my word," his father said. "Thank God you and your brother have spent so much time around your Uncle Meyer and your cousin, Ari. The world could be collapsing and you four would remain calm. You sure didn't get this kind of skill from your mother or me. I have to call Meyer and Ari to tell them."

He smiled and patted Jonah on the head. "Good job helping your brother, Jonah."

He paused for a moment, thinking, then his father continued. "Many years ago, your Uncle Meyer said to me once that he thought the most trusted people in his life were the people he would want next to him in combat. For me, I would want you and David next to me."

"Wow, thanks, Dad."

His dad smiled. "I am so lucky to have such fine sons. Ethan the musician, David the future doctor, and you, Jonah, the future brilliant whatever-you-decide-to-be."

He went toward the kitchen where Jonah's mother was. "Hey, Michelle. You're not going to believe this."

Chapter Thirty-Two ~ David and Linda, Anna and Michael, plus David Linn

MICHAEL DROVE LINDA AND David over to the hospital to bring Anna and the new baby home. When they arrived, Anna was sitting in a chair and had her little bundle of joy all wrapped up. He was awake and moving his tiny arms and legs, nestled in his mother's arms.

"How's Philip?" Linda asked.

Anna smiled and looked at Michael. "We decided to name him David Linn—after the people who helped deliver him. Linda, I'm tired of holding him. Will you hold him for a while?"

"Oh, wow, just look at this precious little guy." Linda carefully cradled tiny David Linn in her arms. "Hi, David Linn. I met you yesterday."

David smiled, as Linda seemed to be walking on air while she carried baby David Linn around the room. As she walked, she started singing, "David *Melech Yisroel, chai, chai Vekayom,*" an old Hebrew melody about King David.

After four trips around the room, Linda turned to David. "Your turn."

David took the warm bundle in his arms and started singing Stevie Ray Vaughn's "Love Struck Baby." He nodded to Linda and she started singing with him. They engaged in scat singing during the bridge. David and Linda—and little David Linn—moved together in time to the song.

Michael smiled at Anna. "Only two-days-old and look what joy he's already bringing to the world. Just look at their faces."

"He seemed to calm right down as soon as they started singing."

"Do you think Linda will want to babysit for him?"

Anna laughed. "I think she'd move into our house, if we let her."

"Can I?" Linda asked with a big grin.

"Maybe we'll start with a date night for Michael and me, once we're settled into a routine, and we'll go from there."

Linda chuckled. "It's a deal."

David Linn started back to fussing. "It sounds like he's hungry," Anna announced.

"Should we leave the room?" Linda asked.

"Stay right here. The nurses showed me how to do it in a modest way, so it's no problem. Besides, other than Michael and my doctor, you two have seen more of me than anyone else."

Everyone laughed, except David Linn, who was too busy with lunch.

***

The day after Anna arrived home with David Linn, her grandmother flew into town. They had decided not to tell Grandma about the baby coming early and surprise her when she arrived in Meridian.

Anna didn't want to go out in the cold with the baby, and Michael wanted to stay home with them, so David, Linda, and Andrew offered to go pick Grandma up. Michael and Anna agreed and let David drive Anna's big pickup to the airport.

They waited at the baggage area, Andrew holding the sign he'd made with the name of Perla Cortez on it, and soon they were approached by an older, gray-haired woman who had Anna's warm smile.

Linda decided that she would have recognized her without the sign.

"Hello," she told them. "I'm Perla Cortez."

"We're neighbors of Anna and Michael," Linda said. "They asked us to pick you up and drive you over to their house."

David smiled and introduced everyone. "Hi, I'm David. This is Linda and her brother, Andrew."

He gestured to a nearby bench. "Why don't we sit down until the luggage starts coming out?"

"It's nice to meet you, David, Linda, and Andrew. Do you kids have a last name to go with those wonderful first names?" Perla asked as she sat down.

Linda smiled happily. "Actually we do—that's why we asked you to sit down."

"What? Well, now I really don't understand."

"Tell her, Andrew," Linda said.

Andrew proudly stepped forward. "Well, David's last name is Kaplan, but my sister and I have the last name of Schulman."

"Shulman? Oh, my word," Perla said. "What a coincidence. Why, my father was—"

"Sam Shulman," Linda finished.

"How did you know?" Perla asked.

Andrew grinned. "Our father has been tracing our family tree, and he found out that our great-great-grandfather was Sam Schulman. You are being greeted here today by the children of your nephew."

Perla just stared at them for a while, shaking her head. "Are you sure?"

"If your mother was Carrie Yoselovitch, we're sure," Linda told her.

"She certainly was." Perla beamed. "You couldn't have given me a nicer surprise. And you, Mr. Kaplan, are we related?"

"Not yet," David said with a wide smile. "Linda and I have only been dating for three-months, but it looks promising."

Perla laughed and looked admiringly at them. "Well, I can't believe I'm meeting three new family members in one day! That will be hard to top."

Just then, the baggage started coming out, so they walked over to the conveyor. As Perla pointed out her bags, she looked amazed to see eight-year-old Andrew easily remove her rather large suitcase off the conveyor with one hand.

Linda saw her surprised expression. "He's quite strong for an eight-year-old."

"My father, Sam, was strong like that. Andrew has his warm smile, as well—so do you, Linda."

"You guys wait inside here, where it's warm," David said. "Andrew and I will go get the truck and bring it over."

"I have orders to call home as soon as we get to the Levins' house, so my parents can come over and meet their aunt," Linda told Perla while they waited.

When they arrived at Michael and Anna's home, Michael greeted Grandma Perla with a hug. He took her coat and directed Andrew and David to put her luggage in the small bedroom.

"Have a seat over here. Anna will be out in a moment. She has a surprise for you."

"I've already had a wonderful surprise, meeting my three new relatives." Grandma told them.

"How about four?" Anna floated into the room with joy radiating from her face, carrying her new son. "Hi, Grandma, I have someone for you to meet."

She walked over and placed David Linn in his great- grandmother's arms.

"Anna, he's beautiful," she said. "Does your mother know?"

"Yes, she does. Seeing as he came early, we decided to surprise you."

"What a day of wonderful surprises."

"His name is David Linn," Linda told her in an excited voice.

"He was born in a pickup truck during a snowstorm," David stated.

Then Andrew announced, "He was named after the two people that helped deliver him." Andrew proudly pointed at David and Linda, who were both grinning from ear to ear.

"Born in a pickup truck in a snowstorm?" Perla asked. "You two helped deliver him?"

"Yes, they did—he's in perfect health, and so am I," Anna reassured her.

"David Linn—what a fine name you've given my great- grandson. He really is a precious little bundle, isn't he?" She looked to the heavens. "And thank you, Lord, for letting me live to see this day."

Anna gave her grandmother a hug.

She smiled brightly. "How I would love to be able to call my father and mother to tell them—I've just met their long-lost, great-great-grandchildren, and I'm holding their newborn great-great-grandson."

As if right on cue, David Linn made a cooing sound in Great-Grandma Perla's arms.

Anna looked from her baby boy, to her grandmother's happy face, to the white stippled ceiling above. With her arm still draped over her Grandmother's shoulder, she gave a gentle squeeze. "I have a feeling they know."

~ ~ ~ The End ~ ~ ~

If you enjoyed this novel, please leave a review at the online vendor where you made your purchase. Thank you!!!

Don't miss out!

Visit the website below and you can sign up to receive emails whenever Richard Alan publishes a new book. There's no charge and no obligation.

https://books2read.com/r/B-A-XUNH-WBLX

BOOKS 2 READ

Connecting independent readers to independent writers.

Also by Richard Alan

Meant to be Together
Finding a Soul Mate
The Couples
Finding Each Other
Growing Together

Watch for more at https://villagedrummerfiction.com.

About the Author

Richard is a 101st Airborne Division Vietnam veteran. After an education in mathematics, 17-years in manufacturing engineering then 22-years as a software engineer, Richard embarked on a career in writing. His debut series, Meant to Be Together, is a tender and heartwarming, multigenerational family saga about relationships, love and life. This was followed by a series of historical fiction novels, set in 1847 – 1900, about the predecessors to the characters in his Meant to Be Together series. Expertly researched, American Journeys: From Ireland to the Pacific Northwest (1847 – 1900), Volumes One and Two, details the family's struggles during the Great Irish Famine, emigration from Ireland to Boston, the journey across the United States, the Oregon Trail, and the Panama Canal. A Female Doctor in the Civil War follows Dr. Abby Kaplan, trying to become a surgeon during the Civil War. She was first introduced as a little girl in Volume One of American Journeys. Being a lifelong learner, Richard loves pursuing the research for his historical fiction. It is frequently accomplished while RV traveling with his wife, Carolynn, to libraries, museums, and historical sites around the country. Having a career that is portable permits traveling to many spectacular areas of the United States. It also provides opportunities to visit our adult children, grandchildren, other relatives, and friends.

Read more at https://villagedrummerfiction.com.

www.ingramcontent.com/pod-product-compliance
Lightning Source LLC
Chambersburg PA
CBHW060914210726
48293CB00006B/2102